Jayne Hargreave

All the Seas Between

Nicola Kearns

GW00457667

This novel is dedicated to the memory of

Jonathan Southfield

Master Sergeant, United States Air Force

1971 – 2017

Acknowledgements

There are some people who have given assistance in my journey of writing *All the Seas Between* and to whom I wish to extend my appreciation. Tony O'Connell, author of *Atlantipedia* and *Joining the Dots* has, once again, been invaluable with his advice and proof-reading. His friendship and support kept me going when sometimes the task seemed too great.

I also wish to acknowledge the support of my family, especially my two sons Darragh Mc Shane and Adam Curley-Kearns, whom I love with my whole heart.

This is the third novel which designer, Steven Weekes, has worked on for me and his expertise is second to none. Thank you Steven for your unlimited patience.

A very significant credit goes to my father, Nicholas Kearns, for once again painting the beautiful cover of my third novel. Thank you Dad and I love you. I extend my deepest gratitude to my mother, Mary Kearns, whose support, guidance and gentle coaxing is one of the main reasons that this book was completed. Thank you Mum from the bottom of my heart. I love you very much.

PROLOGUE

Forli, Italy. March, 1944.

'Marius,' Signora Inglima called with vexation. Where had the child got to? These tireless games of hide and seek every time they needed to leave the house were maddening. Usually indulgent with her youngest child, this time she had no patience for his frolics. Serenella had always been the one to eventually find her brother in some cupboard or under a bed, giggling mischievously to himself. The study door was open which was unusual, but the weeping she heard from inside was not her son's. Tentatively pushing the door open, she saw the sorrowful sight of Rachele, leaning with her hands across the ornately carved desk.

'Rachele,' she whispered, concerned. 'What is it?'

Her friend shook her head and turned to face Maria-Angela. 'This,' she replied, holding a piece of jewellery on the ends of her fingers. 'He's had yet another *puttana* in here.'

Maria-Angela took the necklace out of Rachele's trembling hand.

'Can I get you anything?' she enquired gently.

To try and sympathise was futile. This was a

7

common occurrence and platitudes only added salt to the wound. Rachele shook her head and together they left the room silently. As Signora Mussolini walked towards the kitchen, Maria-Angela stalled in the hallway and examined the piece of jewellery in her hand. It was a long gold chain with the links roughly snapped, as though pulled violently from somebody's neck. Cheap gold she believed, typical of a working class woman. Opening the clasp she gasped out loud, recognising the face which looked back at her from inside the locket. But how? Then realisation dawned. Her daughter had owned this chain and had been in this room. When? It was a recognised fact that Il Duce took his many women visitors in here for one reason only. 'Oh my God,' she cried, suddenly comprehending. 'My poor, beautiful daughter. What have I done?'

Sixty Years Later
Malta. October, 2004.

Jessy hadn't thought about where she was running to
until she arrived at the blue door. Why? Why had she
come here? Panting for breath, she leaned her two
palms against the coolness of the wooden frame, as
though she was trying to push the door open. Her legs
felt like jelly, unused as they were to running so fast.
Beads of sweat ran down the front of her dress as the
strap of the brown leather handbag slipped from her
arm. Pressing her forehead against the coolness of the
door, Jessy gradually felt her heartbeat slow down. She
waited until her breathing calmed, then picked up her
bag. Opening the small zipped compartment inside, her
fingers felt the jagged edges of a key. She pulled it out
and inserted the key into the lock. It opened easily. The
door creaked a little.

The hallway smelled instantly familiar. Jessy heard
the click behind her as the bolt sprang back into place.
She bent down and picked up the letters under her feet,
holding them in her hand as she ascended the spiral
staircase. Her breathing was normal now, but her
mouth felt dry. Walking into the long narrow kitchen

she reached onto the open shelf for a glass. There was bottled sparkling water in the fridge. She poured some into the glass and swallowed it quickly. It made her splutter and cough. The water was freezing and felt like it burned her chest. She replaced the bottle and closed the fridge, then noticed the photo stuck to the front. She, Billy and Neil smiled back. Jessy ran her finger over the smiling face. His blond hair was shorter then.

Chapter 1

Italy. June, 1940.

The Inglima family was highly respected in Sicily. Their home in the hill-top city of Ragusa Ibla was positioned in the south-east of the large island, situated in the middle of the Mediterranean Sea, just off the toe of mainland Italy. Serenella's father, His Excellency Giovanni Francesco Inglima, held the position of the only judge in the Province of Ragusa. He also owned numerous businesses and had a hand in almost every type of produce you could think of, from wines to linens. The family was also staunchly Fascist, devoted to Benito Mussolini, who was both Prime Minister of Italy and the National Fascist Party Leader.

The Inglimas were regular visitors to Mussolini's home in Emilia-Romagna on the mainland, often taking the children, including Serenella, there for holidays. They would socialise with Benito's younger teenage children, Romano and Anna-Maria. Il Duce and Giovanni were long-time friends. Likewise, his long-suffering wife Rachele and Giovanni's wife, Maria-Angela, were close friends. Serenella Inglima was the Inglimas' only daughter and was often taxed with the job of entertaining the younger children or helping with their studies. There were strict time-tables to adhere to and classes they were expected to attend, run by Fascist groups for Italian adolescents. These were held in the nearby town of Forli. The young men were required to attend camps where they were taught military practices, from marching to the use of guns. The young women were encouraged to join classes on domestic duties, ranging from cooking to the values of motherhood. These classes were compulsory, as was the uniform of black shirt and trousers for the young men, a white blouse and black skirt for the young women.

Serenella was just sixteen years old when on 4th June 1940, she journeyed to what would turn out to be a four year long stay in mainland Italy. Her pleas to be left at home with their servants in Ragusa for the summer were ignored by her parents. She cried silently as the ferry sailed slowly out of Catania, en route to the port of Livorno, on the western coast of Tuscany, Italy.

'Serenella,' her mother called sternly. 'I will not tell you again, young lady, to go to your cabin and stop parading yourself on deck like a commoner.'

Signora Maria-Angela Inglima had no idea that her

12

young daughter was in love. The family was accustomed to Serenella's docile manner and her uncharacteristic show of defiance against going to Italy was greeted with annoyance by her mother. It was a mammoth task to prepare the large family to vacate the humid city of Ragusa, for the cooler climate of Emilia-Romagna during the summer. Her daughter's sullenness had made the whole experience even more stressful. In the last year, her once obedient and placid child had turned into an un-cooperative young woman. Signora Inglima hoped the holiday in the countryside would shake Serenella out of whatever ailed her. It would not be long before she could marry the girl off to a local man chosen by her husband and she would be out of her mother's hair, once and for all.

Daughters were of no use. As an only child herself and persuaded into an arranged marriage to provide an heir, Maria-Angela never hid her distaste for either married life or motherhood. It was inconceivable to her that unless she had married, her family wealth would pass to a male cousin on whom she would be completely dependent. Sons were what mattered - sons who would carry on the family name and keep their fortune safe, both that of her own lineage and her husbands. Thankfully she had given birth to four sons, assuring Maria-Angela of her own financial security. Serenella would have to be married into a prosperous family, if she wanted to be kept in the comfortable lifestyle to which she was accustomed.

Ascending the steps towards the family's suite of cabins, Serenella put her hand under her pink cotton blouse and grasped the small gold locket that hung on a chain between her budding breasts. Pausing on the last step and lifting the chain out of its confines she opened the clasp, revealing the photo of the young dark haired man concealed inside. She kissed the image before snapping the locket shut and returning it under her blouse.

'Giorgio', she whispered. 'Giorgio.'

Just saying his name out loud seemed almost blasphemous. If Mama had even an inkling of her relationship with him, Serenella knew she would be whisked off to a convent for wayward girls until she was to be married. So far she and Giorgio had managed to keep their burgeoning romance a secret, but this dreaded holiday would keep them apart for the next three months. It was going to be hard not seeing Giorgio and his family every day and extremely difficult to even get a chance to write to him - but Serenella vowed to try her best not to let this separation part them forever.

The housekeeper, Sophia, ran Villa Carpena, the home of Il Duce, in the Northern Italian Province of Forli-Cesena, like a jailer. Her wizened, pale pock-marked face seemed to pop up everywhere Serenella went. A bunch of keys dangled on a chain from her waistband, which even further enhanced her prison warden look. She hated the Inglimas' pretty young daughter simply for being beautiful. The extra workload caused by the arrival of the Inglima family to Il Duce's house, set her teeth on edge. It was the reason for the migraine which stubbornly refused to leave, despite her frequent spoonfuls of morphine stolen from *la padrona di casas'* medicine cabinet.

Sophia had to admit that the five children of the Inglima family, Angelo, Lorenzo, Marco, Serenella and Marius were extremely well behaved, as were the two youngest Mussolini children. Both sets of parents were strict about discipline and the household was run like an institution. The children were expected to be up early, to make their own beds and get washed and dressed before being at breakfast for seven o'clock sharp. Their day was quite industrious, consisting, as advocated by Mussolini, of various classes in the nearby town run by the local Fascist youth group. Assorted recreational activities run in the evening kept the youths busy until late. After an evening meal and some leisure time they were then in bed by ten at night. If they wanted to read after that they could do so, but usually they were asleep quite soon after a busy day. The family had been visiting at Villa Carpena for many years and the two Signoras were respectable women who accepted that a woman's sole occupation was to be a good mother and wife.

The abhorrent behaviour of Il Duce towards his wife and his disgusting animalistic desire for a profusion of women was never spoken of publicly, but it didn't need to be. The frequent vociferous arguments between Mussolini and Rachele were a regular occurrence and kept the entire household privy to their most intimate rows. Il Duce was not at their country estate very often. Both he and Giovanni Inglima were frequently away dealing with affairs of state, but when he was home the atmosphere immediately changed. Children were quieter and the domestic staff even more so. Maria-Angela kept to her room unless summoned by her husband. Rachele Mussolini either dressed more elegantly and danced fond attendance on her husband, or screamed with rage, literally pulling her own hair out with fury.

Mussolini would often charge furiously down the staircase after one of their altercations, loudly shouting orders for his car to be made ready and would storm out with Rachele running after him, issuing threats of suicide. These rows usually concerned Mussolini's mistress, Claretta Petacci, or his wife's discovery of yet another of Mussolini's female conquests. The next morning the Signora would be in the kitchen wearing her apron and making pasta, as though nothing had happened the night before and the rest of the household would follow suit. Like Rachele's ragu sauce, the ambiance in the house was always that of a bubbling pot ready to boil over at any moment.

Every other year Serenella looked forward to their annual holiday, but not this year. Not now that she had a very good reason to stay in Sicily. She wasn't quite sure when she and her childhood friend fell so hopelessly in love. The young woman knew her mother would have one of her turns if she had any idea of this, for Giorgio was not only the son of their gardener - his

17

mother was also one of their cooks. He was somebody who was most definitely not suitable for the daughter of the respectable *Signor Presidente della corte*, the esteemed Giovanni Inglima.

There was never a time that Serenella could remember when Giorgio was not part of her life. Her chubby little legs as a child would follow the older boy as he helped his father in the Inglima family's extensive palatial gardens. At just six years of age he was already assisting his papa, gathering up leaves and weeds, throwing them in the wheelbarrow. The family gardener would then lift the two children on top of the day's collection and Serenella would cling on to Giorgio, squealing as they were sped down the hill leading to where a bonfire would be set, ready to be lit as usual every Friday afternoon.

As a sickly child prone to chest infections, Serenella was encouraged by the family doctor to play outdoors for fresh air as often as possible. This gave her freedom to play at leisure with Giorgio when he had time for games. He was a dark haired, skinny boy who was quite tall and serious for his age. Growing older, his thin arms turned into hard muscle, as he eventually took over the heavier work from his father. Likewise,

Serenella's slim frame changed as she reached adolescence, her once bony shape suddenly became softer and rounder, with long slender legs giving her the appearance of young colt. But still she played with Giorgio.

Innocent days were spent with the young boy and his father, as he patiently taught them the names of every flower in the splendid botanical gardens. Serenella by the age of twelve could identify every plant, shrub and vegetable that their gardener Carlo, had sown. Sunny afternoons were spent climbing trees to shake down their citrus fruits - lemons, oranges and prickly pears. Fingers were stained purple as they deftly pulled fat wine coloured grapes from their vines, or strawberries from their beds. Many happy days were also spent climbing the steep hill to Giorgio's home at the top of Ragusa Ibla, where his mother Valentina always greeted Serenella with a motherly welcome, even allowing both children to lick out the bowls of whatever she had been baking that day.

But the grape harvest was Serenella's most favourite time of all. Always held at the end of August, the Inglima family was back in time from their annual vacation in Italy for this yearly occasion. Although

19

never taking part in the harvest themselves, the family liked to preside over the *festa* which took place afterwards and Maria-Angela enjoyed having yet another occasion for which to buy a fashionable new dress.

With Mama always busy at this time of year shopping for clothes for her sons' return to boarding schools, Serenella had unsupervised freedom to join Giorgio's family as the grape picking began. It was scorching hot. With a white cotton scarf tied around her head and borrowed peasant clothes, Serenella didn't even notice how her skin was turning darker and darker. Every night she fell into bed exhausted, but happy in the knowledge she had performed a good day's work. Well able to keep up with the other girls working in the vineyards, she enjoyed the companionship and chat. Sometimes she had to veil her discomfiture at the coarse jokes the local *ragazze* shared with the workmen they toiled alongside.

***

Ragusa Ibla, Sicily. August, 1939.

It was during some of this flirtatious banter a year ago

that Serenella first felt a stirring in her heart for her friend Giorgio. With her sunburnt skin and farmhand clothing, she passed for just another of the country labouring girls brought in for the harvest. Bending over to reach the bottom grapes, she suddenly found herself shoved head first into the bushes by the force of somebody slapping her very forcefully on the behind. With her cheeks flaming and tears embarrassingly smarting in her eyes, Serenella turned to reprimand her attacker. But somebody had got there first. Giorgio appeared out of nowhere and she was flung back as he lunged himself on top of the burly local man, who must have been the one who had struck her. With his fists he punched the unsuspecting young man, until several other workers hauled him off. Pointing at the dazed Serenella, he bawled at the man in front of him, who was being helped to his feet by obliging rescuers.

'If Signore Inglima was here, he'd have you shot,' he bellowed and with the back of his hand, wiped the blood from the one blow the other man had managed to get in.

All faces turned in her direction and immediately Serenella's assailant began to screech his defence.

'I didn't know it was the Signorina Inglima. I

didn't know,' he beseeched, touching both hands together as if in prayer, shaking them up and down in front of Serenella begging to be forgiven. Her father could indeed arrange to have him shot if he wanted to, or his whole family thrown into prison if he so wished, just for insulting one of his children.

Once again incensed with rage, Giorgio made another swipe at the whimpering man but was heaved back, this time by his father who was called when the skirmish broke out.

'Don't ever touch her,' Giorgio roared. 'Don't ever bloody touch her again or I will kill you.' He placed his left forefinger under his left eye in a threatening gesture, indicating that he would be watching his opponent from now on.

'*Ti sto guardando*,' he warned.

As the workers reluctantly returned to their various posts and continued gathering their grapes, they whispered with glee about the welcome diversion the scene had created. Serenella tentatively walked up to where Giorgio was standing with his father, being given a terse reprimand.

'Giorgio,' she whispered nervously. 'Thank you.'

He turned and nodded his head. She could see a

cut above his eye where he had been hit. Taking her headscarf off, Serenella dipped it in one of the many barrels of water and gently wiped the dripping blood from his cut.

'You are very brave,' she whispered softly. 'My hero,' and kissed him impulsively on the cheek, ignoring the audible gasps of the onlookers.

Giorgio's face flushed and he winced as Serenella lightly dabbed at his injury. Aware that every eye was on them, he stepped back from the girl's hand and with a flick of his fringe he stomped off, returning to his own work. After watching his retreating figure for a few seconds, Serenella then pushed the soiled cloth into her apron pocket and also returned to her grape picking. The matter was over.

Yet between them it had just begun. For that very evening her friend, Giorgio, fortuitously came to her aid once again.

Maria-Angela had been utterly furious to be publicly told of the alarming events that had occurred at her property, whilst enjoying midday lunch at the home of her neighbour. She was especially annoyed when the story was divulged by a sneering acquaintance, who had heard every exaggerated detail from her young kitchen maid that morning. Serenella had witnessed her mother's violent outbursts before, but never once had they been directed at her. Incensed with rage to have been informed by her contemptuous neighbour, Signora Russo, of her daughter's unruliness, Maria-Angelo issued a vicious attack on her adolescent daughter.

'You were behaving like a provincial servant-girl,' she shrieked, slapping her crying daughter sharply across the face. 'Signora Russo told me the whole town is talking about it - how you kissed that dirty boy's face and threw yourself at him. You deserve to be whipped and by God you will be.'

No amount of protestations from Serenella was listened to. Nothing was more important to Maria-Angela Notarbartolo-Inglima than the respectable reputation of first herself and second, her family. That her arch enemy, Signora Russo, was the person to gleefully make known to her about the scandalous behaviour of her own daughter had stung the proud woman tremendously. It will be the gossip of the year that she had raised a daughter to behave so improperly. If it hadn't been for the gentle persuasion of her best friend, Margarita, she would have struck the unbearable Russo woman.

'*Mio amico,* don't let her trouble you,' she had whispered cautiously into Maria-Angela's ear. 'She would get so much satisfaction if you retaliate. Don't let her win.'

Maria-Angela nodded. That did the trick. She had no intention of letting Signora Russo get the better of her. Even as a child, Margarita could always calm her down during one of her terrible rages. She had always been more of a sister to the young Maria-Angela than just a childhood friend. Margarita's gentle reassurance had got the young Signorina Notarbartolo out of many situations when her temper threatened to cause conflict. Her status as being the sole heir to a fortune had turned the young girl into a spoiled woman and it was her family's wealth which prevented anybody from ever chastising her. The only person who ever could do so was Margarita.

Margarita's family, wealthy Jewish aristocrats, owned the impressive Sacca family villa at Ragusa Ibla and was renowned for their exquisite jewellery production. Margarita was a suitable choice of companion to the young noblewoman, as she was genteel and of good birth. As was the custom of the time, it was not acceptable for young women of Maria-Angela Notarbartolo's and Margarita Sacca's status to be outside alone and the two young women had been inseparable until their respective marriages. Despite their lives now being on very different paths and Margarita living on the neighbouring island of Malta, the two women still kept in contact and visited one another whenever possible.

'*Grazie* Margarita. You are saving me from yet another embarrassment,' Maria-Angela replied, clenching her fists in temper. 'But I will punish my daughter severely when I go home.'

By the time she reached Casa di Inglima her temper had only increased - feeling as she passed every window on the short journey home that people were looking out and laughing at her.

'Do you know the irreparable damage you have done to your good name?' her mother shouted, furiously. 'What man will want you when he hears of your performance?'

'I didn't do anything wrong Mama,' Serenella cried desperately. Tears stained her face which bore the red imprints of Maria-Angela's fingers.

'You didn't do anything wrong!' Maria-Angela

yelled. 'Apart from acting like a *puttana*, you were picking grapes like a disgusting farmhand. Show me your hands.' She roughly pulled her daughter's arms up and after investigating her stained palms, she once more struck Serenella hard across the face. This time the force of the blow knocked the young girl to the floor.

'You are a slut,' Maria-Angela screamed in temper. 'You are a disgrace to this family.' Blindly her arm reached for the first thing at hand - a tennis racquet. She picked it up and ignoring the screeches of her young daughter, rained the first blow down on the fragile girl cowering at her feet.

It was Serenella's screams that alerted Giorgio Cavallo who was working late in the garden.

It was he who wrenched the broken racquet out of Signora Inglima's hand and carefully lifted the almost unconscious Serenella into his strong arms.

It was his mother, Valentina, who took care of the young Signorina and saw to her severe injuries, just as the young lady had seen to her son's earlier that day.

And so began a chain of events that would change all their lives forever.

Chapter 2

Malta to Sicily. October, 2004.

Jessy descended the slope at Valletta Waterfront leading to the huge ferry bound for Sicily. Gosh, she thought, this boat is massive compared to the one that goes to Gozo. It seemed more like a ship. The doors to the hold of the ferry were open, awaiting the long line of cars queued up outside. Jessy thought it looked for all the world like an enormous shark, with its mouth waiting to gobble people up. The similarity with the smaller Gozo ferry was that people here pushed and shoved just as much to get on - exactly like they did when getting on the buses. The Maltese hadn't yet become skilled in the art of forming orderly queues.

When finally on board, the young woman sat people-watching as she sipped from her Styrofoam coffee cup. It was a favourite pastime of hers and one that always made a journey, or any time spent in waiting, go by much quicker. It was easier to do with sunglasses on also, so nobody could accuse you of staring. It was fun daydreaming about where each person was going to end up. At work? At home? On a lover's tryst? Were they happy or sad? What were their homes like – big or small? Even while on a bus going through busy towns Jessy liked looking voyeuristically into people's gardens and windows, imagining what kind of life they might be living.

On a recent occasion Jessy had been an unintentional observer of the kind of daily life she looked forward to with Salvatore, when they were married and had their own home. She had been on a bus waiting in the usual traffic jam on her journey home from work. It was dark, but only about six in the evening and there was an unusual light shower of rain at the time. Looking into the kitchen of somebody's apartment, her attention was grabbed by a domestic scene. A woman who looked quite well dressed, as though she worked in a professional job, was wearing a black suit with a red blouse that had a bow tied at the neck. Her hair was long and dark and she looked very attractive. Perhaps in her thirties, Jessy guessed. She was chopping something on a table or counter-top.

A man walked into the room. He had a beige coloured trench coat on and he had obviously been caught in the rain, as he shook his head when he entered the kitchen. Jessy was so close to their apartment window that she could see droplets of water fall off his head. The woman swung around and hugged him and they kissed on the lips - then she returned to her chopping and the man reached up to a shelf, lifted two wine glasses and placed them on a table. He stretched up to what must have been a high up cupboard or shelf and took out a dark coloured wine bottle. Jessy watched as he extracted the cork, then poured red wine into the glasses. He tipped the lady on the shoulder. She turned around once more. He gave her a glass and lifted one for himself. They clinked glasses and smiled at each other. The bus drove off.

Jessy found herself thinking back to the pair all evening, wondering if they were married or engaged or just a new couple in the early days of a romance. Had the woman invited him around for dinner? Had they children? Perhaps not, because if so where were they? In another room? No. Surely a Dad would have gone to say hello to them, just like he did his wife. Where did they both work?

Jessy passed that apartment block every day, twice a day on her way to and from work, but the bus never stopped at that exact spot again. But every day she hoped it would.

Now she sat once again watching other people.

There were several groups of families with young children running about noisily. Others, obviously tourists, excitedly ran from window to window taking photos. There were a lot of couples. Some of whom, mostly the older ones who were huddled together, sat with an arm linked into each other's, or had an arm protectively across their partner's shoulder. It made Jessy feel a bit lonely. It would have been nice to have a friendly arm draped across her own shoulder right now. The majority of the passengers seemed to be Italian. They were easy to spot by the simple fact that they were louder than anybody else and waved their hands around a lot more. Franco did that, but then he was half Italian.

I don't know much Italian, Jessy thought. Well, except for the odd word that I picked up from Salvatore and Franco. *Certo, Mio Dio*. But the Vellas didn't speak Italian frequently in Malta. Franco wasn't completely fluent. He mostly just spoke phrases he had picked up from both his Italian mother and his Italian wife. The only time she heard Salvu speak it was when he was arguing with his older brother, Marco. She guessed that was because they didn't want her to understand. Their Italian gestures were quite expressive with arms and hands waving about dramatically. Franco sometimes mumbled in Italian, especially when he was worried or upset about something. Thinking about Franco caused Jessy to sigh anxiously. He didn't seem to think her impulsive decision to be with Salvatore today was a good idea.

'You won't know anybody,' he had said. 'Salvu will be too busy to introduce you to all the extended Inglima family.'

Jessy had felt agitated then and a bit put out. 'He is my fiancé. I should be with him at a family funeral and I am going,' she'd said stubbornly.

Franco had looked at her intently then, trying to read her mind with his eyes and causing Jessy to blush a little. It was as though he knew she was using the death of Marius Inglima as an excuse to meet Salvatore's Sicilian family. Franco had said he wasn't going to make the trip to Ragusa, citing his reason was due to the fact that he and the *famiglia Inglima* did not see eye to eye. The last time he had seen any of his in-laws was when they had arrived *en masse* to Malta in the company of funeral directors, after the death of Franco's wife Serenella. They had come without being asked, to take her body home to be buried in the family vault in Sicily. Only two of Franco and Serenella's children kept in touch with their mother's side of the family – the eldest, Marco, and Salvatore – the youngest. It was as though there was some big family secret which prevented Salvatore ever taking Jessy to Sicily, a place she had been longing to visit with him.

An old woman next to Jessy tipped her on the arm and asked a question in Italian. Jessy smiled kindly and answered, *'Non capisco,'* but the woman who was entirely dressed in black, pushed a plastic container of *arancinis* in her direction and indicated that Jessy help herself. *'Mangia,'* she insisted and Jessy understood the word 'to eat'. She nodded enthusiastically and lifted the smallest *arancini* out of the box, hoping that it did not contain meat. The woman smiled an almost toothless grin at her. *'Brava ragazza,'* she said. *'Sono buone.'* Jessy bit into the still warm rice ball and nodded in agreement. With relief she could taste that the *arancini* was a vegetarian one of fried aubergines, with onion and peas.

To Jessy's amusement the old lady watched her as she ate, nodding her head and smiling all the while, until Jessy eventually pushed the last morsel into her mouth. Handing over a paper napkin the old woman continued to nod her head and smile, '*Sono buone? Sono buone*?' she asked over and over and Jessy nodded back. '*Si, molto bene. Grazie.*' Perhaps, Jessy thought, I do know more Italian than I realised. Eventually the old lady gave her attention to the other people in her group. Jessy returned her gaze to the window and the sea outside, feeling full now with the delicious unexpected snack she had just enjoyed.

The sea looked rough, but probably only because of the motion the boat was causing as it sailed the sixty miles across the Mediterranean Sea to Sicily. In the distance the water looked quite calm. I feel like I could simply sit here forever, Jessy thought, watching the ebb and flow of the water, cocooned on this ferry and at this moment not having to do anything but just sit and think and be.

A few hours later Jessy waved and smiled at the noisy family group she'd met on the ferry, as they rowdily walked towards a parking area after they disembarked. The whole family waved back, as though she was one of them. It felt nice. Then she looked about and with horror, realised that she had no idea where she was, only that it was Pozzallo Port somewhere in the south of Sicily. The docks became quickly deserted, with everybody except her seeming to know where they were going. Most people had driven off the boat in cars or had one waiting at the car-park. Others were picked up and a few had bicycles or motorbikes chained up waiting to be reclaimed. Soon the only people about where those who seemed to work at the port.

There must be a bus stop, Jessy surmised and began to walk in the same direction the cars had taken. Turning a corner that led onto a wide dusty street, she shrieked at being almost sprayed by a young boy relieving himself against a wall. A car was parked next to him and a young woman got out. She yanked the boy inside, apologising profusely and loudly to Jessy as she pushed him in the car. It was the same family again. Before she knew it, Jessy was sitting squashed between what seemed like ten people in the back seat of a stifling hot car, which was now driving at full speed to God knows where.

'*Dove*?' she recognised that word. She was being asked where she was going. Jessy pulled the torn page that she had scribbled on that morning out of her bag. She handed it to the woman who had just rescued her feet from an unpleasant accident. The address was read out and it seemed everybody including the young boy knew where it was. They also appeared to know that the place was a house of mourning. Immediately they all began to bless themselves and shake their clasped hands up and down really fast in front of Jessy until she began to feel dizzy. Also, if the hand signals and boisterous arguing were anything to go by, it seemed they all had their own personal opinions on how to get there. Jessy thought she should have felt terrified. For all she knew they could be kidnappers or murderers. Instead she felt strangely safe and shyly glanced from one animated face to the other while a heated discussion took place.

It was difficult to see out the window and it was beginning to grow dark. The only scenery Jessy could make out seemed to be of terrifyingly windy roads and sharp bends. After about half an hour or so, through the windscreen in front, she could see a town full of glittering lights perched high on a hill and she worried that perhaps nobody really knew where they were going. Eventually the car came to a screeching halt and parked. With some difficulty Jessy managed to squeeze herself out onto a narrow road. After several minutes of waving, some kissing and fervent handshaking, she was alone.

Looking upwards Jessy recognised the outside of the building from photographs. So this was the Inglima family home. Another reason why she knew this was the correct address was because of the poster plastered on the wall outside, with an image of an elderly man under the name 'Marius Inglima'. Jessy knew from having seen similar posters in Malta, that the writing in Italian would contain information about his funeral. She pulled the bell on the wall outside. A few minutes later the door opened and a young woman dressed as a maid stood there. Jessy was stunned. An actual maid! She knew the family was rich, but to have a staff member answer the door was unexpected.

'I am here to see Salvatore,' she explained, wondering if the maid would understand her.

The door opened wider. '*Si. Avanti,*' the maid replied. '*La famiglia sta manciando,*' she continued. Jessy understood that she was to go in and something was said about the family eating.

'*Come ti chiami?*' the maid asked, without turning around.

'Jessica,' she answered, thankful that she could understand that question.

Suddenly she began to think that perhaps Franco was right. It all seemed like a great idea back in Malta to travel to Sicily and be with Salvu for his uncle's funeral, but now that she was here Jessy began to wish she was still in Malta. Trying not to gasp at the opulence of the Inglima home, she stared around whilst following the neatly clad woman through the stately hall. Finally they reached a set of high cream doors elaborately decorated with brightly painted cherubs, on the left of a wide staircase. After knocking first, the maid entered the room and spoke rapidly in Italian before ushering the nervous Jessy inside.

Salvatore's mouth gaped wide open when he saw the surprising guest. 'Hi Salvo,' Jessy said, smiling uncertainly.

They were eating. Perhaps twelve or more people were seated around a table that was laden with several dishes of delicious looking food. The cacophony of chatter which could be heard when the door was opened, now quietened into a deadly hush. All eyes turned to see who had just joined them. Jessy stayed standing at the doorway, suddenly feeling very shy and uncharacteristically tongue-tied.

Salvatore recovered himself quickly from the

shock. 'Everyone. This is Jessica McGuill. Remember…'

But he didn't need to finish his sentence. They all seemed to know who Jessy was and for the second time that evening, she found herself smothered in kisses and handshakes from people who were complete strangers to her.

'So this is Jessy,' a voice declared in English from somewhere. She could see a very tall, very old man stand up from where he was seated at the end of the long rectangular table. Again the room fell silent.

'*Zio*,' Salvatore said, ushering Jessy towards where the old man was standing. 'Jessy, this is my Uncle Angelo Inglima.'

They shook hands. The man's hands were the size of the small shovels she used when gardening. He looked the young woman up and down and Jessy felt like she was being inspected for an auction. It made her feel quite uncomfortable.

'Sit,' the man ordered, then clicked his fingers towards another young woman who was already beginning to stand up. 'Francesca, go and get Martina to set a place,' he ordered.

Within seconds Jessy took the vacated seat and an empty plate was put in front of her. Looking around the table she failed to see Salvatore. Where had he gone? Instead there was just a sea of unfamiliar faces all staring in her direction and Jessy once again had an overwhelming wish she'd stayed in Malta. This plan was beginning to seem more and more like a very bad idea. Answering that yes, she would like a portion of whatever was in the huge white serving dish next to her, Jessy took the plate out of the maid's outstretched hand and proceeded to eat. All around her the animated conversation, or conversations, continued and she was relieved to see Salvatore returning to the room.

'Well this is a nice surprise,' he whispered into her ear, as he took the empty seat next to hers. Jessy wondered where the girl who had been sitting in her chair had gone.

'I feel scared to death,' she whispered back. 'I didn't think there would be so many people here.' But Salvatore had no chance to reply as an animated quarrel, or what seemed to be one, had begun on the other end of the table. It was in Italian and all Jessy could make out was the word '*Inglese*'. Her face reddened, horrified to think that they were arguing about her. Confused, Jessy looked at Salvatore, while everybody except her broke into laughter.

'They are trying to decide who has the best English to chat with you,' Salvatore explained, 'and I said that I did. But *Zio* Angelo just told us all that if anybody is going to talk to the pretty woman it will be him.'

Jessy blushed and looked up coyly at the old man seated next to her. '*Grazie*,' she said, and was greeted with another outburst of laughter at whatever his response was. She raised her eyebrows at Salvatore for a translation.

'He said he might be able to speak in English,' Salvatore replied, still laughing, 'but when he talks to pretty women he still thinks like an Italian man!' Jessy blushed even redder and grinned up at this roguish Uncle Angelo.

'I am glad I can't read minds then,' she retorted boldly, which was met with even more laughter from those that could understand her cheeky reply.

Feeling a bit more at ease, Jessy discreetly went around the table with her eyes, trying to guess who was who. She had heard various names from Salvatore of people on his mother's side of the family. Uncle Angelo was one name that came up all the time. She knew he was Salvatore's mother's eldest living brother and head of the Inglima family. It was the youngest brother,

Marius, who had just died and it was Angelo's home that she was now in, which had belonged to the Inglima family for centuries. Jessy also knew that other family members lived in the same house. Surely not everybody lived here, Jessy wondered, for she had counted eleven apart from herself in the room, although the Francesca girl hadn't come back. That would have now made it thirteen present for dinner.

After the meal, coffee was passed around and Jessy accepted the small espresso cup handed to her. Like the other dishes used during the meal, this little cup and saucer looked antique. This was a beautiful room too - like something you would see in 'Hello' magazine showing a millionaire's Italian villa. Magnificent art covered the walls and the ceiling even had fresco paintings like in a church. A huge gold cross also hung on a white wall, which unlike the others had nothing else on it, just the massive crucifix dominating the room. Jessy remembered how Salvatore had told her that his mother's family was very religious.

There were nine men and just three women. No children in the room, which was a bit unusual. Everybody was dressed in black and the women's hair and makeup was impeccable. Thankfully, they were all very friendly towards their unexpected guest and appeared to be on very intimate terms with each other. There was a lot of conversation and occasionally Jessy saw people dab at wet eyes, obviously talking about the deceased. Although Jessy didn't understand most of what was said when they forgot to try and speak English, she had been included in every conversation. All in all, it seemed exactly the type of noisy, close Italian family her fiancé had described.

It was quite impossible to remember each person's name. Looking at the woman who was handing the empty plates to the maid, Jessy recalled that she was Maria. That name, the same as her own mother's, was easy to remember. But where she came in the family, Jessy had no idea. I'm sure I will find out in time, she thought, who everybody is and how they are related to Salvatore. Someday they are all going to be my family too.

She nodded, when catching Salvatore's eye she saw him mouth the words, 'You okay?' in her direction. He then stood up at the same time Uncle Angelo began to rise from his seat.

'Yes,' she mouthed in return. 'I'm fine.' At that moment she was.

Her offers of helping to clear the vast amount of dishes from the table was rejected fervently.

'We have a maid to do that, *grazie Dio,*' Maria told her, rolling her eyes and lighting a cigarette. 'I wouldn't like to face this now.'

'Oh, is the maid that girl Francesca?' Jessy asked. 'The one who didn't come back to the table?'

'No.'

Jessy looked behind her chair in surprise, where the girl in question was now standing. She hadn't noticed her return to the room. The young woman's dark eyes were flashing with obvious insult.

'I am not the maid,' she stated coldly, then launched into a flow of words spoken so rapidly and angrily, that Jessy had no hope of following.

'I am sorry … I …' Jessy said, standing up and trying to apologise for her mistake. Instead she was shot with a contemptuous look, before Francesca flounced dramatically out of the room.

Jessy glanced towards Salvatore hoping he would come to her aid, but he was not looking her way. He was already heading in the direction of the door Francesca had just stormed through.

'Don't worry,' Maria said, putting her hand on

Jessy's shoulder at seeing it slump. 'Francesca can be hot-headed. It is in the Inglima blood.'

Chapter 3

Ragusa Ibla, Sicily. August, 1939.

'She needs to be admitted to hospital immediately.'

Doctor Moretti shut his medical bag with a click and looked around at the sumptuous grandeur of the Inglima master bedroom, where the young Signorina was being cared for after her collapse at breakfast. Serenella had seen the dining room sway around her before she fainted, frightening the other children into screams of terror. Her elder brother, Angelo, hastily rushed to her side and loosened her clothing, while a petrified maid ran for her mistress. The family doctor was immediately summoned.

'Open the window. It is much too stuffy in here with this blasted heat. Signora Inglima, I need to speak with you privately,' the doctor ordered.

His tone was brusque and the older woman felt her face flame. She knew that he was going to enquire about the marks on her daughter's face, as well as the welts on her arms and back, caused by her own firm hand.

'Indeed Doctor,' she answered, amiably. 'We can talk in the study.'

Bartolomeo Moretti had not risen to the ranks he had in the field of medicine, without having been a recipient over the years of various favours. In Sicily there was a tacit understanding that certain courtesies would be adhered to in the upper classes and he was about to indulge.

'Signora Inglima,' he said, bowing quickly to indicate his respect for her status in Ragusa. She nodded her head slightly in acquiescence, already aware that she had to assent to whatever request he was about to solicit.

'Your daughter is very ill. I also suspect that several of her ribs are broken and this is obviously affecting her already weakened chest. Her injuries are consistent with a vicious attack and it is within my professional duty to report it to the authorities.' Holding his hand up to silence the woman who suddenly looked alarmed, he continued. 'I have heard the nasty rumours in town concerning how the young Signorina came to be so badly hurt and I have a suggestion to make.'

Doctor Moretti looked perceptively at the shame-faced woman.

'I submit to anything you propose for my poor

daughter,' Maria-Angela replied. Both were aware of what this statement entailed. It meant that in order for the doctor to keep quiet about the brutal attack that she had made against her own daughter culminating in her collapse, Signora Inglima would give him whatever he asked. Her own and her family's reputation were at stake. For this reason Doctor Moretti was prepared to take full advantage of the situation for a particular cause he had in mind.

'I believe that the young lady requires the sea air and much rest. The complication of broken ribs is dangerous for somebody with her condition. She will need to convalesce for quite some time. Months perhaps. Possibly even a full year.

'Of course Doctor. Where do you suggest?'

'I propose the *Sanatorio della Madonna della Sofferenza* at Marina di Ragusa. The sea air there will be beneficial for her weak chest and the Sanatorium of Our Lady of the Suffering has a highly trained nursing staff, who practice utmost discretion. Of course, I will need to be there to supervise her care.'

'Of course Doctor.'

'Unfortunately,' he added. 'It is a shame that the sanatorium is soon to close due to lack of funding.' He raised his eyebrow cynically.

Signora Inglima inclined her head in agreement. 'I will speak with my husband.'

Bartolomeo Moretti smiled in acknowledgement as he began to move towards the door. He paused and without turning around to face the Signora he said, 'If I had the title of *Professore* I would have a greater influence in the care of the patients at the sanatorium.'

Signora Inglima bit her lip.

'I will see to it Doctor,' she replied diplomatically, closing the door firmly behind him.

***

Marina di Ragusa, Sicily. September, 1939.

'I can't believe you are here,' she shrieked, gently putting her arms around the delighted young man's neck. He smelt the same. A faint, sweet aroma of male sweat and soil. He always smelt like the garden after a rainfall, but with the constant, added perfumed odour of fresh lemons.

Giorgio grinned down at the happy face of the young Signorina he had been missing so much. The last time he had seen Serenella was when he had rescued her from the vicious beating at the hands of her mother. Without speaking a word to Signora Inglima after he had stormed into the room on hearing Serenella's screams, he had simply picked the young woman up tenderly in his arms and carried her to his mother, in the large kitchens of the Inglima pallazzo. It had taken all his strength not to return a similar beating to her vile mother.

'How can she do that to her own daughter?' he had cried to his mother, who was murmuring words of comfort to the moaning girl. 'It was as though she was possessed by some evil spirit. Her eyes looked dark with hatred.'

Valentina had clicked her tongue as she daubed gently at the open cuts on Serenella's face. 'The *padrona* has always had a wicked temper,' she replied. 'It is not the first time I have cleaned up somebody's injuries after one of her attacks.'

'She should be locked up,' Giorgio declared. 'A nasty, vicious woman like that should never be allowed to have children.'

Now Giorgio was thrilled to see how happy and healthy Serenella looked. 'Well,' he replied, laughing as he placed his arms around her slender waist.

'Somebody has to keep an eye on you. You look so healthy and I don't see any marks on your face,' he said, softly stroking her cheek with the palm of his hand.

'But how? How did you end up here? Who hired you?' Serenella asked quizzically, noticing that Giorgio looked much more grown up since she had last seen him. He had a moustache now and his forearms were more muscular. He was taller and broader too. He was a man and the knowledge both excited and saddened her.

'The kind Doctor Moretti,' he replied.

'Doctor Moretti? Why?'

Giorgio brushed some fallen leaves off a white wooden garden seat and motioned Serenella to sit down beside him. Casually he took her tiny hand in his, which contrasted with his rough tanned one.

'I was dismissed by your father after that incident in the vineyard.'

Serenella gasped. 'No,' she said defensively. 'But that was *my* fault. Not yours. Your family has worked for ours for years. Before I was even born. Doesn't that account for something?'

Giorgio shook his head. 'It doesn't matter now

whose fault it was. You know what your father is like – appearances and the family name are all that matter. My parents were permitted to continue being employed by the household even though I had been discharged. I think your mother insisted, out of loyalty, that they remained - but they didn't want to, out of their own loyalty to me.'

'I can't believe it,' Serenella whispered. 'Your parents are more like family than employees. At least, to me they are.'

'It turned out for the best,' Giorgio replied. 'Papa is looking forward to the job here. He will be chief gardener with a full say in the running of the gardens, which are a mess by the way, according to his standards. Mama is delighted with the house they have given us. Which I also may add, is just there.' He pointed to a small limestone house with emerald green shutters, just at the end of the walled grounds, matching those on the sanatorium where Serenella had been staying for the last week.

'But that's wonderful,' she cried. 'You are right beside me. But why did Doctor Moretti give your father the job? Is he friends with your family? Do my family know they are here?'

Giorgio shook his head, laughing at her barrage of questions. 'Who knows? Who cares? Come on. Mama is eager to see how you are,' and he held out his hand which she eagerly took.

Signora Valentina kissed the thin girl warmly. '*Mio Dio*, you need to eat more,' she cried, scanning Serenella's slim frame. 'What do they feed you in there?' she asked, nodding her head in the direction of the sanatorium. 'Never mind. Soon you will be fattened like a calf for market.'

Serenella laughed. 'I have missed your food. The nurses have to do the cooking here because we have no chef. The hospital was going to be closed you know and most of the staff had been laid off, but now it's not,' she added knowingly, not noticing the discerning glance that Valentina threw her son.

'That will soon change,' Giorgio declared. 'Mama is the new cook.'

'I am so happy,' beamed Serenella. 'That is such good news. Oh, I can't believe this. It is like a dream – having you all here like this.' Embarrasingly she felt her eyes moisten. 'Now I never want to get better in case I am sent home,' she added and they replied with much laughter and more loving hugs.

Often we are not privy to how events come about. Naively we accept matters without asking any questions. Serenella believed Doctor Moretti had heard about Giorgio's family being unemployed and took pity on them. She assumed he perhaps had also heard through his work in the sanatorium, that there were positions for both a gardener and a cook. She did not wonder at the correlation. That she appeared to be the only patient at the sanatorium also did not cause her any concern. Wasn't it about to be closed? So naturally patients would have been hospitalised elsewhere. And how fortunate that 'somebody' had decided to fund the sanatorium once again and how lucky that it was her good friends that got the jobs. Serenella agreed when her parents visited that she wouldn't mention that her family's former employees were now working at the sanatorium - supposing to avoid any unpleasant memories.

Doctor Moretti was gratified on receiving his certificate of *Professore di Medicina* in the post. He was even more gratified to be informed that a private account had been set up at the *Banca Della Sicilia* in his name, by Signor Giovanni Inglima.

Signora Inglima would not be arrested for the near

manslaughter of her teenage daughter. The doctor stated on Serenella's medical forms that she suffered from anaemia, causing iron deficiency and shortness of breath which resulted in her bruised skin and inevitable collapse.

Nobody questioned the re-opening of The Sanatorium of Our Lady of Suffering in Marina di Ragusa, or why it never seemed to have any patients apart from the pretty dark haired girl sometimes seen in its beautifully restored gardens.

Chapter 4

Ragusa Ibla, Sicily. October, 2004.

The Sicilians certainly knew how to do death in style, even orchestrating it to rain at exactly the right moments. Every single person was dressed in an expensive black outfit by an Italian designer, managing to make this sombre occasion into more of a display of fashion than a funeral service. Men looked attractive in black woollen coats with tailored suits underneath, their white shirts complimenting tanned skin, with carefully groomed hair and beards. But Jessy couldn't take her eyes off the women. The sound of gold bracelets jangling on arms and the clatter of towering high heels had made her look around, as the female family and friends of the deceased, Marius Inglima, entered the Duomo of San Giorgio, Ragusa's Parish Church.

Immediately Jessy brushed invisible fluff off her own black suit and pushed an untidy strand of hair behind her ear. Some of the ladies even wore black mantillas on their heads, like in the olden days. The women's style was breathtaking. Figure hugging suits and dresses sailed past her in a haze of expensive perfume. Gucci, Versace, Louis Vuitton handbags were draped over arms and flowing scarves trailed around necks also adorned with heavy gold necklaces. All the women were crying loudly, but no tears could be seen with the over-sized dark sunglasses they all wore, even inside the ancient church. Clutching each others arms the women were ushered into seats on one side, leaving the men on the other.

Salvatore sat in the prominent position of front row with his brother Marco and Uncle Angelo. On the opposite side of the aisle, the front seat was taken up by Maria, who Jessy now knew was a first cousin of Angelo's, her daughter Marianna and grand-daughter Francesca, (with whom Jessy had had the uncomfortable exchange the night before). Again, there were no children. Wondering who the other women were, Jessy sat half way down the small church on the side she now realised was for the men. Looking around, she saw that every pew was completely full. The Inglimas had been a well-known and respected family for generations. Angelo Inglima was the last of his generation. He was now in his late eighties and in ill-health. Marco and Salvatore were the only male descendents, as their mother Serenella had been the only family member to have had children.

A procession of priests, led by a bishop, came out of the sacristy onto the beautiful baroque altar, as a male soloist began to sing. It was not a song that Jessy had ever heard before and she didn't understand most of the words, but the haunting air made tears fall from her own eyes. They were not tears for Marius Inglima, whom she had never met, but tears in memory of the last funeral she had attended, for her grandmother Ana. Looking forward, she could see the top of Salvatore's head as he stood next to his uncle. He hadn't invited her to sit with the family, although she had travelled in the long black funeral car with them to the Duomo. Jessy had the unwelcome feeling that her boyfriend wasn't completely thrilled at her impulsive trip to Sicily yesterday, to be at his side.

***

It had been almost an hour following his dash after Francesca the previous night, before Salvatore returned - at which stage Jessy had been struggling to keep awake, as she sat on a terrace overlooking the wonderful views of Ragusa Ibla. From her position she could see right down into a wide piazza with a wonderful old church at one end. The church was illuminated by lights that showed its magnificent spires soaring majestically into the sky.

'Where did you go?' she had asked him, as he took a seat opposite her and sighed.

'I needed to sort something out for Angelo,' he'd replied.

'It looked like you were going after that Francesca girl.'

Salvatore raised his head. 'Francesca? No. Why do you say that?'

'Because you went after her when she left the room, when I stupidly asked if she was the maid. I feel mortified about that,' Jessy said, her cheeks reddening at the memory.

Salvatore shrugged. 'Oh, she will get over it.'

'Do you mind my being here?' Jessy asked, half afraid of what the answer might be. Because if he was annoyed about her turning up at his uncle's house unexpectedly, she was still stuck here until morning.

Once again he shrugged non-commitedly. 'What made you come over?' he asked. 'You didn't mention you would be travelling here when we spoke this morning.'

So he *is* annoyed, Jessy realised. 'I just thought I should support you. Be here for you.' She gazed out over the panoramic view of orange roofed houses which looked as though they were piled one on top of the other. Lights began to be turned off from many windows and the air was chilly. Glancing at her watch, Jessy couldn't believe that it was almost midnight.

'Where will I sleep?' she asked.

To her exasperation Salvatore shrugged once again.

'There are lots of empty bedrooms.'

She wanted to shake him. 'But which one will I sleep in? Will it be with you?' she asked.

He looked horrified. 'You can't sleep with me. Not here,' he said. 'Come on. I'll take you to a room.'

She followed him in silence along several marble tiled hallways until finally he pushed open a door, looked inside, then gestured for her to enter. The room was quite long and very narrow. There were medieval slits cut into the walls as windows, but there was a comfortable looking bed and the room seemed quite airy with very high ceilings.

'There is a bathroom at the end of the corridor,'

Salvatore said and yawned dramatically, stretching his arms over his head, as though letting her know he was exhausted.

Placing her bag on the bed, Jessy put her arms around him and he circled his own arms about her waist, then kissed the top of her head before saying goodnight. Jessy felt her heart sink as she watched the door close behind him. Something was definitely wrong and she didn't think it was the passing of his Uncle Marius that was the problem.

***

The next morning, as the funeral cortege wound its way to the cemetery, Jessy noticed people stop and bless themselves, just like in Ireland. This time she went in the car with the female relatives. Marianna had lit a cigarette as soon as they got into the back seat. Maria had taken a compact mirror out of her Gucci handbag and began touching up her red lipstick. Francesca on the other hand was tapping a message into her sleek mobile phone. As the car approached the cemetery entrance Jessy couldn't believe that the women, as if on cue, began to suddenly sob loudly as the driver opened the door and they got out, once again clutching each others arms as though for support. Unbelievable, she thought, surprised at their insincerity.

Also as though it was prearranged, the sky suddenly darkened as Marius Inglima's decorative coffin was lifted out of the hearse and carried to the ornate family vault. Outside were plaques inscribed with Italian print, including names of those buried inside. Jessy saw the name of Serenella Margarita Rosalia Inglima Vella. Oh, she thought, both Salvatore's sisters names. She had supposed that Salvatore's sister, Margarita, had been named after Franco's mother. Then she recalled that Salvatore had told her both his grandmothers had been friends as girls. Maria-Angela, if I recall, Jessy thought. Salvatore had confided how he had been born after the death of his grandmother, when his mother was almost fifty. Franco said he had been the only baby his mother had ever really shown any affection for. Jessy thought this was terribly sad for his older brother and twin sisters.

Salvatore, along with his brother Marco, Uncle Angelo and four other men who had been at the previous night's dinner, were the only ones who went inside the family vault. When they came out, closing the elegant gates behind them, people who had been huddled outside under large black umbrellas began to disperse and make their way to waiting cars. Jessy looked at the three Inglima women who were also walking in the direction of their car, then looked over at Salvatore who was in conversation with the other men. She caught his eye and he nodded towards the women. Jessy bowed her head under the deluge of rain, wishing she had brought an umbrella of her own and also wishing once more that she had stayed in Malta like Franco had suggested.

There was a lavish banquet held at the Inglima palazzo afterwards. Long trestle tables were laid out under a covered pergola in the courtyard and waiting staff served so many variations of courses that Jessy felt she was going to burst afterwards. Like at a wedding, the top table was for family members, where this time, Jessy was included. It seemed as though the whole town had been invited and Uncle Angelo's meal had been interrupted many times by people coming up to give their condolences. Jessy smirked, thinking it was like a scene from the Godfather movie. Especially the way almost everybody handed him an envelope, presumably a sympathy card. Salvatore also was frequently approached and Jessy watched as he gave the customary kiss on both cheeks to each guest.

Jessy was seated at the far end of the table, next to Maria. At the other far end sat Francesca, next to Marianna. Jessy felt as though both she and Francesca were almost like bookends. Neither she or the other young woman, who was probably Jessy's own age, had spoken to each other since the night before, despite being in close proximity all day. On seeing Francesca at breakfast the next morning Jessy had said *Buon Giorno,* but her greeting was determinedly ignored. She didn't bother to try again.

A face in the crowd caught her eye. Then another. She smiled. It was the family that had given her the lift yesterday. Jessy grinned widely and waved, relieved to have found some friendly faces. They didn't see her. Immediately she rose from her chair and made her way to where the old lady waited in a line to offer condolences to Angelo Inglima. She was clutching the hand of the little boy who had also been with the group yesterday. It was he who noticed Jessy first.

'*Nonna, Nonna,*' he shouted, pulling at his grandmother's arm. '*E la signora Inglese,*' he squealed, pointing over at Jessy who was by now almost at his side.

'*Ah, si, si,*' the old lady replied, then launched into a stream of Italian that Jessy could not understand. The woman had gripped Jessy's arm and seemed intent on taking her with them to the top table, to also give her condolences. Jessy gestured towards her seat, trying to explain that she was part of the funeral party, while all the time the old woman held tightly on to her hand.

'*Nonna,*' a voice said out of nowhere. With relief, Jessy looked up to see the mother of the young boy whom she had also met yesterday.

'Please,' the woman said. 'My grandmother has no English whatsoever. Let me translate for you.'

Jessy laughed. 'Good to see you again Alessia.' She was glad she had remembered the name. 'I wanted to say hello, but it seems I am being taken along to give my condolences also - but I am with the family.'

Alessia explained to her grandmother who reluctantly dropped Jessy's hand.

'She said to come over and join our table, until she gets back.'

Jessy looked over to where Alessia pointed, then glanced over at the top table where Salvatore was once again greeting a guest. Maria was engrossed in conversation with one of the black suited men, one Jessy didn't recognise - and Francesca was glaring daggers in her direction. 'Okay,' she replied. 'I'd love to.'

Alessia introduced everybody to Jessy, then added something in Italian. 'I was just telling them how some of us met you yesterday on the ferry and then gave you a lift,' she explained. 'We didn't realise you were one of the family. We thought perhaps one of the staff to be honest. We are old neighbours of the Inglimas. We are the Cavallo family and that old lady, Nonna as we know her, is Annunciatia Cavallo – her parents once worked for the Inglima family.'

Jessy laughed. 'I am not one of the family,' she replied. 'I am engaged to Salvatore - Angelo Inglima's nephew.' Mistaking their look of confusion for misinterpretation, Jessy accepted a glass of red wine and agreed when one of the men at the table voiced the opinion that the Inglimas sure knew how to throw a party.

'*Saluti*,' they chorused and Jessy clinked glasses with the family, feeling for the first time in Sicily that she was welcome there.

Chapter 5

Italy. June, 1940.

As May gave way to June and the warm Sicilian sun grew hotter, the Inglima family were once again making plans to leave for Italy. Serenella needed to be fetched from the seaside town of Marina di Ragusa, over an hour's journey away. A driver was sent to collect the young lady. She was not to be taken to her home in Ragusa, but deposited at Catania on the east coast, where the rest of the household would meet her at the busy harbour town. This slight did not go unnoticed by Serenella. Despite the two visits by her parents to the sanatorium in the last nine months, Serenella was quite aware that it was more out of a sense of duty than the fact that they missed her. She was now classed as a troublesome child and their affections toward her had changed irrevocably.

Maria-Angela found her daughter sullen and distant. Signore Inglima no longer looked on her fondly as a loving daughter, but instead as a wanton, rebellious young woman who needed to be handled firmly. On their first visit to Marina di Ragusa at Christmas, they had remarked that Serenella admittedly looked much better. She had put on weight and Signora Inglima had audibly gasped when she saw her daughter. She had developed into a beautiful young woman. Her hair hung loose, which Maria-Angela immediately reprimanded her for - but her face was luminous. She looked quite stunning. Her skinny frame had changed into curves and her mother realised she needed to buy her daughter clothes more befitting a young lady and no longer clothes for a school-girl.

The visit was strained. Coffee and cakes were laid out in a sunny dining room overlooking the Mediterranean sea. The conversation was stilted and after initial enquiries about her health, they lapsed into an uncomfortable silence, punctuated only by the stirring of spoons and sounds of the waves crashing against the shoreline outside. Afterwards, Serenella was told *verbatim* how the conversation had gone between Doctor Moretti and her parents, by Valentina Cavallo who had unashamedly listened from outside the doctor's surgery door.

'Doctor Moretti told them you needed to stay here

another couple of months,' she told Serenella. 'He said that the winter air in the city was not good for you and they seemed content to leave you here.'

Serenella breathed a sigh of relief. She had been terrified at the thought of being sent back to Ragusa and away from Giorgio and his family. After dinner, Serenella was permitted to have an evening walk, or *passeggiate* along the seafront with Giorgio. As chaperons, Valentina and Carlo Cavallo would both walk a short distance behind, discreetly ignoring when the two young people's hands intertwined.

Of course as Giorgio's parents, not to mind his being their only son, the Cavallos had serious concerns about his relationship with Signorina Inglima. However, her innocent misdemeanour in the vineyard meant one thing – she would no longer be a suitable match for any young man from a respectable Sicilian family. Instead, she most likely would be married off to a widower friend of her father's, someone who would be eager to accept a young bride despite her questionable conduct. The only other alternative was she would be obliged to enter a convent. In both of these cases a handsome dowry would accompany her. Both Valentina and Carlo loved Serenella as a daughter and would not want this to be her fate. For this reason they were ready to accept any repercussions from the Inglima family when their son decided he wanted to make her his wife. With the Cavallos under the protection of Doctor Moretti, there was not much the Inglima family could do. They too were now beholden to him. However, as happens often in life, a series of events conspired to change the course of people's destinies.

On Saturday the 1st June 1940, Giorgio Cavallo accepted his conscription papers from the Italian army. He received the official green postcard by registered post. Giorgio was fortunate that he received the postcard in time. As few people in Ragusa knew where the Cavallos now lived, the postman had a difficult task in locating him. Giorgio was to attend a medical examination over a period of three days in Ragusa, beginning that very afternoon.

After discussing with his parents, the young man decided that he would marry Serenella Inglima on his return from the medical examination and before his compulsory two year military service began. He did not inform Serenella of his plan, as he first wished to purchase the ring he had been saving to buy while in the city of Ragusa. The Cavallos hastily packed some belongings and left Marina di Ragusa by horse and cart for the military barracks in Ragusa. Valentina and Carlo would use the opportunity while their son was having his medical assessment to visit their daughter and other relatives.

On the afternoon of 1st June, an elderly gardener at the sanatorium succumbed to a sudden and fatal heart attack. The letter he had been asked to deliver to the young signorina in the sanatorium was found several days later in his small workman's hut and returned to the Cavallo home. Giorgio swore when he received it.

On the morning of 2nd June, Signore Inglima made a phonecall to the sanatorium to inform Doctor Moretti that he was taking his daughter to Italy for the summer. He did not tell him that it was because she was needed to help his wife with the younger children.

Doctor Moretti, needing some time off from his professional duties, for his other interests, agreed – but he insisted that Serenella needed to return to the sanatorium in August. Signore Inglima gladly concurred.

On the afternoon of 2nd June, Serenella was informed by her doctor that she was being collected the next morning to make the journey to the harbour town of Catania. Distressed at having to leave so suddenly, she quickly went to the small limestone house at the end of the walled garden, where she was met with a locked door.

On the evening of 3rd June, Giorgio and his parents returned to Marina di Ragusa. Entering the small house, they almost missed the envelope pushed under their door. It was for Giorgio. He flung the letter Serenella had written him on the table in exasperation after reading it. Beside it he placed the small red velvet box with her ring inside.

'I will have to wait until August,' he said sadly to his sympathetic parents.

Meanwhile inside the car, Serenella gazed out from the back window. Under her blouse was the birthday present Giorgio had given her in April. It swayed on its chain to the rhythm of the black motorcar as it sped along the dusty Sicilian roads, en route to Catania and a ferry bound for Italy.

Chapter 6

Malta. March, 2003.

Neil had sounded quite anxious on the phone. The whole conversation was very mysterious and Jessy felt more irritated than excited about meeting her half-brother here in Malta again. Her questions about what it was all about were answered cryptically by Neil, saying that he would tell her when they met. Then he told her to keep it a secret before ending the call rather abruptly. Jessy stood in the kitchen, just looking down at the phone still in her hand, before Franco walked in and asked if she was alright. Jessy jumped when she heard the elderly man's voice and put her mobile down on the dining table.

The Azure Window, Gozo's famous attraction, wasn't that easy to get to. It was even harder for Neil. He would have to fly to Malta from San Francisco where he'd been visiting his mother for the last five weeks. This would include a stopover in London, then a bus from Malta International Airport to the harbour at Cirkewwa and a ferry to Malta's neighbouring island of Gozo. He'd then have to get to Dwejra where the famous Gozitan landmark was situated. Jessy would need to take the ferry from Malta too. So why had he picked there, she wondered? Was it because it was a poignant place for both of them? Neil had been her knight in shining armour when they were on Gozo in January. He had helped her when she had stood, completely frozen with fear on that precipitous cliff face, frightened to death of falling into the turbulent sea below.

'You look like you have seen a ghost,' Franco said worriedly. 'Are you okay *imħabba tiegħi*?' he asked.

Jessy picked up the tea-towel and continued with the dishes she had been drying before the strange phone-call.

'Yes. I'm fine. It was just a wrong number,' she answered cheerfully, feeling a bit guilty telling a lie. But since Neil has asked that she kept his visit to herself, she had no choice.

Franco breathed a sigh of relief. The last time he had seen that look on Jessy's face had been two months ago, when news came from Ireland that the identity of her father had been revealed. That night she had looked exactly as she did now – pale and stunned. Until then, the only person who had information about her father had been her mother Maria, who had died in 1979

74

giving birth to Jessy.

'Okay, good,' Franco replied, giving her shoulder a squeeze. 'You worried me. I thought it was bad news from your Ireland.'

Jessy shook her head. Franco always referred to her home country as '*your* Ireland.' She thought it was so cute. Giving him a quick hug she answered, 'No. Everything is fine Franco,' and with a reassuring smile added, 'Don't worry.'

But Jessy *was* worried. It was all very strange and why did she have to keep it a secret that Neil Wilson was back in Malta? Billy would love to see him. Her grandfather, Billy Cortis, had been Neil's guardian when he was a child and was presently staying here on the island. He had flown from England with Neil after Christmas to meet his grand-daughter Jessy for the first time. At the moment Billy was living close by at his townhouse, in what used to be the small fishing village of St. Julian's where he was born. He had been living primarily in London since the end of World War II, when he had served as a fighter pilot in the Royal Air Force. His wife Katie, who had been tragically killed with their two babies during the war in Malta, had been from London. Visiting her family after the war, Billy had become so involved in the lives of his in-laws that he had never left. He became a guardian to Neil, whose father had been Katie's nephew Jimmy. Neil's mother had abandoned her husband and young child for the hippy trail of the sixties and Jimmy was often away from home during his training as a pilot.

It was only a few months ago that Jessy and Neil had both found out that his father Jimmy was also Jessy's father. This revelation had come as a huge shock, especially for Neil who had been falling in love with Jessy. The disclosure had prompted his sudden leave of absence from the Royal Air Force in Britain to San Francisco, to visit his mother who still lived there.

Jessy wiped the counter next to the sink with a tea-towel then opened the washing machine door and flung the wet cloth inside. Franco had opened the narrow wooden door which led from the small kitchen out onto the terrace and was now walking towards the back wall, which was waist high and looked out over the impressive city of Valletta. Along the tops of the wide limestone walls were dozens of plant pots, festooned with various types of flowers and plants. He tut-tutted at seeing the withered heads of the daffodils which Jessy had failed to keep alive in the warm Maltese sun.

'That funny girl,' he mused, shaking his head and began to pluck the dead leaves out with his hand.

Franco thought it was amusing when Jessy had been so thrilled to open a parcel received in the post and find daffodil bulbs inside from her grandmother's friend, Joyce. Like a child with a new toy she had immediately ran outside and began filling plant pots with the soil Franco had ready and waiting for this very occasion. Not bothering to put on gardening gloves, Jessy had filled each pot and pushed the bulbs down safely into the earth. Her hands and nails had been filthy by the time she had finished and Franco had helped her carefully water each pot. All the while, Jessy prattled on beside him about how beautiful the flowers would look once the yellow buds finally opened.

'Gran always had rows and rows of daffodils in our garden,' she told him. 'Each side of the pathway up to our front door was lined with them every spring and our back garden was always full of daffodils too. They are my most favourite flower. I always think they look so cheery. Almost as if they are smiling and nodding at you.'

Sadly the daffodils didn't grow very well in Malta. The green shoots burst through the soil and some of the buds did flower, but immediately died thanks to the heat of the sun much to Jessy's disappointment.

'I don't understand it,' she had lamented. 'I looked up information on the internet about daffodils and they *do* grow here in Malta. Well, ones called Sea Daffodils do anyway. I watered them well and there's obviously been no frost like we would have had at home, so why won't they grow?'

Franco just shook his head bewildered, and threw his arms up in the air in defeat. Gardening had never been his thing. That has been his deceased wife's speciality. He preferred to spend his time on the sea rather than on land. Serenella would have been annoyed to see he hadn't looked after the beautiful plants and flowers which had once adorned their large balcony and terrace. When Jessica came to live with them in the first terrible months following her grandmother Ana's death, she began to take an interest in brightening up the outdoor area with colourful plants and flowers. She had told Franco how she missed the huge gardens in her home back at Ireland.

'I never took much interest in the garden really,' she explained to Franco. 'I loved sitting out there to read, but I didn't pass much heed to how it was maintained. The priests in the parochial house where we lived had a gardener who did all the heavy work, but Gran was the one who chose what flowers to grow and looked after them. I miss it. I miss the colours and smells. I even miss the grass.'

Franco noticed the sadness that came over Jessy from time to time and knew she got homesick for Ireland and the life she had left behind. Sometimes he would catch her looking into space with a melancholic look upon her face. He wracked his brains each time to come up with some way to make her smile again. On one of those occasions he had suggested she could 'jazz up' their outside living space in whatever way she liked. Then she could sit out there and read, like she had at home. To his delight Jessy had jumped at the idea and he was only too happy to ferry her around several gardening shops and centres where she picked out shrubs and seedlings for her new project.

Now both the balcony and terrace once more boasted a riotous mixture of colour, with inexpensive garden pots covering their walls and tiled floorings. She had transformed them both and Franco was happy to fulfil the little jobs that Jessy assigned him. He had hung multi-coloured fairy lights on little hooks around the railings which could be turned on from the kitchen, enabling Jessy to read outside when it got darker but still warm enough for sitting outdoors. There were mismatched cast-iron chairs that he and Jessy had painted in vibrant red, blue and yellow.

The old wooden table which had also been painted, was once again used for family and friends to sit around for *al fresco* meals. At the moment it was covered with a pretty yellow and blue chequered tablecloth which Jessy had unearthed from some wardrobe in the house and washed. Fringes hung down from the edge of the tablecloth and Franco recalled his children when they were little, twisting these pieces of cloth around their fingers while they waited impatiently for meals to be served up. It was nice to see this item of their family history being used again.

Franco took great pleasure in small touches like these, which Jessy had made in their home. Since his wife had died almost twenty years ago, the place had slowly become somewhat neglected. He and his youngest son Salvatore, two men living together, simply used the house as a place to sleep. Both of them spent most of their waking hours in the family restaurant. Although they kept the house relatively clean and neat, it lacked the essence of a homely feel. It was only when Jessy moved in and began to make subtle modifications that Franco realised Jessy had gradually turned the house once more into a home. New tea-towels replaced the old worn ones and small changes like soap dishes appeared in the bathroom and en-suite, rugs appeared on the floor, cushions on the sofa. Franco noticed each little alteration and valued them all. This is what he had been missing - a woman's touch.

Franco Vella was well aware and not a bit put out by the knowledge that Jessy had wrapped him around her little finger. He saw so much of his old sweetheart in her. Finding Ana again after sixty years apart was a miracle in itself and losing her so suddenly, so soon afterwards, was a huge loss. Jessy's desire to stay in Malta after Ana died had eased Franco's heartache a little. Her now being engaged to his son Salvatore made him feel secure that she would always be part of his family. For this he was thankful every day. It was almost like having Ana, his one and only love, still part of his life – the girl to whom he had become engaged during the war while she was here with her father.

Wing-Commander Laurence Mellor had been

stationed on the island at the outbreak of what later became known as the Siege of Malta, during the Second World War. It was this man who had cruelly ordered Franco's exile from Malta for being an enemy alien, due to his being born in Italy. Mellor believed a Maltese fisherman was not a suitable match for his daughter. Franco had been sent on a naval ship with other Italian prisoners to spend the rest of the war in the far away islands of Orkney, off the North-West coast of Scotland. To Franco, it might as well have been on the other side of the world.

Sixty years later Franco set eyes on Ana Mellor again. A lifetime. A life in which both of them had married others and had children but never forgotten the love that they had shared. Both had thought the other dead. Both had grieved for decades, for a love that was lost. One memorable day in 2001 they had unexpectedly met again. Here in Malta while Jessy and Ana were visiting the island they had been reunited, until death had taken Ana suddenly and once again she and Franco were torn apart. Franco's intense grief had been a matter of great concern to his youngest son Salvatore. He was aware that having Ana's grand-daughter in his life was a huge comfort to his father.

Jessy now looked out at the terrace, completely oblivious of the vibrant colours of the flowers and shrubs she had planted. Her mind was far away, wondering what on earth Neil was up to and what the puzzling phone-call could possibly mean.

Chapter 7

Malta. March, 2003.

He would love a pint. A beer would relax him a bit and take away the nervous churning in his stomach. Just the mere thought of seeing her again made him feel literally weak at the knees. Would she even turn up, he wondered? Why had he hung up the phone so quickly? Jessy won't know what to think.

'You bloody idiot,' Neil shouted out loud, his spittle hitting the window-screen in front. He banged his palms against the steering wheel of his rented car and shook his head angrily. 'What am I doing?' he asked himself out loud, then quieter this time. 'What the hell am I doing?'

It was good to hear her voice again. Her funny Irish accent could always make him smile. He had missed hearing it. Part of his plan to take some leave from the R.A.F. and go to San Francisco included not ringing Jessy. He had planned on not having any contact with her at all and if he could manage it, on not even thinking about her. That bit hadn't been so easy. Every time he sat opposite a woman and listened to her brainless chatter he thought of Jessy, comparing every single woman to her. Jessy had made him laugh out loud with the things she would say, things that she had no idea were so funny. It was the way she would talk nineteen to the dozen about everyday matters, unaware that her endearing brogue completely captivated him. She didn't try to impress or be anything other than her completely beautiful self. The innocent ability to just be so normal was refreshing, unlike the high maintenance women he was used to finding himself with. Jessy didn't mind if her hair was unruly or if her makeup wasn't perfect. She dressed fashionably but could just as happily open the door in her pyjamas and bare feet if company called. Neil was absolutely infatuated with her. Discovering that he was in fact her half-brother had completely devastated him and no amount of women or alcohol had so far managed to erase his anguish.

***

San Francisco. February, 2003.

It had been a relief to leave her behind that day in London. Jessy and their father Jimmy had come to see him off at Heathrow where he was getting a direct flight to San Francisco. The few days they had spent

85

together in London talking with Jimmy and hearing the story of his relationship with Jessy's mother Maria had been tremendously stressful for Neil. It had felt like he was acting a part that he had not yet been given a script for. It was only as he sat on the plane and it soared into the sky, that he felt the tension leave his body. In truth he had surprised himself by getting the sudden feeling of wanting to cry. Not just have a little sniffle to himself, but he actually wanted to yowl. He wanted to open his mouth and let his body do what it had needed to do just two months ago, when he heard the unbelievable news that the woman he had fallen in love with, was his sister.

Up until now he realised he had been holding himself as though coiled into a tight ball of wire, careful so as not to let his real emotions show. It had been absolutely exhausting emotionally, physically and mentally. Regardless of how much he hated leaving Jess, his whole being needed this time away from her. He needed to recap, recover and then hopefully forget.

Nobody had any idea how much that revelation had affected Neil. He had admitted his feelings to Jessy who had surprised him by acknowledging that she had guessed. But that was not as surprising as her declaring that she loved him too. That had been a huge affirmation. But of course he realised she meant in a sisterly way. Within forty minutes of the eleven hour flight, Neil was pleasantly drunk. Within two hours he was hammered and fell into a blissful sleep, not wakening until the plane touched down at San Francisco International Airport. Descending the steps of the plane, Neil scrunched his eyes as the strong sunshine temporarily blinded him. His head felt as though somebody had hit it with a brick.

On reaching the terminal, Neil pulled the woolly jumper up over his head and shoved it into his small rucksack. It was February in London and freezing cold when he'd left, but the temperature was about twenty degrees in San Francisco at the moment. Luckily he hadn't bothered wearing a coat or else he'd end up carrying it around. His bag held just enough gear to do for a night or so, a razor, toothbrush, underwear, phone charger and the latest Dan Brown novel. Jess had lent him that, saying she hadn't been able to put it down till it was finished. He thought it a bit far-fetched, but was reading it purely because Jess had. He was thrilled knowing he was following the same story that she had read. Seeing a chocolate stain on the odd page made him grin, imagining her chomping on the dark chocolate she was so fond of while she read. Gosh he had it bad. This very thought made him walk more quickly and look for the nearest bar.

Wakening the next morning in his mother's house, or *condo* as she called it, it had taken him a few minutes to remember where he was. His first question was what the heck the noise outside was. He could hear the deafening sounds of workmen drilling and even louder traffic. A plane could also be heard flying noisily overhead. His mouth was as dry as a desert. The bedside locker was white. He noticed roughly applied brush strokes of paint and a badly hand-decorated brown leaf painted onto the corners. The only person he knew who would do that to an otherwise decent piece of furniture was his mother. He blinked, so that's where he was. In San Francisco and by the other kind of noise of somebody snoring too closely behind him, he was obviously not alone.

Neil didn't move. Both for fear of discovering who owned the foot he could feel pressed against the back of his leg and also because if his head was already spinning whilst lying still, he feared what it might be like if he actually moved it. The bedside lamp was comfortingly familiar. It had always been *his* lamp and part of *his* bedroom furniture in whatever home his mother lived in. Despite her frequent moves around various parts of *San Fran'* as she called it, she did manage to always ensure there was a spare bedroom for Neil and each time set his room up in the same way. As a result, wherever or whenever her son turned up at her place even as he grew into a man, he always felt that in some way he was coming home to a familiar place.

The lamp had a round brass base with a cream shade. As it was one of those sensor lights which he had thought really cool as a teenager, he knew that if he touched it, it would immediately come on. As would the one that he knew without looking was on the other side of the bed, on the matching locker, undoubtedly now sporting newly painted brown leaves. That was the only thing that did change. From time to time his mother would renovate furniture by using whatever paint she had left over from other projects. Neil wished he had thought to bring a glass of water to bed for the morning. He also wished he could remember who was lying next to him.

Patches of memory from the night before began to come back. The airport. He remembered that. He had hit the first bar he saw on disembarking, which ironically had been an Irish one. He'd had a bit of a fuzzy head. Burger and fries. Good. At least he'd lined his stomach with something before what obviously had turned out to be quite a bender. There'd been lots of pints of Guinness … and whiskey chasers. Oh no, he grimaced in remembrance. Whoever was in the bed with him was Irish. He knew that for certain, because that was what had attracted him. Her accent.

He'd been four pints in at that stage and it was she who had initiated both the conversation and the whiskey drinking.

'Are you Irish too?' she'd asked, pointing to his pint of the black stuff.

His head had swivelled in her direction. She sounded just like Jess. Shaking his head he took in the tall red-head with too much dark orange foundation on her face. But it wasn't a bad face, if it wasn't for the part above her lip which was sweaty and whiter than the rest of her fake skin tone.

'Nope,' he answered lazily, turning back to his drink.

He could feel her getting up on the high bar stool beside him and watched her through the mirror opposite, behind the bar counter. She saw him looking and winked.

'Caught ye,' she said, nudging him in the ribs. He grinned self-consciously despite himself.

They continued their conversation that way, as a kind of joke. Speaking to each other via the reflection of the mirror. It was easier that way, he found.

At some stage, after the whiskey part, they had obviously moved on to more face to face exchange. Sometime later he could remember holding her up as they tried to wave down a cab and telling her to try to look sober or they'd never get one. They must have managed to hail one at some stage because now they were here, but he had no memory whatsoever of the journey, or what happened afterwards. There was a blank when it came to arriving at his Mom's and the same of even getting into bed, never mind what may or may not have happened in it. Neil groaned. How was he going to get her out? It turned out to be easier than he imagined.

'Just swear to God if you ever see me, anywhere with anyone, you'll ignore me right?'

Neil held the cab door open, more to hold himself up than in trying to be gentlemanly.

He nodded.

'Sure.' That suited him fine. Thankfully she was in no rush to repeat the performance of last night.

'Man of few words, eh?' the red-head answered sassily. 'A bit different from last night!'

Before he could reply she pulled the car door shut, then rolled down the window.

'I hope it works out with that Jess,' and she was gone.

He never did remember her name.

The rest of the day had been spent sprawled on his mother's futon trying to piece together the previous night, drinking gallons of water and eating bag after bag of potato chips. Thankfully the medicine cabinet was full of all kinds of drugs for his banging head and not all of them legal, but he wasn't going there no matter how bad he felt. Neil felt wretched. A few Ibuprofen was enough for him. He had done a lot of crazy stuff in his life but his hatred of drugs had kept him well away from them. Not to mention instant dismissal from the R.A.F. if drugs were ever discovered in one of the random blood tests. Looking at his watch he sighed and pulled the mobile phone out of his pocket.

'Dad, it's me. Just to let you know I've arrived safe and sound like you asked.' He listened to his father's light lecture for not ringing the night before and squirmed when he thought again of what he'd been up to instead. 'No,' he responded, when asked if he had rung Jess yet. 'In a day or two.'

But it took five weeks before he made that call, at which point he'd already booked his flight to Malta.

Chapter 8

Malta. March, 2003.

She'd forgotten her sunglasses in the rush out the door. In her mind's eye Jessy could picture them sitting on the window ledge in Franco's kitchen, her cream glasses with the gold bar at the side. She liked those ones. They were the first designer pair she had bought about a year ago and it was a miracle she still had them. Usually she lost things like sunglasses and umbrellas within in a week or so of buying them. Not that there was much need for umbrellas in Malta, thankfully. That was the reason she never spent much money on things like that, until on impulse she'd bought the cream Gucci shades at a sale in Valletta. Jessy remembered feeling quite independent as she handed over her debit card. Just knowing that she had enough money in her current account to pay for them gave her a frisson of pride. Simply carrying the little Gucci gift bag had made her walk a little taller. Jessy cringed, remembering how after replacing her cheaper sunglasses with the new ones, she had put them into the Gucci bag so she would still have a reason to carry it around, dangling from her arm. She was sure that salesgirls in the stores would take her a little more seriously now that she was obviously a designer gear shopper.

Annoyingly her eyes had begun to water with the glare of the sun. Casting a glance across the road where the souvenir shops had low-price glasses on stands outside their stores, Jessy looked quickly at her watch. Five minutes until the bus arrived. She had time to run over and make a speedy purchase, but fortunately she noticed there was no need to cross the busy street. Lining the promenade on Jessy's side of the road were benches for weary walkers to sit and take a breather. On one of these a street-seller had laid out his wares for sale. There were fake designer handbags and conveniently he also had several pairs of fake designer sunglasses. Ironically Jessy spotted the exact same pair as her own, although at less than a quarter of the price. However, this time there was no fancy Gucci bag to carry them in. They were unceremoniously put into a small clear plastic bag like one would use for putting sandwiches into. They were then handed over with a cautious look around by the seller to ensure no *pulizija* were watching. Putting them on, Jessy realised also that although they kept the harsh glare of the sun out, they weren't half as good quality as her own authentic pair and made everything have a blue tinge. Just as well, otherwise she'd be quite maddened by the difference in price.

As usual when the bus arrived, there was the usual chaos of squeezing past all the people who were huddled at the front near the driver's seat, yet on walking down the aisle she noticed that there were plenty of empty seats. This was something Jessy never could understand in all her time in Malta. Why did the passengers prefer to stand, hanging on to the ceiling straps for dear life – when they could be sitting down? Obviously the bus driver had the same thoughts, for he spent the entire journey to Cirkewwa shouting at his passengers to 'move down, move down. There are vacant seats,' and sounding quite exasperated. But, as was the custom, he was completely ignored and could be heard swearing under his breath as he shook his head in frustration.

It was roasting on the bus, although the narrow windows on the roof were opened wide. Ordinarily Jessy enjoyed bus rides – it was a cheap way to see around the island. In spite of Malta being only seventeen miles long and nine miles wide, due to the heavy traffic it took hours to get from one part of the island to the other. A journey from Valletta on the east of the country to Cirkewwa took almost two hours by bus with all the stops, or even longer if it was rush hour. By car it was about an hour long journey. The last time I was making this journey Jessy thought, was with Neil, when we made that trip to Gozo in January. That seemed like ages ago but it's been only two months.

In that short time so much had happened. She had discovered who her father was and met him in London, acquired Neil as a half-brother and got engaged to Salvatore. At this thought Jessy looked down at the modest diamond ring on her finger. Apart from today's sudden phone-call, Neil hadn't kept in touch as agreed after he went to San Francisco. Not even a postcard, which had disappointed her as he'd promised to send one of the well-known Golden Gate Bridge.

Jessy tugged at her waistband, feeling it dig uncomfortably into her skin. She had gone up a whole dress size since arriving in Malta. It was because of all the rich food, especially eating regularly at Franco's restaurant, L'Artiste. It was more Salvatore's restaurant now since his father had handed him the reins, after Ana's death in 2001. A big advantage to eating there meant not having to pay, but it did encourage her to eat more greedily. The food was just so good. I need to walk more Jessy mused, instead of hopping on a bus so quickly. Otherwise I will be a fat bride! I don't want that!

The reality of walking down the aisle, of actually being married seemed surreal to her. Being engaged didn't seem quite real yet at all. It had happened so suddenly and even wearing an engagement ring felt bizarre – like it was all pretend. Jessy always imagined it feeling more sort of … well, just different. None of her friends back in Ireland was engaged or even in a steady relationship yet, so there was nothing to compare it to. Nevertheless, she always thought being engaged would involve much more excitement, a big party – something to mark it as the huge occasion it was. Or should be.

In fact, her friends didn't even know that she was engaged yet. Jessy was waiting to tell them in person on her next visit home. Actually she was planning to say nothing and wait to see how long it would take the girls to spot her ring. If she knew them, it wouldn't take long at all. Her grandmother's best friend, Joyce, and the priests she and Ana once lived with had been told the news already, on the very day that Salvatore had proposed to her, even before he had purchased the ring.

Jessy had been too excited to wait and Joyce had received the news with a mixture of delight and apprehension.

'Well, Ana liked him so that's good enough for me,' Joyce had said sincerely. After speaking with an embarrassed Franco for a while she found herself very relieved to hear that there was no reason for a hasty wedding. He had assured her that the young pair were in love, but in no rush to have their big day just yet. Joyce admitted Salvatore Vella seemed a nice young man, but she had a few genuine concerns about Jessica.

'That young one isn't ready to settle down yet,' she said worriedly to her husband Patsy, who replied without looking up from his paper.

'That's what your Da said.'

'I know. He was right,' Joyce answered, 'and remember the trouble there was.'

Patsy nodded. 'How could I forget?' Indeed he did remember, for after two months his young wife had decided she was fed up being married and subsequently disappeared off to England. It was the sad and dishevelled appearance of her husband months later at the coffee shop where she was working that made her return with him to the farm. Prompted by

Joyce's mother, Patsy didn't waste any time in giving his wife another reason to stay home and motherhood soon loomed. But they had been happy. Eventually.

'That Salvatore is her first real boyfriend. She's only twenty-three and she still has itchy feet.'

Joyce had known the young woman since she was born and had a feeling that marriage at a young age and settling down in Malta to start a family wouldn't be enough for her. Not yet.

'She was all talk about going off to university before their trip to Malta. She might still want to go yet.'

'Don't be worrying woman,' Patsy said, shaking his paper noisily to let Joyce know that the conversation was over.

His wife got the hint, but he hadn't managed to soothe her concerns. Jessy is too full of brains to be kept at home minding babies, she thought, and that Salvatore lad seems the traditional type to me.

Jessica and Salvatore had been thrilled at receiving their one and only engagement present in the post from Joyce. It was a painting.

'It's Aghameen,' Jessy had whispered softly when they unwrapped the gift. At Salvatore's quizzical expression, she explained that it was a painting of her home village.

'Look,' she pointed to a decaying stone building. It was a very old kind of church on a hill, with stone walls and overlooking a small village with another ancient, rectangular shaped church set just on the outskirts. Next to this church was a different old stone building. It was quite a grand house, with a lake behind it. It looked like this house was inside a walled garden and the artist had painted a colourful array of flowers within the walls, which had green ivy climbing them. On the lake there were even two white swans and a boat. Everything looked so peaceful, unlike the busy hustle and bustle of Malta.

'That is the old abbey from the 16th Century ... and there,' Jessy pointed to the house. 'That's the parochial house, where I live. Lived,' she corrected.

Salvatore lifted the painting in his hands and turned it toward the light.

'It is beautiful. But in my opinion not done by a professional.'

Jessy nodded. 'No. Look,' she said again, and pointed to the name at the bottom right hand side. 'It's by Conor. Joyce's son. He likes to paint in his spare time. Same as you.'

'He certainly captured the stillness and the greenery. But you can see where he obviously painted over something and there are few inconsistencies with the scale. Do you see how the church on the hill is the same size as the one in the village? That's not right.'

Jessy carefully took the painting out of Salvatore's hands and put it back on the table.

'It's an abbey, not a church,' she replied quietly, re-wrapping the picture once again. They would hang it someday. Somewhere.

She did place the engagement card in the centre of the kitchen table and even put a little flower in an espresso cup sitting ceremoniously beside it.

'At home cards always go on the mantelpiece,' Jessy explained to Franco who was moved when he saw her little presentation. 'But there's never a mantelpiece in the houses over here,' she continued.

'If you want a mantelpiece my love, I am sure Salvatore will build you one in your new home some-day,' and he gave the startled looking woman an indulgent hug.

It had never occurred to Jessy that they might not continue living with Franco. This was her home now and it felt as such. But she felt a little sensation of excitement in her tummy at imagining herself and Salvatore having their own place. But how could they leave Franco all on his own? Suddenly issues that she had never thought of before popped into her head and it made her feel slightly panicky. How could they afford their own place? Her wages at the library just kept her in shoes and clothes. Would she have to stop spending and begin to save? Gosh, they probably do need to start to save now, she realised, for the wedding.

Jessy sat down uncertainly on the kitchen chair. She and Salvatore had never talked about serious things like that. They were just getting used to being engaged. Jessy had no idea how much her ring had cost him. She looked down at it and slid the band off her finger. It was definitely gold. There was the stamp and the delicate diamond looked real enough. She assumed it was. Pushing the ring back on her finger Jessy wondered if her fiancé had had to borrow money for it. He never seemed to have a lot of money and indeed still drove the battered old motorbike he had when they first met.

The restaurant was certainly doing extremely well. She knew that. There was a steady stream of customers and a new kitchen had been put in since Salvatore took it over from Franco. Not an especially elaborate one, but it was new all the same. She'd have to talk to him about money. It made her feel quite grown up. But she *was* grown up now. She was getting married and today was the first time that she realised she had no idea how they were going to pay for a wedding or a house.

Salvatore laughed when she voiced her concerns to him over a delicious *spaghetti marinara* in L'Artiste that evening.

'You will have whatever kind of wedding you want and house you want,' he assured her, playfully pinching her cheek then rubbing the spot with his finger which he then kissed. It was just one of the many endearing little ways he touched her that made Jessy feel special.

'But where will we get the money?' she asked worriedly, childishly wiping at her chin after spooning another forkful of the creamy tomato sauce into her mouth.

'Jessy,' Salvatore looked at her very seriously. 'It is not for you to worry about. Okay?'

'But, what about the account?' She had suggested to Salvatore that they open a joint bank account for savings and he had reiterated that she was not to worry about money.

'You keep your money for all those clothes you keep buying,' he replied teasingly. 'And let me worry about everything else. Okay *hanini*?'

And that was that.

***

I forgot to tell Salvatore where I was going! Jessy sat up straight on the plastic ferry seat with a bolt of alarm. After finishing up in the kitchen that morning, she had gone to the other end of the house where her bedroom was and had a quick shower. The outfit chosen to meet her brother Neil was purely for comfort. Jeans, flat brown knee boots, soft navy sweatshirt and a light red rain-jacket, just in case, as there was rain forecast. Her hair was tied up in a high ponytail, remembering from the last trip what the wind on the ferry did to her long curls. Pulling out her mobile phone Jessy scrolled through the contact list and pressed the green call button. Voicemail. Typical, she thought. 'Hi love, it's me. The weirdest thing. I got a call from ...' She hesitated and hung up, remembering that Neil had curiously asked her not to tell anybody he had been in touch, so she'd better keep her word. Biting her lip Jessy opened up the message screen and began to type.

Sorry about my garbled voicemail – I'm meeting a friend so won't make dinner this evening. See you tomorrow if you are late home tonight. Love J x.

I will explain all tomorrow, she decided. By then I will know what Neil is being so secretive about. As the white cab sped towards the Dwejra Point Cliffs, Jessy chattered amiably to the taxi driver while close by, a young man stood waiting, his eyes squinting as he watched for the first sign of the woman he had failed to forget.

Chapter 9

Gozo. March, 2003.

She looked so young and strikingly natural. Neil had forgotten how much so. He had become accustomed to being in the company of what he termed, 'high maintenance women' during his last few months of mindless flings. Women, mostly blonds if he recalled, who looked like they'd just stepped out of a Playboy magazine. They all had the same bland appearance and figures like Barbie dolls, with their perfect makeup and elegant long straight hair complete with skimpy outfits to match. Jess looked completely different. Stepping out of the car she waved, then opened her bag to take out a purse as she stood next to the driver's rolled down window. She had a red jacket tied around her waist. Neil took in her long shapely legs in brown boots, the curve of her breasts in a tight sweater and long messy hair tied up in an even messier high ponytail. Even from where he stood he could see that Jess had no makeup on, apart from her trademark red lipstick. Dark freckles peppered her face and he felt his heart beat faster, believing that she was the most gorgeous looking girl he'd ever seen.

'Here let me,' he shouted, running over to the cab. 'I'll get it.' But the driver was already pulling off.

'It's paid,' Jessy laughed, opening her arms to him. 'It's so good to see you.'

She was in his embrace at last and smelled exactly the same. A subtle hint of White Musk perfume assailed his nostrils. He'd even bought himself a miniature bottle at The Body Shop in the airport on his way to San Francisco, just so he could remember her scent. But it smelled so much better on her. She was beaming broadly up at him and Neil felt his heart contract. God she is stunning, he thought, already feeling arousal just looking at her. This instant reaction made him drop her hands suddenly and stand back, on the pretence of wanting to get a better look at her.

'You have even more freckles,' he declared, pointing at her with a chuckle as he lifted the sunglasses from his head and put them on.

'Cheers big brother,' she replied convivially, also looking him up and down in the same way as he was appraising her. 'You look very well yourself!'

Immediately his face clouded and Neil began to walk in the direction of the renowned Azure Window, with his head bent against the ever present wind.

'Hey,' Jessy called, running now to catch up with him. 'Where are we going? Wait for me!'

He turned around slowly. 'Look Jess. There's something I need to tell you.'

'Me too. I have something to tell you too. Me first,' she answered, excitedly. 'Look.'

And to Neil's absolute horror, Jessy held her left hand out proudly and he saw the glittering, taunting sparkle of her engagement ring. He was too late.

'Well?' Jessy asked coquettishly, waving her bejewelled finger in front of his dazed looking face. 'Aren't you going to congratulate your little sister then?'

Neil could barely speak, feeling winded as though he'd just been punched in the gut. Jessy was by now jumping up and down, clapping her hands like a kid on Christmas morning when Santa had arrived.

'Can you believe it?'

He couldn't. Jessy ran towards him and once more threw her arms around his neck hugging him tight, while he swayed, feeling as though the air was sucked out of his lungs. Still dazed, he followed where Jessy led towards the rocky precipice with her arm tucked companionably under his. Neil wished he could jump in to the turbulent sea below and away from the words he had just heard come out of her mouth. Jess was engaged to Salvatore. Bloody hell. He hadn't been expecting that. Not for one minute.

'Oh it's so lovely to tell somebody that is family. I mean, I don't really have many family and I didn't want to tell Dad before telling you. But you never wrote to me like you said and I'd no address for you. Why didn't you write to me?' she questioned, pummelling him playfully in the ribs to get his attention when he made no reply.

Neil stopped walking and pulled her arm out from under his.

'Let's see this rock then,' he said teasingly, lifting her hand up closely to his eyes. 'Where is it?'

'Oy,' Jessy answered acting as though she was insulted. 'That is an actual real diamond you know.'

'Can I bite it to see?' he teased once more, pretending to pull the ring from her finger.

Jessy laughed, pulling her hand away and to his surprise enfolded it into his own, in a totally innocent display of affection which only served to increase his distress.

'I was dying to tell you,' she said, swinging his

arm as they continued to walk towards the cliff edge. Then she dropped his hand and spread her arms wide shouting elatedly out to the wind, making other people standing nearby clap and wave in their direction 'I'M GETTING MARRIED' she cried, spinning herself around like Julie Andrews in The Sound of Music movie. 'WOOOOOOHOOOOOOO!' she squealed and Neil actually couldn't decide if the tears he felt come to his eyes were out of genuine delight at her joy, or sorrow at his own loss.

***

'What did you want to tell me?' she asked.

'What?' Neil had to come up with something quick.

'You said there was something you needed to tell me. Earlier. Before I told you about getting engaged.'

'Oh yeah, I'd forgotten. It can wait.'

'No tell me now,' she insisted. 'And why did you want me to come the whole way out here? To Gozo and back to this place?'

He opened the boot and lifted out a six pack of water, handing a bottle to Jessy. Opening the top of his

111

own bottle he took a long slow drink, while hastily trying to come up with a plausible answer.

'I wanted to surprise Billy by us two arriving together at his house.'

'But why not just meet on Malta then instead of here?'

Neil spotted his camera lying in the boot. 'I needed to get a photo of you at the Azure Window. For Billy.'

Jessy looked puzzled. 'Why?'

'Remember we told him about how scared you were that day when we were last here and you thought you were going to fall in?'

Jessy shuddered. 'How could I forget?'

'What did he say to you?'

'He said I had to get back on the horse.'

'Exactly,' Neil replied, strangely proud of how quickly he could lie through his teeth.

'So, you need to go back out there and I'll take a photo of you to show Billy.'

'No way,' Jessy shook her head resolutely and opened the passenger door of the car to get in.

'You told Billy you would … get back on the horse like he said,' Neil reprimanded.

'But not today,' she replied, obstinately.

'Yes,' he said firmly, pulling Jessy gently back out of the car. 'Today.'

Reluctantly she once again took his hand, walking silently back towards the area where the huge arch jutted magnificently out into the Mediterranean Sea. The top of the arch was much wider than she remembered. The last time she and Neil were here Jessy had lost her footing and it was Neil who came to her rescue, gently leading her onto more solid ground. The strong wind made her feel a bit nervous. What if she got blown away by a big gust of wind? But remembering what Neil had said to her the last time, about people diving off here just for fun and how good he was at swimming, she felt a bit calmer. This time she didn't feel as scared, as Neil held tightly onto her hand. Looking up at him, Jessy was surprised to see him staring at her fixedly.

'Hey,' she declared. 'Keep your eyes on where you are taking us, Mister. I am relying on you to keep me up here, instead of down there you know.' She pointed to the crashing waves below.

Neil grinned. 'Just making sure you are okay.'

She nodded. 'Yes, but only because I am trusting you. Is this not far enough?' They had reached half way across the arch now and Jessy had no desire to go to the edge, where it would be easier to get blown over.

'Okay. Now, to quote Madonna,' he joked. 'Strike a pose.'

His first photo was of Jessy giving him a reproachful look to let him know what she thought of his witty repartee. Then he clicked away as she childishly acted out a variety of different Madonna poses, with her arms placed like an Egyptian over her head, pouting and even copying some of Madonna's Vogue dance moves in the famous song. Neil laughed his head off at her bad impersonations until a sudden downpour of rain caused them to make a quick run for his car.

'You are a nutcase,' he laughed, leaning over the back seat to retrieve his camera cover.

'I just knew it would rain today,' she told him. 'One of the advantages of being Irish is expertise in predicting when a rain shower is due. Well, that was fun,' Jessy giggled. 'Will you send me some of the photos when you get back?'

He nodded. 'Sure,' and started the engine.

'No, wait,' Jessy said, putting her hand on the steering wheel. 'Let's just sit here. I love hearing the rain and watching it when I am all snug inside. Can we just stay here?'

'Okay weirdo,' he answered, turning the engine off. 'We can do that.' So they did - watching as the heavy deluge turned the now empty car-park into a muddy river of mud and stones. They didn't chat. Instead they sat in silence, listening and watching.

Neil decided it was the best time he had had in weeks.

***

'Hey Mom.'

'Neil, good morning. How are you? Where are you?'

'In Malta and it's almost ten at night here. I told you I was coming over.'

'And?'

'And I have decided not to say anything for now. To anybody. Got it?'

'Sure honey, I got it. But are *you* sure?' his mother asked concerned.

'Yep,' Neil replied decisively. 'For now at least.'

As he continued their chat Neil's mind was elsewhere. He'd already made up his mind that after a quick visit to Billy he was going back to England tomorrow evening and back to work. It was time for some normality in his life.

Billy was upset at Neil's flying visit.

'At least stay till Sunday,' he'd asked. 'Spend the weekend here.'

But Neil was resolute. 'No. I've had enough time off and I've things to do before I get back to Base on Monday.'

'What?' Billy asked.

'What do you mean *what*?'

'What do you have to do that is so important you can't spend a bit of time with this old codger?' asked Billy, raising his eyebrows questioningly.

Neil felt bad. He missed Billy too. For as long as he could remember the old man had been like a father to him and when Billy was home in England, they saw each other almost every day. There was still even a bedroom for Neil in Billy's house. The same room he'd had as a child before moving out for a bit of freedom when he turned twenty-one. But he still called round to Billy's almost every day to see how he was and in many ways the old man was his best friend. Their shared career of flying with the R.A.F. gave them much to talk about and Billy was a great sounding board for good old fashioned advice when needed. Right now Neil really needed some of that fatherly guidance, but was sure the solution he'd already come up with for his problem would be the same as Billy's. To get out of Malta and leave Jess alone. And that was exactly what he intended to do.

Chapter 10

Malta. December, 2003.

Lights twinkled in the miniature Christmas trees dotted all around the restaurant. Jessy sat outside so she could watch the view of Spinola Bay as she ate. Although it was December, it was still comfortably warm enough to eat outdoors, even though the sun had gone down some hours ago. She kept her red winter coat on, but unbuttoned. Her fiancé Salvatore never understood her reluctance to dine indoors where it was warmer and where the service was usually better. Table staff often forgot about customers eating outside, especially in winter. But Jessy didn't mind that. She wasn't in any kind of hurry.

The picturesque town of St. Julian's was busy tonight. Christmas shoppers and tourists wrapped snugly in warm scarves walked past where Jessy sat, with their gloved hands clasping those of a lover or child. It was sixteen degrees according to the weather gauge on the restaurant wall. In Malta this was considered cold, especially with the strong winds coming in from the sea and the locals were dressed for the drop in temperature. At sixteen degrees in Ireland, everyone would still be walking around in a t-shirt Jessy thought, as she perused the menu handed to her by a waiter. Her hand felt cold as she reached out for the glass of white wine he had just placed on her table. The wine was cold too. The sharpness of the first taste bit her tongue, then her insides immediately felt warmed as she could feel the alcohol hit her stomach. It growled. She hadn't eaten since breakfast. That was the reason for the slight headache which had tapped against her left temple all afternoon.

It had been busy at work in the library today. She kept intending to nip out and get something to eat, but before she knew it, it was time to finish for the day. The bus was so packed this evening that by the time she had made it to the door to get off, it had passed her usual spot. She had no choice but to stay on board and disembark further up the road, just outside the door of the restaurant where she now sat. The smell of fresh fish cooking had been too hard to resist and the waiter had smiled when she asked if she could have some bread to eat now, while she read the menu.

'Of course Madam,' he replied, handing her a menu. 'This evening's special is the rabbit stew.'

Jessy grimaced and shook her head. She never ate

meat. 'No thanks,' she answered, 'and butter please.' She knew from experience that butter served with bread was still a novelty in Malta. The waiter nodded and walked away.

It was just three days until Christmas. Jessy was a bit annoyed that she had to go in to the library at all today. The impressive National Library of Malta situated in Valletta was an interesting place to work and at Christmas it was beautifully decorated as was the rest of the capital city. It was always quite busy but Jessy had presumed, or hoped, as all of the staff had, that they would have finished work before now. What was the point in opening for one day? But the last working day before Christmas proved to be an extremely hectic day to Jessy's surprise and she had been rushed off her feet. Some of the staff were going for drinks at the trendy new bar close by on Republic Street and Jessy was joining them.

The first year working in the library she had been caught out by being unaware of the Christmas drinks tradition. The other women had come prepared to work. Before leaving the building they had all made a beeline for the Ladies' Room where they had pulled glittery dresses and high heels out of what seemed like

Mary Poppins handbags. Jessy had simply to make do with brushing her hair and applying fresh lipstick and felt very Cinderella-like. But this year she too was prepared. She had worn a simple black shift dress to work that morning with a larger than usual black handbag, but adding a red fur shrug and heels themed with a thin red diamante belt had turned her little black dress into a sexy party one.

The two glasses of champagne at the party had gone straight to her head, especially on an empty stomach and the painful tapping on her temples had moved up tempo. There had been plenty of food on offer at the restaurant/bar earlier but it all looked extremely fattening. Several delicious cakes had been set out for the library staff, richly adorned in chocolate Christmas decorations, but Jessy had not succumbed to temptation, intent as she was on losing weight for the New Year. As the others began to pull on coats to go home, Jessy sent a text to Salvatore to ask if he could pick her up and take her for something healthy to eat. Now, almost an hour later as she sat waiting for her meal to arrive, he still hadn't replied and Jessy was furious. Her message showed both sent and received ticks. It takes seconds to reply and he had chosen not to.

Jessy picked up the phone again and firmly pressed the on/off button at the side. Two can play at that game, she fumed.

Just a few miles away, Salvatore hit Jessy's number and put the phone to his ear. Her phone was turned off. He sighed. She must be having a good night, he thought. As his fingers began typing out a message, his older brother Marco shouted, 'Salvu, quick. The sauce is bubbling …' He pushed the phone back into his pocket and darted back into the restaurant kitchen. He'd ring her later.

Jessy picked up her handbag where she had placed it beside her chair when she'd sat down a few moments ago. The red fur shrug was sticking out from the top. She felt around underneath it until she found the small package she had taken to work that morning. Jessy laid it on the table and took another sip of her wine before opening it again. She had only a chance to have a quick look in work. Now she wanted to savour the opening of it. She had already opened the envelope inside that morning but she wanted to read the words again. Slipping the card out, Jessy stared for a few seconds at the picture in front. It was a simple Christmas tree, with Happy Christmas written above it. Nothing very special. Inside were the printed words, 'Wishing you a Happy Christmas'. Again, nothing special. He had written .... *To you, love from me xx.* Jessy gently removed the bubble wrap and held each side of the small photo frame in her hands. Once again she smiled on seeing the image. It was the Azure Window. A photograph taken by Neil.

He had captured the wildness of the sea that day beautifully. Smiling at her own comical pose in the photo, Jessy picked up her phone, turning it on again. It took a few seconds, then she quickly scrolled through her recent text messages and finding her last one to Neil, she deleted it and sent another. *Got my photo. Love it. About time. How's you?* xx Then she turned her phone off once more. She knew that he wouldn't reply straight away. He would usually send a message whenever he managed to get near a satellite, or whatever it was that made him able to send the random text messages she received in the last few months. Jessy hoped he would get in touch at Christmas, just because, well, just because he was her brother and it was Christmas soon. Since Neil's return to England in March she hadn't seen him. Her initial daily texts to him became once a week, then less, after he never bothered to reply.

On questioning Billy, who had told her Neil was on 'deployment' somewhere, Jessy felt a bit mollified, as she was beginning to think he was purposely ignoring her. Then on her birthday in September he'd sent a text simply saying, *Happy Birthday sis xx* and she had surprised herself by bursting into tears. Her reply asking where he was and how he was went unanswered, then one night in October, about two in the morning she had woken to another text saying, *Miss you xx.* Immediately she had sat up in bed and called the number and patiently listened as it rang out once more. Billy had told her how the R.A.F. on duty sometimes got satellite coverage wherever they were based but surely if the phone rang, it meant he could answer it? But, he didn't.

The tips of her fingers felt cold. Jessy took another sip from her glass. Would it look weird to eat with my gloves on, she wondered? The rest of her didn't feel cold though. Her Gran used to say, '*Cold hands, warm heart.*' Gosh she was starving. She could feel and hear her tummy rumbling loudly. I feel a bit tipsy, she realised, wishing the waiter would hurry up. As if he had heard her, he came out just then and Jessy ordered her favourite, *Spaghetti Vongole*. The waiter smiled. It wasn't the first time she had eaten there, or ordered the same dish. Leaving the bread on the table, with butter, he wondered once again why the pretty young lady always ate alone.

Salvatore was having a bad night. His brother Marco's recently joining the restaurant staff was supposed to be a help, not the hindrance it had turned out to be. Puzzled as to why he even wanted to work here when accountancy was his business, Salvatore had not looked a gift horse in the mouth at the time. The restaurant had continued to be busy during the winter months and extra staff was always needed. Having a family member on board was always preferable to employing outside staff and he accepted his eldest brother's offer of help as a Godsend. Now he had other ideas.

Marco couldn't cook to save his life. He wasn't even able to manage the basic preparation of a salad dish. He was worse on the floor, mixing up orders and was rude and quite dismissive to customers. The only thing he did seem to be good at was doing the accounts at the end of the day. But that just took an hour at most. The rest of the time he lounged around close to the front door, taking up a much needed table and chatting to any attractive women that came in. Salvatore turned a blind eye.

Despite his age, his brother's charm he had to admit, did encourage the ladies in, especially the tourists and Marco encouraged them to eat more and drink more expensive wine. But tonight they were especially busy as it was the local workers' last day before the holidays and the restaurant was booked out, not to mention all the late hopefuls who turned up eager for an available table. He had left his brother for just a couple of seconds while he nipped out to the courtyard to make a quick call to Jessy and in that short time, Marco had ruined a whole saucepan of creamed asparagus sauce.

'How can you be such a bad cook?' Salvatore asked, swearing under his breath as he rescued the burnt pot from the stovetop.

'Maybe because my mother never taught me,' was his brother's curt reply, as he stomped back into the restaurant.

Salvatore sighed. Marco had a long held belief that he was an unwanted child. Their mother admittedly had never been one for shows of tenderness but Salvatore couldn't understand why his brother held such resentment towards both his parents. Franco had made up for their mother's lack of warmth by fervently smothering his four children with affection. Being an extremely tactile father he had more than over-compensated for his wife Serenella's aloofness. Their marriage had been one of convenience rather than love or even friendship.

Franco often felt guilty at his lack of sorrow at his wife's early demise when Salvatore was a young child. She had always been in delicate health and becoming pregnant in her late forties had taken its toll on her health. Their son's premature birth had been difficult and his wife had never fully recovered afterwards. Franco believed that it was almost as though she wanted to die. The only task she enjoyed was working in their rooftop garden which is where he found her one chilly evening. She was sitting in a sun chair with her head down and at first he had thought her asleep, until he saw the waxen look of death on her face. A burst blood clot in the brain had taken her instantly, the doctor assured him.

Franco had been more upset for his children's loss than his own. For years he and his wife at her insistence had slept in separate bedrooms. Ironically Salvatore's conception had been due to the death of Serenella's mother. An event which caused her, in her unpredicted distress, uncommonly to seek comfort from her husband. The next morning Serenella had treated Franco with scorn and repugnance, causing him to feel as though he had committed a violation. Her family had arrived from Sicily on her death and without asking his permission, had taken her body back with them to be buried in the Inglima family vault at Ragusa. There had been no objections from Franco. Serenella had never made Malta her home and he knew that during her whole marriage, she had yearned to be living back in the Sicily she loved and missed so much.

Chapter 11

Malta. April, 2004.

The air in the underground carpark was stifling. 'I'd be better off in the cooler,' Marco thought, shutting the heavy door. His advice to Salvatore to rent one of the walk-in cooling compartments in the carpark had thankfully been taken up. When his youngest brother had been shown the enormous store-room, completely refrigerated, with a huge part as a freezer he got as excited as a schoolboy on the first day of holidays.

'But where did you find out about it?' he asked. 'I never knew this was down here under our feet all this time.'

Marco shrugged. 'That's because you never looked.'

'This will mean we can buy produce in bulk from now on. Pop can fish till his heart is content and we can store the lot down here until we need it for the restaurant. It could save us a small fortune. No, a huge fortune,' Salvatore said, running his hands along the cooling shelves. 'Not that I want to be spending too much time in here.'

'Don't worry *huh ftit*. I know you are

claustrophobic, so I will be the one to come down here. Okay?'

Salvatore grinned. 'Thanks. This will hold an enormous amount of food.'

Marco nodded in agreement. 'Be great if Malta gets attacked or goes to war again. At least we won't starve eh?' he joked. But Salvatore wasn't listening. He was already deciding in his head what dishes he could pre-cook and have stored in the freezing room under the restaurant.

Marco was relieved his suggestion didn't meet with any opposition from Salvatore. In spite of Pop giving the restaurant over to his youngest son to run, Marco was still the eldest and by tradition that meant his opinions had to be taken into consideration.

A screech of tyres made him look up from his mobile phone, which had shown no signal during the time he'd been waiting. It was Manuel.

'Why the hell didn't you answer your phone?' his cousin yelled, hopping quickly out of the car.

'No reception down here,' he answered, aware already that something big was going down. Manuel's two heavies were with him and one stood as lookout while the other went to the boot, opening it with a pop.

'You got a body in that or something?' Marco asked half joking, whilst nervously opening the cold room's door.

Nobody answered. Instead he braced himself against the door, holding it open as the two burly bodyguards carried the huge brown sacks marked FLOUR inside. 'There,' he indicated with his head to where he wanted the supply to go. With a thud the sacks were dumped on the ground and the men went outside for a second load. Marco caught the eye of Manuel who winked at him saying, '*Buon lavoro*.' He felt proud that he was proving himself worthy of belonging to *la famiglia Inglima* eventually and that was all he had ever wanted.

Chapter 12

Forli, Italy. August, 1944.

The first knowledge that his child was growing inside her caused Serenella to vomit, not just from morning sickness, but from revulsion that a part of *him* was still inside her. Left there, festering, growing like poison ivy, choking her until she could no longer eat a morsel. Hoping and praying that the thing would starve to death if she did not eat, Serenella's condition eventually attracted the attention of her mother. It was not pregnancy Maria-Angela suspected, but some dreadful wasting disease. The Mussolini household was not short of food as the rest of Italy was, so the girl was not starving for want of nourishment. Her plates came back empty. But unknown to Signora Inglima, the food was squashed into a napkin and disposed of later by the young woman. No, the girl was ill, Signora Inglima decided. Seriously so. None of the other children showed signs of sickness and in fear that she may be contagious, Maria-Angela decided that Serenella would have to be sent away once again. She was no help to anybody in this condition.

A telegram was sent to Doctor Moretti in Sicily

and his reply stated that it was much too dangerous for the girl to travel, both for health reasons and due to the country being at war. He was due in Italy to oversee a military hospital there and would make the journey to Forli to examine his patient, which he did several days later. To his horror, he found the young woman in the early stages of pregnancy, a condition of which she herself was already aware.

'Will you tell me who did this to you?' he asked in astonishment, when his own analysis confirmed her diagnosis.

Silence.

He sighed, then tactfully continued. 'I will ask you some questions and you can just simply nod or shake your head. Is that alright?'

She nodded.

'Do you know the man that did this?' She shook her head up and down once again.

'Was it by force?' She nodded her head silently, but looking at him all the while.

'Did it happen in this house?' When the girl's head bowed he clenched his fists by his side.

'Was it him?' He pointed to the framed picture of their Dictator found in almost every Italian home.

Once again, she nodded her head in affirmation.

***

Three months previously ...

There was a light, but it did not look like that of a candle or a bulb. It was just a small red dot, which moved up and down rhythmically. Serenella squinted in the dark of the night. A soldier, she thought. But was it an Italian soldier or a Nazi one? Either was bad for she was out after curfew. But the Italian soldiers were more lenient with their own people. A German one was more likely to enforce the full law and arrest her. Her heart beat rapidly. She had been so close. It might be one of Mussolini's own bodyguards, she surmised. If so, then she will be alright.

'Did you get lost little one?' a voice asked.

It was him. It was Il Duce.

Serenella gulped. She walked slowly, uncertainly, towards the master of the house. He threw a cigarette down on the ground and stamped on it with his foot. So that's what the light was.

'Have you lost your tongue?' he asked, his voice sounding as though he joked.

'No,' Serenella answered nervously, now reaching the place where he was standing.

'You lost track of time?'

Serenella nodded. 'Yes Signore Mussolini,' she answered.

He laughed. A loud throaty laugh, with his head reared back.

'The whole world calls me Il Duce and here in my own home a girl calls me Signore. Why not call me Benito? Or better still, Ben?'

Serenella hesitated. 'I mean no offence, Il Duce.'

He laughed again. 'Call me Ben.'

She stayed silent, staring at him anxiously. It was her mother that Serenella feared even more than him, if she discovered her daughter was out at this time. Il Duce was bound to tell of her misconduct.

He was much smaller up close. In actual fact, Serenella was amused to notice that she was taller than him by a fraction. He was powerfully built with an exceptionally broad chest which deceptively made him look taller, but he also had an extremely authoritative aura. Everybody she knew, male and female, spoke of how handsome he was. Serenella didn't agree. Up close he had quite a fat face and pudgy lips. Impulsively she smirked, with his bald head and jowly cheeks, he looked just like a pit-bull dog.

'You think I am being funny?' he barked, making her jump.

Serenella shook her head, afraid to speak for fear of addressing him wrongly. She hung her head submissively, hoping to be ordered to her room. Instead she felt his hand on her arm as Mussolini steered her towards the house. It was in darkness, apart from several dimly lit lamps. Even this home had to abide by the blackout rule. She was being guided in the direction of his office. Serenella had seen this room before, from the doorway only, but had never been inside. She had also peeked in at it from the window outside with her siblings. It was out of bounds to everybody but Mussolini. Not even Rachele was allowed in here. But his wife and everybody else knew that he sometimes entertained his lady friends in this room. She had even heard Mama say that for a woman to enter his office was like entering the gates of hell and nobody ever went in there willingly.

It was a darkly furnished room with a large ornamental walnut desk, elaborately carved with writing in bronze on the front. In the light, Serenella could not make out what it said. The Italian flag and the flag of the National Fascist Party, including the Nazi flag stood to attention behind the desk. Serenella had learned about the Fascist symbols in the classes she attended. She knew that the perched eagle on the flag carrying a *fasces,* signifying a bundle of sticks tied together with an axe, is an ancient Imperial Roman symbol signifying the power of life over death. Serenella looked around cautiously as she sat on the straight backed chair in front of the desk as directed. She had an ominous sense of something menacing in the room, causing her to tremble.

'You are cold?' Mussolini opened one of the glass display cabinets along each wall. He took out two tiny crystal tumblers and a carafe of brown liquid on a silver tray. It looked like cognac. Positioning himself on the desk opposite where she nervously sat, he poured the drink. Serenella could tell by the smell that it was definitely brandy.

'No,' she answered timidly.

'Ben,' he said, looking at her closely with his dark beady eyes.

Serenella's eyes widened, questioningly.

'No, *Ben,*' he ordered.

She remained silent, holding the small cold glass nervously in her hands.

'Say it,' he ordered again, more insistent this time.

'No … Ben,' she whispered.

'So you are warm?'

'Yes.'

'Yes what?' he hissed.

'Yes, Ben.'

Once again his head went back as he chuckled loudly. Then, just as suddenly his head snapped back again and he stared intently at her. Serenella felt her skin prickle under his gaze. 'You will be warmer after a taste of this,' he suggested, emptying his glass greedily in one gulp.

'Your turn. Drink.'

She did, also drinking the whole glassful in one swallow. The potent alcohol tasted like a liquid flame and instinctively Serenella coughed. Embarrassingly, some of the cognac spilled on to her chin. Lifting her hand to wipe it, she jumped as he shouted heatedly. 'Leave it.'

With her hand poised mid-air Serenella sat still as a statuette. Her eyes were locked onto his and she could feel a drop fall gradually from her chin onto her neck.

'Warmer?'

She nodded, her blood beginning to pound loudly in her ears as the man in front of her stared covetously at the glistening drop, which was now slowly running down her chest. It burned like acid. The young woman's whole body chillingly primed itself for attack.

***

Doctor Moretti squeezed Serenella's hand. 'You are to do exactly as I say. Do you trust me?' Serenella nodded and he continued. 'The next time you hear from me may be through a second party but if you are told that I have sent them, you are to obey any command. Understand?' Serenella indicated that she did and the Doctor stood. 'I will speak to your mother now, but don't worry,' he added, on seeing the look of dread on her face. 'I will say nothing about what you have just confided. But I will help you,' and he took his leave.

Signora Inglima was relieved to hear that her daughter's condition was not contagious.

'But what is it she suffers from Doctor?'

'Anaemia is a chronic condition,' he explained. 'Loss of appetite, lethargy and even depression are common symptoms.'

'Are you telling me that Serenella is *depressed*?' the woman asked, with disbelief. 'Depressed about what? She has an idylic lifestyle here compared to what is going on out there,' she said, gesticulating towards the window with her hand.

'It is part of her condition,' the Doctor continued. 'I have a suggestion, if I may, which I believe will cure her.'

'Yes, yes, whatever she needs,' Maria-Angela replied exasperated.

'I know that your family is deeply religious and I would advise on the counsel of a priest. A priest to call to her regularly, to give guidance and spiritual support.'

Signora Inglima looked at him aghast. 'A priest? Really? This is what you say will help her? Get her better?'

Doctor Moretti nodded his head. 'I am most sure of it Signora,' he replied.

Doctor Moretti did not waste much time in finding the Father Antonio he had mentioned. Aware that the man was presently hiding in a monastery on the outskirts of Rome, he began the journey there after leaving the home of Il Duce. The young man was surprised to see him.

'I thought you were still in Sicily,' he said.

'I had urgent matters to attend to here,' the Doctor explained, 'but I need to go back today. There is a very serious affair I need to discuss with you.'

Giorgio Cavallo (or Father Antonio as he was known in disguise) looked at the serious face of his friend and leader. 'Tell me,' he said. But he was not prepared for the awful information imparted to him.

'It was Mussolini,' Moretti informed him. 'He violated her.'

Giorgio thumped each pew hard with his fist, as he paced the small chapel like a caged wild animal. 'We have to silence that man forever,' he roared. 'I will kill him with my own hands.'

Doctor Moretti stood up, putting his hands on the young man's shoulders. 'Sit,' he said. 'This is what I propose. But it is all depending on how you still feel about Serenella.'

Soon the Inglima family had taken possession of an empty house in Rimini, less than an hour away from their friends, the Mussolini family in Forli. Giovanni Inglima, tired of not being master in his own home, had ordered his wife and children to move into the lavish villa on the seafront at Rimini. He discreetly left out the information that the house once belonged to a respectable Jewish family, who had been conveniently moved elsewhere.

Like princesses in their towers, both his wife and Signora Rachele Mussolini were unsullied by the actuality of events occurring in the world they inhabited. Busy with children and running households they only were aware of what went on in their own worlds, their own lives. Eager to please husbands, they turned away eyes from seeing what they did not want to and they believed what they were told. Of course husbands will misbehave. Then they must be reprimanded and forgiven in one breath by wives who knew too well, that they and their children would not survive in a country at war without these important men.

***

And so it was that Father Antonio Pisano began to visit the patient. He was humble, quiet and came and left by the servants' entrance at the back of the house.

'The priest is here,' Sophia, the housekeeper, was

practically hyperventilating because of having a man of the cloth in the house. As she showed the young bearded Padre into Serenella's bedroom she quickly glanced around, checking that the room was in order. It was. His being a priest was the only reason he was allowed into the young lady's bedroom. Having declined offers of refreshments, he had seemed anxious to see to the 'patient' as he called the young Signorina. With his hooded robe pulled over his head, he silently crept up the stairs behind the chattering woman.

'Oh she has been very ill Padre,' Sophia told him. 'Your pious direction for the soul I am sure will be of great benefit.'

Serenella was sitting up in bed reading when they entered the room. She looked up. He gasped when he saw her pale thin face. Signorina Inglima was agitated at being interrupted. Serenella studiously ignored any presence of the priest and asked Sophia why he was here.

'Doctor Moretti sent him,' she answered. 'He said spiritual support would help you.'

Serenella sat up straighter in the bed. 'Thank you Sophia,' she replied, remaining silent, as the priest did, until the housekeeper closed the door.

Swiftly the priest ran out. 'We are not to be disturbed,' he called, then locked the room from the inside with a key which he deposited under his robe. He pulled down his hood and Serenella gasped, until he covered her mouth with his hand.

Chapter 13

Malta. September, 2004.

'He's here,' Jessy squealed, shaking Billy's arm excitedly and jumping out of her seat where they had been sitting waiting for Flight LN762 to arrive from England. Slipping under the roped off area and totally ignoring the signs not to do so, Jessy bounded towards Neil, almost knocking him over with her hug.

'Steady on girl,' he laughed, hugging her back. 'You almost did me an injury then.'

'It's been ages,' she said, slapping him playfully on the shoulder. 'Why haven't you been in touch?'

'Hey, wait, where is she?' Neil asked, spinning around and obviously looking out for somebody.

'Where's who?' Jessy asked, also looking around, though she'd no idea who she was looking for.

'Ah, here she is,' Neil said, putting his arm around the most stunning woman Jessy had ever seen who sidled up beside him smiling. 'Jess, this is Mia. My partner.'

Jessy was stupefied. Neil had a *partner*. He'd never said. But then he hadn't said anything, because she hadn't heard a word from him since receiving his card

145

and gift at Christmas.

'Wow! This is a surprise,' she said, offering her hand to the blond vision in front of her. 'You are a dark horse, Neil.'

But her handshake was rebuffed as she was folded into the softest cashmere sweater ever. Mia wrapped her arms around Jessy and exclaimed how excited she was to meet Neil's little sister.

'Oh you are just like he said,' she gushed. 'So pretty and so *cute* looking. Not like a puppy at all!'

Jessy grimaced, unamused. 'Not like a puppy! What does that mean exactly?'

Neil and Mia both laughed, like it was some kind of private joke and Jessy felt her ears literally burning. 'I was trying to describe you and she …' Neil pointed to his *partner*, 'said I'd just described you like a puppy.'

'Oh,' Jessy said, raising her eyebrow at him and folding her arms defensively, 'and what exactly did you say?'

'He said,' Mia replied for him, proprietorially tucking her arm into his, like Jessy usually did, 'that you had loads of hair and big brown eyes and were kind of cuddly. And I laughed because it did sound just like you would describe a puppy. Don't you think?'

Jessy glared at him. *'Kind of cuddly?'* she repeated. 'Gee, thanks bruv.' Jessy was mortified. So he thought she was fat did he?

Mia giggled again. 'He did say that you wouldn't like to be called that. Or called a puppy either.'

Jessy grinned sarcastically but privately fumed. 'And did he tell you that he is the worst big brother ever?' she asked. 'He didn't contact his little sister for nine months. What do you think of that Mia?'

'Oh I know,' Blondie (which Jessy decided she was going to call her privately) replied. 'I kept telling him that and to let us have a chat on the phone, so we could get to know each other, but he kept making excuses.'

Jessy glared again at Neil who was looking quite sheepish by now. 'I thought you could never get a signal wherever you were based?'

'Signal? Based?' Blondie repeated. 'But he's been in London all year. Well, apart from that brief deployment in March. Isn't that right honey?'

Neil and Jessy both looked at each other now, one set of eyes flashing with anger and hurt and the other with embarrassment.

'Billy,' Neil called, gladly spotting the older man who was waving for attention at the other side of the roped area. 'So good to see you,' he said warmly, climbing over the barrier and wrapping his arms lovingly around the man who had brought him up.

'Who have you got here then?' Billy asked, running his eyes over the vision before him. All legs and bosom from what he could see, with peroxide blond hair cut into a sharp bob at her bony shoulders. Huge baby blue eyes peeked out from under a thick layered fringe and to his delight he too was enveloped in her arms. Oh, she smells so good, he thought. One is never too old to appreciate a good looking woman, though he preferred a few curves on a lady.

'This is Mia,' Neil said once again.

'His *partner*,' Jessy added.

'You kept this young lady as a big surprise for us all, did you?' Billy asked, wagging his finger at Neil. 'I don't blame you. I guess you were worried I might steal her away eh?'

They all laughed, even Jessy who was in a foul mood at this stage. Her excitement at seeing her brother again had quickly turned sour. Feeling small and dumpy beside this athletic looking model beside her, she just wanted to go home. No, not true. She wanted to go on a diet, dye her hair and her eyes and stretch herself to taller than her five foot six inches and just, well, just look like *her*. His *partner*. The word stuck in her throat when she said it to Billy.

'How long have you two been together?' she asked, directing her question at Mia.

The couple looked at each other and both replied at the same time. 'Since Christmas.'

'Christmas,' Jessy repeated. 'So now I know why he hasn't been in touch.'

'Oh,' Mia answered, putting out her bottom lip and pouting like a baby. 'I must take the blame then. We've been sort of in a little love bubble. Haven't we honey?' she purred up at Neil, who looked suitably embarrassed.

'*A love bubble*?' Jessy repeated, making the vomiting sign of putting her fingers down her throat. 'Yuck.'

Billy laughed again and put his arm around Jessy's shoulders. 'Oh don't worry,' he said. 'At least you won't have to live with them.'

Jessy paused in their walk to the booth where Neil was picking up keys for his rental car. 'You are both staying in Billy's?' she asked the couple.

'Actually no, we're not,' Neil replied, looking at

Billy. 'Sorry, I hope that's okay, but we are going to stay in Sliema actually. In a hotel there. Just so as not to disturb you.'

'Whatever you want,' Billy answered. 'Either is okay by me. But I will get to see something of you this time won't I? Last time you were out of here faster than a greyhound chasing a hare.'

'Sure,' Neil replied. 'In fact I was hoping you'd come over to Gozo with us. We'll take the car on the ferry.'

'I might do that,' Billy replied. 'Maybe Franco too?'

Neil nodded. 'Sure, why not?'

'And Salvu,' Jessy added.

'Then where would you go?' Neil asked, winking at her. 'In the car I mean?' He smiled. He could see Jessy adding up in her head how many people that would be, then looking disappointed.

'Okay, no you go Billy,' Jessy said, 'and maybe Franco too. Salvu and I are planning a trip anyway by ourselves.'

'Oh yes of course, you are engaged. How wonderful,' Mia cried, grabbing Jessy's hand. 'Let me see this ring.'

Lifting her hand to give the other woman a better

look, Jessy listened as Billy and Neil discussed places to show Mia on Gozo.

'And the Azure Window,' Billy suggested. 'That's worth a look Mia.'

Jessy dropped her hand and looked over at Neil, but he was busy filling in forms for the hired car. He didn't see the injured expression on her face. But Billy did and it gave him a terrible feeling of unease.

Jessy wasn't in any better humour by the time she got back to Franco's. The Azure Window was *their* place and now he was taking *her* there. She knew it was childish and unreasonable to feel as she did, but she couldn't help it.

***

'Never mind,' Salvatore said, grinning as he wrapped his arms around his moody fiancée. 'We will be going soon. To Gozo. And … staying in that fancy hotel you told me about.'

'The Kempinski?' Jessy squealed, incredulous. 'Really? How come?'

'Come with me and I'll show you,' Salvatore said smiling, with a glint in his eyes. Taking Jessy's hands he guided her towards the front door where outside a shiny new black Alfa Romeo car was parked.

'Whose is that?' Jess asked, running her hand along the gleaming roof. 'It's gorgeous.'

'Mine,' Salvatore answered proudly. 'Manuel gave it to me today.'

'*Gave* it to you?' Jessy asked with surprise. 'Why?'

'Get in.' Salvu opened the passenger door and Jessy climbed in, breathing in the unique odour of new car.

'Oh wow!' she squealed. 'Look at all the buttons,' reaching her hand out, only for Salvatore to slap it away playfully.

'Oh no you don't,' he laughed. 'I know what you are like with controls. You'll press every one and mess the whole thing up, leaving me to sort it out.'

Jessy giggled. 'You know me too well. But seriously. Your cousin just *gave* you a brand new car?'

Salvatore nodded. 'Well sort of. He said I could use it for going over and back to Sicily on the ferry and there was no hurry in paying for it. And … he gave me a large cheque, for he said, *taking care of family business.*'

'Wow!' Jessy said. 'But then you do have to pay for the car? Sometime.'

Salvatore looked at her reproachfully. 'Oh come

on. Don't ruin it for me. The restaurant is doing really well. Manuel isn't going to rush me. I can just give it back to him if I want to at any stage.'

'Okay boss,' Jessy answered, leaning over and kissing him good-humouredly on the cheek. 'Where to driver?' and Salvatore grinned, delighted that she was in a better mood.

'To the car-park,' he said, winking his eye.

'The car-park?'

'Yes. I have something else to show you,' Salvatore said.

On reaching the cool room however, he realised that the key was with his brother Marco.

'What is it?' Jessy asked, looking at the ominous steel door.

'It's a cool room. Like a store-room – it's a huge walk-in fridge and freezer. Marco organised it. I wanted to show you.'

'Is he paying for it?' Jessy asked.

'He … I don't know,' he answered, because Salvatore just realised he didn't know who was paying for it. 'I guess it is rented. Marco does the books now.'

'Hmm,' Jessy wondered. 'I would say it is expensive down here. Even to rent a parking space is exorbitant. Are you keeping the car here too?'

'Don't take the good out of everything,' he grumbled. 'I have just shown you two things I am proud of and you immediately point out the negative points.'

'Oh, I'm sorry,' Jessy replied, putting her arms around his waist. 'I just worry.'

'I told you I would look after anything to do with money. So just let me okay?'

Jessy smiled. 'Okay boss,' she said again, jokingly.

To her surprise Salvatore took her hands in his and looked very serious. 'It is important to me that you let me look after you and my business without you worrying, or asking questions. Okay? Will you respect that?'

'Yes,' she replied. 'Okay, from now on I will. Now can we drop it and go somewhere fun for a drive in that fabulous car of yours?'

But the matter was not dropped for her. A feeling of discomfort came over Jessy. As Salvatore drove them out of Valletta and along Qawra's picturesque coastal road, she pondered on whether this was what she wanted – to not be able to ask questions, or even say when she was worried. To just let Salvatore take care of all their finances without any input from her. Looking over at his handsome face she couldn't help but get a horrible feeling of foreboding.

Chapter 14

Rimini, Italy. September, 1944.

'Shush, quiet my love,' he ordered, slowing removing his hand.

Serenella was speechless. But her mind wasn't. He had called her 'love'. That was all that she cared about right now, at this minute.

'I …' she tried to speak, but once again he silenced her by placing his finger gently on her lips.

'Doctor Moretti told me everything. I am going to marry you.'

They had much to talk about, but first, Giorgio needed to hear from Serenella's own mouth what had happened to her.

'I had slipped out to see the German soldier, the one you told me to give my letters to.'

Giorgio nodded. 'Go on,' he said.

'He was late turning up, so I had to wait and I knew it was after curfew by the time I was walking back to Villa Carpena. I was ever so quiet but it didn't matter because Il Duce was outside smoking. He often went for a walk through the grounds to look at his collection of artefacts. He brought me in to his study and that was where …,' she hesitated. 'That was where he did it. I didn't want to. You know that?'

Giorgio nodded his head once again and he looked quite calm, but there was a pronounced blue vein standing out on his neck and he kept clenching his jaw as though he had a bad toothache.

'Afterwards … he told me to be a good girl and he would look after my family and make sure none of us got hurt. He said that really bad, terrible things were happening to people every day in the war and that it wouldn't be nice if I, or my family, were sent to one of those labour camps. I knew what he was saying. He was telling me to be quiet. So, I said nothing, to anyone. Then after a few weeks, I began to feel sick and I just knew. I knew what was wrong with me.'

Giorgio believed he had got over the shock of what Moretti had told him, but hearing Serenella give her own pitiful account nearly made him sick. He looked at the thin pale arms of the young woman he loved and saw the pain in her eyes. To him she was just as beautiful and innocent as when he had last seen her in Sicily. They didn't know that that would be the last time they would be together in Marina di Ragusa. It was the night before his conscription papers had been delivered by the postman. The night before Signore Inglima had informed the Doctor he would be taking his daughter to Italy for the summer.

Nobody knew then that just a few days later, Benito Mussolini would declare that Italy had joined forces with Germany and was now at war. Subsequently all their lives would change forever. Serenella's letter to him, which she had slipped under his door, informing him that she was leaving for Forli had included the address. But who would send private love letters to the home of Il Duce? Nobody sane. Especially not anybody who was fighting to be rid of the treacherous Dictator. For Giorgio Cavallo and his father, together with Doctor Moretti, were fighting their own private war now - as part of the ever growing Partisan group, better known as the Italian Resistance. Giorgio, before beginning his military training had been posted by Doctor Moretti, the local Sicilian *Partigiani* leader. He was sent to take up arms in the hills overlooking Rome, against the army and Fascist movement run by Il Duce, Benito Mussolini.

***

It was Moretti who had who received the first letter from Serenella to Giorgio at his parents' address in Marina Di Ragusa. Thinking it to be important, Valentina brought the letter to the Doctor, who scanned it quickly and told her he would look after it. It was several weeks before the letter reached Giorgio in Rome, who quickly sent a return letter to Serenella via a reliable source.

Sweetheart, I hope this letter finds you well. The man who has given you this envelope is to be trusted. Never use any other means to reply to me. This is a quick message just to say that I love you and I miss you. I will be in touch again, very soon, Till then, be strong in knowing that with a hopeful heart I tell you that this war will be over very soon and then we can be together. With all my love, As Always, Yours.

Serenella wondered why he hadn't signed his name. Except for the fact that she recognised his small tight hand-writing, she wouldn't have been convinced the letter was from Giorgio, especially as the man who placed it into her hand was none other than a Nazi soldier. It was with a thumping heart that she had approached the tall blond haired man when he beckoned her, while she walked in the grounds of Villa Carpena one sunny afternoon. Handing her the grubby envelope, the soldier looked around with a stern expression on his face. 'If you are asked, you are to say that I was reminding you not to leave the grounds,' he told her. 'This is a letter from a friend. You may reply through me, but you are to burn Giorgio's letters after reading and tell nobody that you received them. You may not mention your name or any other person's name or places in your correspondence. Understand?'

Serenella assured him that she understood his commands and gingerly accepted the letter from his hand, then pushed it into the pocket of her dress. Noticing her brother Marius look over enquiringly at the unusual sight of a soldier speaking with a member of the household, Serenella mumbled her thanks and walked away slowly, with a sombre expression on her face.

'What did he want,' Marius asked. 'Are you in trouble?'

Serenella tut-tutted. 'He is a horrible man. He said we are not to leave the gardens. Just trying to show us who is boss.'

'Il Duce is the boss, not him,' Marius answered candidly.

Serenella made an excuse to go into the house and

once indoors, ran quickly to her bedroom. Reading his words of love over and over it seemed unbearable to have to burn his letter. But she would, because the soldier had told her to. But the envelope – she hadn't been told to burn that. It had been in his hands and at least it was some reminder of the first letter he had sent to her.

The young woman's whole afternoon was spent composing a letter to Giorgio. Sitting up on the bed with pillows behind her, her knees drawn up and balancing her writing set on them, she wrote pages and pages of expressions of love, asked dozens of questions and gave every detail of what she had been doing since leaving Sicily. Just as she was about to sign her name, she remembered the soldier's warning – then warily re-read the words she had just written. She would have to start again, for the letter mentioned not just names of places as she been warned against doing, but also names of her family members.

Carefully she copied the letter out once again, omitting these transgressions. That letter was also discarded when Serenella realised that the paper she was using could be easily identified, if it fell into the wrong hands. It had been a Christmas gift from her parents, paper especially embossed with their family seal. Sighing, she began again. This is so difficult, she thought. I am afraid to write normally in case some family member finds it and recognises my handwriting. Pulling a plain sheet of paper from a drawer, Serenella dipped her pen once more into the inkwell and practised writing with a different penmanship. Finally satisfied, she began her letter again, this time in capital letters which slanted slightly to the left and on rough paper used for classwork.

My Darling, I am so happy to hear from you. Everything is well with me. I am sorry we did not get a chance to say goodbye and I hope we meet again very soon. I do not know where you are but wish you safety as you fight for this terrible war. I hope you are right and that it will end quickly. I want to go back and see you again soon, so much. I think I am going back to the same place we were on return. With all my love forever, yours also, for always.

***

Unbelievably he was now here with her, after all this time. Under her bed, wrapped carefully amongst out-of-season clothes, were over a hundred envelopes.

Some not even proper envelopes, but bits of cardboard or stained brown wrapping paper which had been tied roughly with string or pieces of wool. But inside they had all carried the same treasured letters from Giorgio, the letters immediately burned by her own hand after reading.

'Why are you dressed like that?' she eventually asked, after he had rained kisses on her face and her lips, leaving her almost breathless.

'I am in disguise because if I am seen I will be arrested.'

'Have you deserted the army?' she asked, concerned. 'That will get you in big trouble you know.'

He smiled at her innocence. 'I never joined the army,' he told her. 'At least not the one you are thinking of.'

Serenella was astonished. 'But, all this time, I thought you were fighting somewhere awful with the army. Where have you been? Have you ... you haven't actually become a priest for real?' She asked, horrified.

This made him laugh out loud, then quickly glancing at the door he said more quietly. 'No, *Tesoro*. I am with the Partisans.'

She recoiled from his embrace, her face showing

alarm at what he had just disclosed. All she had ever heard about the unruly Partisans was how heinous they were - how they were preventing Italy from winning the war with their depraved beliefs. Whole classes at their camps in Forlì had been dedicated to warning the youth against these bandits. To think that Giorgio was one of them was preposterous.

'Serenella, listen to me. It is important you understand what I am going to tell you.' When he saw the revulsion on her face he knew that she, like many ignorant people under the rule of Mussolini, believed in the Fascist propaganda as though it was a religion. 'You have been quite sheltered here in Rimini and at Villa Carpena, but you are naïve about what is truly going on in this war. I will educate you.'

The young woman beheld the earnest face of the man she loved and knew that whatever he told her, she would believe. For he had never hurt her or lied to her. In all the years she had known him from childhood, all Giorgio had ever shown her was love, protection and kindness, much more than her own parents had done. So she listened as the young partisan enthusiastically explained their fight for Italy's freedom from both Fascism and Communism. Without giving away any details which might someday bring her danger, Giorgio told of the ideology of their cause, the brave young men and women who gave their lives heroically, living rough in caves and safe-houses. He spoke also of the horror of the labour camps where they had freed hundreds of starving people and of the evil of Mussolini's regime. Serenella quietly listened as Giorgio spoke, gasping aloud at some parts and quietly weeping at others. To think all this went on, sometimes just miles from where they were living such sheltered lives, as Giorgio had said. It was unthinkable.

'I want to go with you,' she pleaded. 'Take me with you. We can say that you are taking me to church or to hospital. Please Giorgio. I want to help.'

Giorgio hugged her tight. As he pressed her head to his chest he could feel the softness of her beautiful thick hair. She smelled so clean and fresh, but he could also feel her ribs under her chemise. 'You are in no condition,' he murmured. He felt her body tense under his hold. 'After the marriage vows are exchanged, Moretti will take you back to Sicily. Mama will look after you until I get back.'

'How can you accept me, knowing what you do?' she asked tearfully. 'I am ruined.'

Giorgio shook his head, lifting her face to his and looking into her sorrowful eyes.

'It is not your fault,' he said softly. 'Mussolini is a tyrant and you are not the first woman he has abused in this way. But don't worry. He will meet his retribution soon. Your baby will be *our* baby. Nobody will ever know what you had to suffer.'

Serenella shook her head quickly. 'No. I don't want to have it. I am not eating in the hope it will go away but ...' Giorgio once again put his finger on her lips. 'Then you will be a murderer too *Tesoro*. This is a child from God. Not *him*. It will have my name, as you will – soon. Trust me.'

And she did. She began to eat and every few days *Father Antonio* would visit her bedroom for an hour or so, for spiritual guidance. Signora Inglima was relieved that the doctor's advice was working and worried less. Their new house in Rimini took up much of her time and she travelled weekly to Forli, visiting Signora Rachele Mussolini whenever possible. The two women had a strong friendship, borne out of a devotion to their Catholic faith, not to mention the shared understanding of being wives to complex and formidable men.

Chapter 15

Malta. October, 2004.

'How beautiful it all looks,' Mia exclaimed, taking the seat which Neil had pulled out for her. Indeed the view from Mdina was breath-taking, even in the twilight of this warm September evening. Built on one of Malta's highest points, the beautiful ancient walled town of Mdina was also known as the Silent City. At night, the eighth century fortified city was lit only by lamps, giving an atmosphere of a by-gone era. The town of Rabat spread out below them and in the distance, between twinkling lights, could be seen the wondrous Mosta Dome. On a hill opposite was the town of Mtarfa, where the famous Naval Hospital could be seen, watched over by its prominent Clock Tower.

'That's where Gran worked as a nurse during the war,' Jessy said, pointing over in the direction of Mtarfa. 'I bet she never thought as she looked over here from the hospital, that one day her grand-daughter would be looking back to where she once stood.'

'No. I bet she didn't,' Franco replied quietly. He also had been thinking of Ana as he gazed towards the hills of Rabat which he had travelled many times, many years ago. It was a journey he made often to see Ana when she was younger than Jessy's age now, to take her out of the busy hospital wards for a day so that they could spend time together. He remembered the many trips he had made in his humble horse and cart with Ana by his side, chattering companionably. He knew every private laneway where they had once pulled in to kiss and cuddle, always managing to get back before Matron Saliba locked the nurses' dormitory doors for the night.

Now Franco sat on the opposite side of Jessy, who was also at the end of the table, affording them both prime seats for the view. Leaning over the table he grabbed one of her hands and squeezing it gently said, 'She would have loved to be here to celebrate your birthday.'

Jessy squeezed back, her eyes moistening. 'I know. I wish she was.'

The old man and the young lady looked at each other warmly, each thinking of their own special memories of the woman they had loved. To Jessy she had been both grandmother and mother. She had been home. To Franco, Ana had been the love of his life, his sweetheart, his hopes and dreams. Sitting here with her grand-daughter, soon to be his daughter-in-law, he looked back once again to the Clock Tower which had been his and Ana's meeting place. It was hard to imagine how those sturdy black hands had turned every day since 1895. It had faithfully given the time every day during Malta's terrible suffering during World War Two and thankfully was one of the buildings never damaged in the almost daily bombardment. The young couple had leaned against the tower's solid limestone wall on many occasions, sometimes in a lovers embrace, other times just enjoying a few stolen minutes together if Ana could get out of the hospital and he had time away from his own work. Ana often remarked how it was impossible to actually read the time on the towering clock unless you were a distance away. One day they had even gone inside the building and climbed to the top. From their vantage point, they had pointed to the citadel of Mdina in the distance and Ana had worried about what damage the bombs could do to the beautiful city. It didn't seem possible that the clock was still ticking on day after day, when Ana was no longer here. She would say, 'Meet me at *our clock*' and to him it seemed wrong that it had outlasted her.

Giving himself a shake, Franco jumped out of his reverie as Billy nudged his elbow. 'Gone back a few years there have you mate?' he asked, nodding his head in empathy when he noticed the wet eyes of Franco. 'Us old fella's spend half our time in the past, the other half trying to feel comfortable in the present.'

Franco nodded. 'One of the disadvantages of getting to our age I guess …' he replied. '…are the frequent bouts of nostalgia that hit you right between the eyes sometimes.'

Billy agreed. 'Yes sir, but when I get like that, I look around to see what is here right now in front of me and it isn't a bad sight. It definitely is not.'

The two old men observed the group gathered around them. There was Jessy, laughing loudly as Salvatore tried to pin a birthday badge on her dress and Neil was engrossed in conversation with Mia. Further up the table was a scattering of relations. Franco and Ana's daughter Rigalla, or Sr. Lucija as she was known, was chatting with Ana's long-time friend, Jeany Castelletti-Borg and her husband Alexander. Franco's other children were also present with their offspring and Billy's nieces and nephews, together with his sister Stephanie. No, Franco thought, life wasn't too bad. This table was surrounded by many people he loved and who loved him and life went on.

'I can't believe I am twenty-five,' Jessy exclaimed. All heads turned in her direction. 'I mean, I don't feel twenty-five. I thought by this age I'd be all grown up and sensible, but I'm not. I still don't know what I want to do when I grow up.' Everybody laughed and Billy slowly stood up, lifting his glass.

'Let's start this birthday meal off with a toast. To Jessica. We all wish you a very happy birthday and many, many more to come.' As glasses clinked together and good wishes were offered, Neil caught Jessy's eye as his wine goblet knocked gently against hers in a toast.

'Happy birthday, old bird,' he winked. 'You look pretty grown up to me.'

'I am a couple of days twenty-five now so I have time to get accustomed to it. We decided to have my birthday meal today as you missed my real birthday. But I forgive you! And, less of the old,' Jessy said smiling at him. And I am really glad you are here.'

They hadn't spent much time together since he and Mia had arrived a few days ago. Apart from the fact that Jessy was working during the day, her brother had been whisking Mia around the island sightseeing and Jessy had been more than mildly put out. That had been her job while Neil was in Malta, showing him the attractions. Now he was using his new-found knowledge to share it with somebody else and it irked her uncomfortably.

'Guess where Salvatore is taking me tomorrow?' she asked, in mock innocence. At Neil's enquiring face she continued. 'To the Hotel Kempinski. We are staying there for the weekend.' After giving this information, Jessy turned to her right to clink her glass with Salvatore, who joined in the conversation.

'Yes. I'm looking forward to getting this gorgeous woman all to myself,' Salvatore said, winking at his fiancée and hugging her tightly to him. 'Two glorious days away from the restaurant. I can't wait.' Despite being relieved at the knowledge that Neil was in fact his girlfriend's half-brother and therefore no longer a threat, with regards to Jessy, Salvatore still felt he fought a territorial battle of ownership with the other man.

Neil wanted to punch the gloating man on the nose. He was furious with Jessy also. The Kempinski was *their* place. That's where they had stayed on their visit to Gozo and he had both fond and embarrassing memories of that night. Following a fabulous meal they had had a really great chat over a few glasses of wine, with Jess pouring her heart out about difficulties she'd been having with Salvatore. Then, he had stupidly tried to kiss her, ruining what had up to then been a wonderful day and night.

His offers of apology the next morning had been silenced by Jess who just wanted to forget it had ever happened, but even now, the memory made his face glow in shame. Thank God it was getting quite dark by this time and nobody could see him blush. But thinking about her and Salvatore sharing a room there together, perhaps in the very bed he had slept in himself made him jealous as hell. He took a long drink of his wine and liberally poured himself another full glass.

'Hey, don't forget you are driving honey,' Mia chastised him.

'Billy, any chance you'll drive us back?' Neil asked, feeling guilty as the old man was probably tired.

'Sure,' Billy replied. 'Once it's not too late. You young ones going to make a night of it then?' he asked, pointing to the ever increasing empty wine bottles on the long table.

'Sure, why not?' Neil answered, looking over at Jessy. 'It isn't every day I get to celebrate my little sister's birthday. Is it?'

'It's the first one you've shared,' Jessy replied sarcastically, 'and I am still waiting on my present.'

'All in good time Sis,' Neil answered with a wink. 'Have patience.'

Neil had good reason to tell Jessy to be patient, because the present he had bought her could not be used for another nine months. Not until June 2005 in fact. But, when he handed over the tickets for the Destiny's Child concert in Dublin the following year, Jessy had screamed so loud that Mia had to put hands up over her ears.

'Oh, wow! Oh wow!' she squealed, jumping up and down, then flinging herself excitedly around Neil's neck. 'I didn't think these were even out yet. I love Destiny's Child.'

'I know you do and the tickets are not out yet,' Neil answered, privately chuffed that she was so happy with his gift. 'I know a friend of a friend,' he winked. 'But I thought Dublin would be the best concert for you to go to, because then you can go visit Aghameen and your friends. Or take one of them since there are two

174

tickets?' He'd prefer she took a friend than invite Salvatore, even though that admission made him cringe at his own selfishness.

'Oh, I'll have to take my fiancé,' she cooed, linking her arm into Salvatore's. 'He still hasn't been to Ireland yet you know. It will be the perfect chance.'

Neil grinned, pleased to see her so happy, then looked at Salvatore over Jessy's head. The other man was staring him in the eye and not in a friendly way. 'Strike one to me Pal,' Neil thought. 'Strike one.'

'I can't believe you even gave me flight vouchers too,' Jessy said to Neil as Salvatore helped her into a jacket. The evening was now getting chillier, as was usual in Malta when the summer was ending and autumn approached. Salvatore then left the group to go inside the restaurant, to use the bathroom Jessy presumed. 'You've been so generous. I feel bad now for giving out about you not being in touch with me. You can go missing again if you like, if you come back with such a great present.'

Neil laughed. 'I'm happy too now that your fiancé is paying the bill for this meal. If I'd known he was going to, I'd have ordered a lot more food and more expensive wine.'

'Salvatore's paying?' Jessy asked, wrinkling her forehead. 'But I thought we were all paying for our own. That's what I told people when I invited them to come for my birthday meal.'

'Nope,' Neil shook his head. 'He said that the meal was on him.'

'But it must cost a fortune,' Jessy said, shocked at Salvatore. 'There were twenty-six people here tonight … that's …' She tried to work out the cost in her head.

'I know,' Neil replied. 'I worked it out too. This is a pretty exclusive place you picked here, each meal costs about seventy euros a head, never mind the wine.'

'Oh no, does it?' Jessy was appalled. 'I would never have asked people to come here if I'd known that.'

'Oh, nobody minds when it's for a family occasion and everybody loves to come to Mdina for a meal, but yes, it was very generous of Salvatore. I would imagine the bill has come to close to, if not over, two thousand euros. L'Artiste is obviously doing very well.'

'But he doesn't have that kind of money,' Jessy said, worriedly. 'And he has a new car that hasn't been paid for and the whole kitchen is being upgraded again. That's why we are going away tomorrow, because the restaurant is going to be closed.'

'To the Kempinski,' Neil said, not able to help himself. 'I always kind of thought of that hotel as *our* place.'

Jessy swung around defensively. 'Well you are taking Mia to *our* window,' she snapped.

Neil drew back in surprise. '*Our* window?'

'Yes,' Jessy continued. 'If the Kempinski is *our place*, then so is the Azure Window ours.'

'Oh, are you two arguing again?' slurred Mia, approaching them both and carrying an open bottle of wine in her hand. Over her shoulders was draped a silver fur box jacket. Suddenly she didn't look so glamorous, Jessy thought, taking in the lipstick smeared across Mia's face and black eye makeup smudged under her bleary blue eyes.

'No,' Neil replied. 'Just my sister being childish again,' he sneered, and Jessy gave him a wounded look.

'Come on, Marco knows a good nightclub in St. Julian's,' Mia said, linking her arm between Jessy and Neil as they walked down the hill, towards where the cars were parked outside the city walls.

'You go,' Neil answered. 'I'm not in the mood.'

'Jessy?' Mia asked.

'Jessy what?' said Salvatore, joining them.

'Is Jessy coming to Pac … Pace …?'

'Paceville?' prompted Salvatore.

'Yes, are you coming with me and Marco?' Mia asked again, nudging Jessy as she spoke.

'No.' Salvatore answered. Both Neil and Jessy looked at him.

'No?' questioned Jessy, sounding annoyed. 'Can't I answer for myself?'

Neil and Mia both stopped walking as Jessy stood still, turning to face Salvatore who was walking beside the trio.

'I just mean that we have an early start tomorrow,' Salvatore explained, not wanting to upset her. 'Of course, go if you want. I'll go with you if you want to go.'

'Yes. I *am* most definitely going,' Jessy replied stubbornly. 'It is my birthday after all.'

Chapter 16

Rimini, Italy. September, 1944.

Serenella felt the cool blades of grass tickle her feet as she walked. The earth felt damp, fresh from the early dawn dew. The morning sun, not yet warm, emitted flashes of light through the canopy of leaves above her head, making her eyes flicker as she looked up. It was chilly. With her left hand pulling a cream lace shawl tighter around her goose-pimpled arms, she paused from her hurried walk and looked back. Their family house looked so much smaller, even from this short distance. Insignificant. Her right hand tightly clutched a small valise, stolen from under Mama's bed the night before. Inside were some clothes, undergarments, a little money also pilfered from her mother and one pair of shoes. It had been purely by accident that the idea had come to make the getaway barefoot across the lawns, at the rear of the house. Otherwise her high heeled shoes would surely make indentations on the grass, giving clues as to the direction she had taken. It was also for this reason that Giorgio did not come to meet her. They couldn't risk footprints or tracks of a motorcar showing on the dusty driveway to the Inglima house. Instead he would be waiting as agreed at Tempio Malatestiano, the cathedral church in the old part of Rimini town. Here a priest would marry them both and from then on she would legally belong to Giorgio. No longer would she have to live under the totalitarian control of her parents.

The air was still, the only sound was that of her own laboured breath due to the exertion of her brisk step. It was a walk she had often undertaken with her brothers, or *Father Antonio*, when Mama on occasion ordered her out of bed for some air, but then she usually walked at a much slower pace. Eventually meeting the road on the outskirts of their property, Serenella was both surprised and relieved that there seemed to be nobody about. There was a peculiar quietness. Not even a dog barked. Stopping to put on her shoes, she wiped the sole of each dirty foot with the back of her hands. Imagine getting married with dirty feet, she thought. This was not the wedding day she had dreamed of. It would have been an elaborate affair if it hadn't been for this dreadful war and the entire family all back in Sicily. Mama would have thrown herself into the preparations, with no money spared for the marriage of her only daughter. Months would have been spent shopping for a trousseau of beautiful clothes, linens, shoes and jewellery. Instead Serenella had a stolen suitcase and no wedding dress - just dirty feet and carrying another man's baby.

How could it be that her Giorgio could still love her after she had been defiled so sordidly? But he did. Just thinking of him made her quicken her strides. The silence was eerie and reminded her of when the townspeople had been forced to watch a horrific execution at the Piazza Cavour, in Rimini's main square. It was a young man, just around the same age as Giorgio. He was naked, apart from a sackcloth tied around him by the older women to preserve his modesty, with the word *Traditore*, roughly printed in black paint across the front. It had only been possible to make out the letters TRADI … as the rest had been soaked in the blood which ran down from the angry red slashes across his chest. But they all knew what it said. The young man had shaken his head at attempts by a German soldier to cover his eyes with a strip of material. Instead he kept his eyes open, defiant in the face of death. It was horrific to think that Giorgio would suffer the same fate if arrested.

As the firing squad began to prepare their rifles,

the reluctant audience looked on in disbelief and horror when the young man began to loudly sing out the words of the rebellious Italian partisan song, *Bella Ciao*. *'Oh partisan carry me away, because I feel death approaching. And if I die as a partisan, oh bella ciao, bella ciao, bella ciao, ciao, ciao and if I die as a partisan then you must bury me'* – and the shots rang out.

Afterwards there had been a deathly silence, just like now and under her breath Serenella began to sing the words of the same song. *'Bella ciao, bella ciao, bella'*... and shots rang out once more. Falling to her knees she dropped the valise, her shawl falling to the ground as Serenella put her hands protectively over her head.

The noise was deafening. Crawling on her hands and knees she crouched between two trees. The ground shook with the sound of approaching army tanks. Even her teeth chattered with the vibration as the heavy artillery trucks slowly passed by. Suddenly there was a yell and Serenella heard something shouted in German. Peering out from her hiding place, she saw a soldier with the swastika symbol on his uniform. He had picked up her valise with the dropped shawl and was looking around, gesturing for the other men with guns to search the roadside area. It didn't take long to find her. Roughly she was dragged out by her hair and Serenella screamed with fear, as the soldier pushed her in front of a stern faced commandant.

Serenella could not understand the angry foreign words he was shouting at her. Her knees stung where they had been dragged along the dusty gravelled road and her legs were scraped and bleeding. He ordered the men to lift her onto the back of a truck, together with her shawl and case. She was flung like a dead animal onto the floor of the vehicle. Lined on each side were Nazi soldiers sitting on steel benches, all holding guns. To her terror, one of the men ran the muzzle of his gun along her leg, lifting her skirt high to expose the tops of her thighs while some of the others looked on and laughed. What are they going to do to me, she agonized, trying to pull the dress back down and tucking it under her legs. Please God don't let them hurt me.

She closed her eyes, then suddenly there was a cracking sound and Serenella, who by now was shivering with fright, looked up to see that her attacker had been hit on his face with something, or by somebody. Blood was pouring from his nose and his head was flung to one side. There was shouting, but one voice was louder than the others and it was a voice she recognised. It was the soldier Giorgio said she could trust, the one who delivered their letters. She didn't know his name, but Serenella was filled with relief to see him. Seeing her recognition, the soldier quickly shook his head and the young woman understood that she was not to acknowledge him. Instead Serenella sat uncomfortably, using her case as a seat. She covered her scratched legs with her shawl, silently praying that somehow she would get to Rimini, to marry Giorgio as they had planned.

The truck trundled along noisily in procession with a long line of tanks and infantry. Soon they were on the outskirts of Rimini. They passed by the uniformed apartment blocks or *colonie* buildings built by the Fascist Movement for Italian families in the 1930s. Serenella saw the Fascist flags hanging from windows, while people also had faces pressed against the panes of glass, watching as the German soldiers marched by. Nobody was outside. Plumes of smoke could be seen beyond these high rise structures from behind the surrounding trees, which led the way into the busy town.

Rimini was unrecognisable. Serenella covered her

mouth with her hands, willing herself not to scream out loud as the horrifying sight of dead people lying along the road met her eyes. In some places there were human mountains of bodies in various stages of decay, bodies of both uniformed soldiers and civilians.

The stench of death was overpowering. Hanging from lamp posts and on makeshift scaffolds swung corpses of men, but also women with their heads shaved. Serenella's heart was beating so fast that she felt it was going to burst right out of her chest. She could never have imagined such horror. Why did Giorgio tell her to come here? To this horrific place? How was she to find him? Would he be at the Cathedral as promised?

Giorgio had not known that one of Italy's greatest battles along the Gothic Line was to take place in the week running up to the day of his hoped for marriage to Serenella Inglima. The Resistance had been fighting fiercely all week, hoping to run the Nazis out of this part of Italy once and for all. In the areas around Forli and Bologna they fought valiantly and had good reason to expect victory. On a tip-off from a loyal fellow Partisan fighter, the partisans were aware that the Nazi convoy was expected to enter Rimini. This was their next target. The German succession of tanks, trucks and infantry approached the Porta-Montanara Gate. Built in the first century, it allowed entry into the city. Resistance fighters in hiding were waiting to detonate several landmines which they hoped would blow the whole lot to Kingdom come.

Giorgio Cavallo anxiously paced the steps of Tempio Malatestiano, praying and hoping that his bride-to-be would somehow miraculously make it to where he and the priest were waiting. His attempts to get a message to her home to postpone, were thwarted by not being able to get hold of Franz, their go-between and his comrade in arms. Although serving with the Nazis, Franz had been the eyes and ears for the Resistance since he was posted at Emilia-Romagna. Giorgio trusted him with his life. The last time he had seen Franz was two weeks ago, when he had given him charge of a letter to Serenella, stating when and where their marriage was to finally take place. Giorgio was unsure if she had received his message as he had heard no reply.

Franz was well aware that he was in danger of being blown to bits, along with Giorgio's girl, if he did not get them off the truck. As they neared the town gate and the truck began to slow down, he pushed the stunned Serenella off the moving vehicle and then jumped down quickly. Darting between the bullets fired in their direction, Franz dragged the screaming girl into the shell of a nearby building and flattened them both on the ground. Seconds later, a thunderous explosion sent debris flying through the air around them. As he lifted himself from her cowering body, Franz looked out.

Through the dense smoke Franz could see the body parts of his fellowmen scattered around the road outside. Roars of dying men could be heard and he flinched to see just inches from where he sat hunched was a bloodied head, with eyes wide open looking in his direction. By now Serenella was completely shell-shocked. Beyond being able to scream, she was rocking to and fro among the dust and dirt of the bombed out building. Unable to stand or walk with clothes almost ripped to shreds, Serenella's face was blackened with soot. Franz lifted her over his shoulder and began to walk in the direction of the church, where he hoped Giorgio would be waiting.

As they came onto the Piazza Cavour, the town clock struck seven in the morning. Serenella was by now limping alongside him, her tattered shawl wrapped over her head for it was a cold blustery day. Under the portico of the Palazzo dell'Arengo, the majestic Romanesque-Gothic style palace in the town square, were Greek soldiers of the Third Greek Mountain Brigade. Franz stopped to watch the historical spectacle playing out in front of them. A man, who declared himself the Mayor of Rimini, read out a document in Greek, Italian and English stating that he was handing the city over to its latest conquerors, the Greeks. From on top of the Palazzo, a Greek flag was hung over the walls. A loud cheer went up. It was not the victory they hoped for, but better the Greeks for now than the Nazis forever.

They were almost there.

From the Cathedral doorway. Giorgio saw the pitiable sight of Serenella stumbling across the square with Franz holding her up, his arm around her waist. He started to run.

'Look,' Franz said, lifting the young woman's head and pointing.

'Giorgio,' she cried, letting go of Franz's hand and running.

The light came out of nowhere, blinding her. She

felt only a thud as her head hit the ground and then blackness. Nothing but darkness. There was a piercing scream Serenella didn't know was her own.

Chapter 17

Malta. October, 2004.

'This is brilliant,' Jessy shouted, trying unsuccessfully to be heard over the deafening sound of Beyoncé's 'Crazy in Love' booming out of the night-club's speakers. Not understanding a word she said, Mia screamed in reply, holding her umbrella-festooned glass high above her head and waving it in the air in time to the musical beat. Within seconds bouncers were by her side and Jessy found herself gawping in disbelief, as Neil's girlfriend was hauled ungraciously from the dance-floor, amidst her disregarded shrieks of apology. Indignant at their dancing being cut short, Jessy squeezed herself through the sweaty crowd and meandered her way back to the bar where Salvatore was keeping their table.

'Did you see what happened to Mia?' she giggled, pointing in the direction of the entrance door. 'She got pulled off the dance-floor by two bouncers.'

'What for?' Salvatore asked bemused. His first impressions of Mia had been 'Bimbo', even if she did have a killer figure.

'Having a drink on the floor,' Jessy told him,

standing up and trying to see over the many heads for a glimpse of Mia. 'I better go look for her. Neil will be mad if we lose his *partner*.'

Before Salvatore could answer, Jessy got up and wandered among the tables dotted around the edge of the heaving dance-floor, looking out for a tall blond woman who was still dressed in a silver fur box-jacket. How can she wear that with the heat in here, Jessy wondered? It didn't take long to find her. It was Mia's long falsely tanned legs that caught her eyes. The skyscraper high heels now resting on a low glass table led her to Mia - who was now kissing the face off Marco - Salvatore's eldest brother. Jessy stood still, her mouth hanging open in disbelief. Oh my God, she thought. What am I going to tell Neil?

'Mia,' she yelled, shaking the woman's shoulder furiously. 'What are you doing?' Two sets of eyes looked up at her and Mia had Marco's saliva still wet on her chin.

'Shush,' Mia giggled, putting a purple painted fingernail coquettishly on her lips. 'You saw nothing, right?' And to Jessy's astonishment, Blondie turned back to an inebriated looking Marco and took up where she had left off.

'I don't believe what I just saw,' Jessy cried, climbing over another pair of entangled legs, before taking a seat beside Salvatore who was on the verge of falling asleep. 'I just caught Mia snogging your brother Marco.'

'Good for Marco,' Salvatore mumbled, getting to his feet. 'Come on. Let's go,' he said, offering an outstretched arm to Jessy. 'This place is a dump.'

'He must be twice her age. And what am I going to tell Neil?' Jessy was outraged. She had suspected that Mia was no good for her brother and her two-timing antics were proof of that.

'Don't tell him anything,' was Salvatore's advice. 'It's none of your business.'

Jessy dropped his hand. 'Are you serious? He is my brother and I just caught his girlfriend cheating on him.'

Salvatore sighed as he reached for her hand, eager to get out of the packed venue. 'Whatever you think then Jessy.'

The air outside was a relief from the smoky stifling atmosphere of the nightclub. Crowds were gathered outside, mostly people trying to get in for the last forty-five minutes of dancing, but also others who were hoping for lifts home. While Jessy pulled on a jacket, a group of about three or four men approached Salvatore, shaking his hand, apparently delighted to see him. Jessy looked on, wondering who they were and not recognising anybody she had ever seen with him before. They were smartly dressed men, kind of business-like in appearance and they seemed to know her fiancé quite well. Salvatore on the other hand, didn't appear to know them at all. To her surprise they followed, as she and Salvatore walked to his car which was parked on a narrow side street. Salvatore opened the passenger door for Jessy to get in.

'Wait here,' he ordered. 'I just need to chat with these friends for a moment.' He shut the door. Jessy watched through the rear-view mirror as the guys walked to the back of the car. She heard the boot being popped open. With the lid of the boot blocking her view, she waited, until minutes later Salvatore jumped in beside her.

'Who were they?' she asked, watching as the men walked away. One of them seemed to put something inside his black suit jacket.

'Friends of Marco's,' Salvatore replied, turning the key and revving the engine noisily. 'From work.'

Jessy nodded. 'I thought they looked like rich business men,' she answered. 'I am going to have a word with Marco when I see him,' she added crossly.

'So am I,' Salvatore replied, furiously pushing the car into gear and speeding off towards Valletta. 'So am I.'

***

The first person Jessy saw at the terminal at Cirkewwa was Billy. He was waving his walking stick in the air as he saw their car pulling up at the very back of the ferry, having almost missed it altogether. Neil's car was at the front. She could see Franco climbing out from the back seat and then Neil also getting out of his hired car. Waving out the window, Jessy waited until Salvatore had turned off the ignition. She too got out and zigzagged through the cars. People were now making their way towards the steps up to the ferry's seating area.

'Billy,' she called. 'You have good eyesight.' Billy laughed, still shaking his stick.

'I was looking out for you two,' he replied. 'You nearly missed the ferry.'

Salvatore looked sheepish. 'I know,' he answered.

'Something came up at the restaurant that I had to see to first.'

There was no sign of Mia. Looking over at Neil, Jessy wondered if he already knew what his girlfriend had been up to last night. However, he seemed in good form and gave Jessy a quick hug.

'Good night?' he asked, taking Billy's arm as they neared the steps. Billy quickly shrugged him off. Neil and Jessy smiled knowingly at each other.

'Kind of,' she answered. She didn't want to tell him what she had witnessed in front of the others.

There was only a scattered number of empty seats left. Jessy followed to where Salvatore had found them one outside on deck, while the others remained inside.

'Are you going to tell him?' Salvatore asked, putting his arm around her. She snuggled in beside him on an uncomfortable steel bench.

'Yes,' she replied, emphatically. 'I have to.'

'Why?'

Jessy looked up into his face. 'Why? Because his girlfriend cheated on him. With your brother. Did you see Marco this morning when you went to the restaurant?'

'No,' Salvatore lied.

***

But he had seen his brother that morning. He had made it his business to, after Marco ignored Salvatore's many attempts to call him. Eventually he found him at the restaurant, in the company of a very hung-over looking Mia, who was still wearing the same clothes and hugging a cup of coffee. Beckoning Marco outside to the small courtyard, Salvatore wasted no time in laying in to his brother.

'I want to know what *you* know about those packages in the boot of my car,' he hissed, jabbing his finger angrily into Marco's chest.

'Packages?' Marco repeated. 'What packages? I thought you were here to give me a hard time over Mia.'

'I couldn't care less about Mia,' Salvatore said angrily. 'I want to know how your friends knew about some 'gear' in my car and what you have to do with it.'

'It's your car, not mine. Or should I say Manuel's car?' Marco answered defensively, turning to leave. Salvatore swung him around. Marco was strongly built, but small and no match for Salvatore's towering height.

'What's going on?' Salvatore demanded, squaring

up to the older man.

Marco laughed. 'Don't play the big innocent with me *Salvucio*,' he sneered, using the family pet name. 'You are up to your neck in it.' Seeing the look of confusion on Salvatore's face he continued, 'Hah! You are so bloody innocent. You don't have a clue. Do you?'

Salvatore stayed silent, his mind whirring with a myriad of scenarios.

'Ask Manuel,' Marco jeered. '*Arrivederci* brother,' and with that he left.

Salvatore slumped on one of the wooden seats used by his staff for a break from the kitchen, where they could have a cigarette and get a few moments peace. He felt sick. Around him were the building materials, ready for the men who would soon arrive to start the restaurant's extension. Marco, thanks to his connections in the council planning office, had somehow managed to gain a permit for a new seating area above the kitchen of Ristorante L'Artiste. The building would now be two storey instead of one. The downstairs area would boast a new wine and tapas bar and Salvatore's cooking area would also be upgraded with state of the art pizza ovens. These changes would make their business one of the most modern and trendiest in that area of Valletta. The only condition made in respect of the planning permission for building an extension, was that the exterior was to remain unchanged, so that it would blend in with the other historical buildings in the UNESCO World Heritage City.

Salvatore ran his hand over the top of the expensive Italian marble tiles carefully piled up against one wall. Marco had also known somebody who could get him these at cost price. Now Salvatore was wondering exactly what that cost was going to be.

Jessy hadn't noticed that Salvatore was completely in a world of his own on the car journey to Cirkewwa. Still incensed at Mia's betrayal of her brother, she had talked of nothing else on the drive, while Salvatore ruminated on what he had gotten himself into with his cousin, Manuel Inglima.

The group met up again on reaching Gozo's busy harbour, Mgarr. After much hugging as if being parted for eternity instead of a day, each car sped off in its separate direction. It was a beautiful warm September morning with the bright yellow sun already promising a gloriously hot day. As Salvatore's car drove the quiet winding streets along the coast, Jessy flicked through a guide book, circling places she had not yet seen on this idyllic island.

Fiddling with the radio controls, trying to find songs in English, Jessy repeated the same question she'd already asked Salvatore a minute before. He seemed to be in a world of his own. 'Which is the one you had on yesterday, you know, the English music channel?'

He sighed, pushing her hand away and immediately the recognisable sounds of Katie Melua's 'The Closest Thing to Crazy' came on.

'Oh, I love this one,' Jessy crooned, turning the volume up. 'Oh, this is heaven.'

Salvatore looked across at the young woman beside him. As usual she had the window wound down fully with one arm hanging carelessly out. Her eyes were closed as she lay back in the seat and he couldn't help but smile. She looked so pretty. Glancing at the shapely legs crossed over each other, he placed a hand on her knee while carefully steering the wheel with the other. With a grin he cheekily slid his fingers underneath her short flowery dress. Her skin was as soft as silk. Immediately Salvatore felt a longing for her that he hadn't felt in a while.

'How do you fancy stopping at the beach first?' he asked, hopefully. 'Have we ever even been to the beach together yet?'

Jessy sat up. 'Oh yes. I'd love that. And no, we haven't. Shame on you,' she admonished him, playfully. 'And we have towels in the boot. I put them there this morning. Just in case.'

Straight away Salvatore's mood changed and he snapped his hand back. That bloody boot. Imagine, he thought, if she had gone to the boot yesterday. It would have been packed to the blooming top with packages of what I now know are drugs. Knowing Jessy, she would have opened one to see what was inside. Then, well then it didn't bear thinking about.

'We'll go to Mgarr ix Xini Fjord,' he said. 'It is beautiful there.'

'Wherever,' Jessy replied, a bit saddened that he had taken his hand away so abruptly. 'Once I am with you, I don't care where we go.'

Mgarr ix Xini Fjord was spectacularly beautiful. The little horse-shoe inlet with its small watch-tower and shimmering shore was a haven away from Malta.

'Listen. Can you hear?' Jessy asked, after she had laid what was really a table-cloth instead of a rug out on the sandy beach.

Salvatore sat down, pulling her down with him. 'Hear what?' he asked. The only sound he could hear was the gentle rhythmic lap of the waves and in the distance, the only noise was from the twittering of birds. 'I can't hear anything.'

'Exactly,' Jessy whispered. 'No noise. No traffic, or building sounds. No people. Nothing but quiet. Oh, I missed this so much.' She lay back, once again closing her eyes, continuing her reverie. 'In Ireland I could walk out into the garden in the morning and this is just what I would hear. Nothing, except Mother Nature at her best. Birdsong. The rustle of leaves on trees. The odd splash of a fish jumping in the lake behind our house. I miss the quietness. The stillness. Lie back Salvu. Lie back and just listen.' Jessy put out her hand without opening her eyes and drew him down beside her. 'Just close your eyes and listen.'

So he lay. Suddenly he sat up to take off his shoes and socks. A moment later Salvatore sat up again and took out the wallet which was uncomfortably digging into him. The sun shone on his face as he lay, jaw clenched and fists tightened by his side. Even his toes were curled up rigidly. Opening one eye he looked in

Jessy's direction. She looked serene. Dead even. Black hair spread like a halo around her head. Her eyes were shut. A peaceful smile was on her face. Her palms faced downward. Lifting his head a little, Salvatore looked at her bare feet. Even they looked asleep. *How I wish I could simply let go like that,* he thought, laying his head back and closing his eyes tightly again. Remembering the feel of the cool Italian marble under his hand, Salvatore clenched his fist. He recalled the accusing face of his brother when he spoke of Manuel and he thought about the tools ready and waiting to knock down the walls of Franco's restaurant and break into the roof above. If his own suspicions were correct, and all the money for the renovations had been illegally obtained, then it all had to be stopped. Salvatore had to find out what was going on. He had to find out what his cousin and Marco were up to, before it went too far.

'I have to go Jessy,' he declared, jumping up and already dusting the sand from his jeans. 'I have to go back to the restaurant.'

Jessy sat up, resting her elbows on the sand and watching incredulously as Salvatore began putting shoes and socks back on.

'What are you talking about?'

Salvatore put out a hand to help her up and Jessy swiped it away.

'I'm not going anywhere. We just got here. What is wrong with you?' She watched in disbelief as Salvatore already began to walk quickly towards where he had parked his car, pushing his wallet back into his pocket on the way.

'For goodness sake. Salvu, wait,' she called. Running after him and flinching as sharp stones jagged her bare feet, she finally caught him up as he opened the driver's door.

'What is going on?'

'Are you coming or what?' he replied impatiently, inserting his key.

'Salvu?' Jessy couldn't believe what was happening. What on earth was he doing? 'Wait,' she answered. 'I've to get my things.' And she rushed towards the sand, quickly gathered their belongings in her arms and threw them haphazardly into the back seat. Before she had even buckled the strap on her sandal, he was driving back up the steep hilly road and back towards the ferry.

Chapter 18

Rimini, Italy. September, 1944.

'I can tell you now, *exactly*, what is going to happen to you,' her mother spat. 'You are going to marry the father of that baby, whether you like it or not. You will also give me his name this minute, or I will beat it out of you and with any luck, that *bastardo* you are carrying too.'

'I can't Mama,' Serenella begged. 'I can't tell you his name.'

Not caring anything about either herself or the baby she carried, Serenella's only fears were for Giorgio Cavallo. Oh God, where was he? Less than two hours ago she had woken to find herself inside the cool Cathedral, with a concerned Father Ignacio looking over her worriedly. Serenella had repeatedly asked where Giorgio was. Nobody knew. It was Franz who had taken the weary and bedraggled girl home on a stolen motorbike, depositing her at the gates of the Inglima home that was situated on the promenade facing the Adriatic Sea, before rushing back to what was now the battleground of Rimini City.

The startling image of her daughter, who was

bleeding and covered in grimy dust from head to toe, had caused Maria-Angela to slice her finger on the secateurs she was using to prune her roses.

'What on earth,' she cried, rushing to where the young woman staggered shoeless up the driveway. 'What has happened to you? Where were you?' She slapped her daughter then pushed her roughly towards the house. 'You ... you are deviant,' she yelled. 'You tell lies, you go with disgusting men. You are a disgrace to the Inglima name.' Following quickly behind her daughter who now raced up the stairway, she continued her tirade of questions and verbal ranting. 'What am I supposed to do with you? With a child like you?' she screamed.

'I am no child,' Serenella replied, defiantly. 'I am having a baby...' She stopped, realising that if she gave Giorgio's name, her mother would waste no time in having him charged with treason for departing the Italian army. She would tell her husband Giovanni, whose official contacts would no doubt find him, then have Giorgio shot as a traitor. Serenella knew she could not reveal his name or where he was.

'You are what?' her mother screeched.

'I am pregnant,' Serenella said, holding her hand

over the small bump that was now quite obvious to Maria-Angela.

It took every ounce of restraint for Maria-Angela not to grab hold of her daughter's hair, drag her from the wide landing out onto the balcony and throw her like a bag of rubbish over the side. Better for her to have died in an unfortunate accident than to carry on living as the *puttana* she obviously was. Signora Inglima castigated herself for taking Serenella with them to Italy. She should have left her behind in that sanatorium at Marina di Ragusa, where no men could entice her wanton daughter. How could a once dutiful and compliant child turn into the indecent creature she had become? Maria-Angela could only blame herself. If she had kept a more vigilant eye on her only daughter, thwarted her friendship with that Cavallo boy and ensured she spent no time with the local coarse labourers, she was sure Serenella would not have been so improperly influenced.

Her own self-blame did not lighten her anger. If anything, it only infuriated the woman more to think that others would likely lay the blame on her bad mothering skills. What would Il Duce think? And Rachele? Their entire family would be completely ostracized in Italy and without Mussolini's influence and support – the Inglima family would be finished. Banished. There was no sense of pity whatsoever for her own daughter's predicament. Signora Inglima's only concern was the welfare of the rest of her family and their name.

'Stay here,' she ordered.

Serenella stepped towards her mother with her arms outstretched. 'Mama, please …' she whimpered. The only answer was the loud slam of her bedroom door and a sharp click as a key turned in the lock.

***

'I promise Mama,' Marius stammered. 'He is the only one.'

Maria-Angela shook her son violently by the arms. 'This is a most serious matter,' she implored. 'You must tell me everything you know.'

'Mama,' Angelo shouted, running over to where his mother was shaking his little brother as though he were a mat somebody was trying to beat dust out of. 'What are you doing?' he demanded angrily, rushing to Marius's side and thankful that for once he was here to thwart his mother's physical anger towards his siblings. 'Leave him alone.'

'What are you doing here?' his mother asked, startled to see that her son was back in Rimini. She was even more startled to notice that he was dressed like a simple peasant. Where was the smart Italian Fascist uniform he once wore so proudly?

Angelo, who towered over his mother, held his whimpering brother to his side and pointed a finger furiously into Maria-Angela's face. 'I am a man and I no longer answer to you,' he snarled. 'I am only here to give you and my family fair warning that you need to think about leaving Rimini. There is going to be serious trouble here soon.'

'Pah! I follow orders from nobody but your father. There is already serious trouble here,' his mother spat. 'Your darling sister is pregnant.'

Angelo reeled back in horror. 'Pregnant?' he repeated. 'Who did this to her? I will kill him with my bare hands.'

'That is what I am trying to find out from this stupid boy,' his mother replied. 'Marius. Tell Angelo what you told me.'

Marius was sobbing uncontrollably by now, both

in fear of his mother and disbelief that his adored sister was having a baby without being married. He was also now worried about the serious trouble coming, as his older brother had just mentioned.

'It's okay *piccolo*,' Angelo murmured gently. 'Tell me.'

'I already told Mama,' he answered, timidly. 'The only man I saw Serenella talking to was the German soldier who guarded our grounds. He used to give her letters. They whispered together all the time.'

Angelo glared. 'What is this German's name?'

'I don't know his name. He is very tall with blond hair. He is the man who brought her back here.'

'That could be any one of those Nazis! I have to find out his name,' Angelo hissed. 'To think that Serenella has been dishonoured by a bloody Nazi soldier? Where is she?'

Maria-Angela simply pointed to the ceiling, indicating that the little sister he loved was upstairs.

Within seconds Angelo was striding quickly up the marble staircase and yelling Serenella's name. Her door was locked but there was no reply to his shouts. Without bothering to return downstairs and get the key from his mother, Angelo kicked the door open. Inside he found his sister Serenella's lifeless looking body half hanging out of her bed. Vomit drooled from her mouth. Roaring her name Angelo lifted his sister, noticing as he did the empty morphine powder sachets on her bedside table. Serenella's eyes rolled back in her head. His wails of despair now mingled with those of his mother and Marius who were by now also in the bedroom, having followed his hasty ascent upstairs.

'My child, my child,' Maria-Angela cried. 'What has happened to her?'

'Ring for an ambulance. NOW!' Angelo roared, jolting his mother into action. Then he added quickly, 'No. No, we can't do that.'

'Why?' Maria-Angela cried. 'We need to get her to a hospital quickly.'

'They are looking for you. For anybody connected to Mussolini,' Angelo answered, all the while trying to coax Serenella to wake up. He patted her hard on the back with the palm of his hand, as though trying to wind a baby, to induce more vomit. 'If the wrong people find out where our family is, we could all be dragged off and killed.'

Marius began to roar loudly with fear, until Maria-Angela slapped him hard across the face. Angelo glowered as this mother. 'Leave him ALONE,' he shouted, heatedly. 'You go. You go and get Moretti.'

'Moretti?' she replied, in panic. 'I don't know where Moretti is.'

'He is at Our Lady of Graces, at Covignano Hill. You need to be quick. The truck I came in will be waiting outside. Tell Pedro the driver that I said to take you to Moretti.'

'At the monastery – but why is he there?' Maria-Angela asked, wringing her hands. 'She is trying to talk.' Pointing at Serenella, she made to cross the room where Angelo was gently wiping his sister's mouth while listening carefully to the words she was attempting to say.

'Go,' he ordered his mother. 'Go now and hurry.'

Marius looked between his mother and Angelo, not knowing who to trust. 'Marius, fill a bath,' Angelo demanded, 'maybe we can shock her into wakening.'

Serenella whimpered hoarsely as her brother lowered her gently into the freezing water which was still pouring out from the tap. A sodden nightdress clung to her slight frame and Angelo could clearly see the small swelling of her tummy. He hoped that whatever his sister was going through she would survive, but that the German's illegitimate child would not.

By the time Moretti arrived, to Maria-Angela's relief, Serenella was still alive, though barely.

'She has not taken enough morphine to kill her,' Moretti told the Inglimas, 'but her heartbeat is fast and I am worried about her pallor. She is still quite blue.'

'Maybe I shouldn't have given her a cold bath,' Angelo said worriedly.

Moretti shook his head. 'You did right. No, it is more to do with her weak chest I would say, being worsened by the morphine.' He showed them the empty sachets in his hand. 'She took three of these. I would imagine she had intended to take more but probably passed out. That glass is only half full,' he said.

Angelo looked down at his sleeping sister and his heart ached with pity and love. He was supposed to look out for her and he had failed. So badly. She was pregnant, probably raped by a Nazi and now had tried to take her own life. Glancing accusingly at his mother he used a tone which for the first time, made her think he sounded just like his formidable father.

'We need to get her out of Italy. If it is discovered

she has been with a Nazi she will be shorn and tarred, or worse, she will be killed. Strung up like those other Nazi whores in the town square.'

Maria-Angela gasped. 'Then take her. Take her with you?' she implored the doctor.

'She will die if we move her now,' Moretti warned.

'Mama,' Angelo said, seriously. 'As soon as she begins to recover you must send her back to Sicily.'

'No,' Moretti shook his head. 'Further away if you can do it. It is best out of Italy completely if possible. You must trust me on this.'

'Malta,' Maria-Angela said. 'I can send her to Malta. To Magarita's family. They will take her I am sure.'

Chapter 19

Malta. October, 2004.

'Do you love me?'

Salvatore was looking out to sea. The sky had darkened somewhat and the air was heavy. Thunder loomed, he guessed. Even the water below had changed colour. Like a chameleon it seemed to change with the mood of the weather. Now it looked grey, even black in parts. He sensed Jessy move beside him. Tense a little. But she didn't look at him.

'Yes,' she replied. 'Do you love *me*?'

He nodded. Then realising she might not have seen, he said it aloud. 'Yes, I do. Of course I do.'

'What is wrong Salvu?' she asked tentatively, half afraid of his answer. Was there somebody else?

'Did you ever want to just get away?' he asked. 'Where nobody knows you. Where you can start afresh. Be who you want to be?'

Jessy looked up at him. His face was set hard. It wasn't a look she had ever seen on his face before. He looked like a man who had reached a difficult decision.

'Yes.' There was so much more she wanted to say, to ask. But somehow the words in her head wouldn't reach her lips.

'Marry me.'

Jessy gasped. 'But I already said I would marry you.'

'I don't want to wait.' Salvatore turned around and pulled her tightly into his arms. 'Let's go away together. To America. I have relatives there who are always asking me to go. They said they could set me up with an art gallery. That's always been my dream as you know. Why not go? You and me?'

Jessy clenched his jacket tight in her fists. 'Why?' she asked. 'Why now? What's happened?'

He kissed her lingeringly on the lips. It was a long time since he had done that, she thought. For a long time his days have been spent working, working, always working. She too worked, but in the evenings she was free. And lonely. Always waiting on him. Waiting on him to come home early for one evening. Waiting on him to take her on a date, to take her on a holiday. But there never was any time. She felt that the restaurant was his mistress and that she was the clinging demanding wife. Always wanting more of him.

'Today, on the beach,' he lied once again, 'I just

wanted to run back to the restaurant and tell Pop to let Marco take it over completely. It has become too much for me. For us. When was the last time I painted, or we spent time together. Just you and me?'

Jessy felt her heart lift in hope. Yes. This is what she wanted more than anything.

'Could we?' she asked, afraid to even voice her desire. 'Could we just go? To America?'

'Why not?' Salvatore answered. He stroked the side of her face gently. 'We have our whole lives ahead of us yet, Jessy. If it doesn't work out, we can always come back. But I think we should get married here first. If you will have me?'

'Oh yes Salvu,' she cried, flinging her arms around him and planting kisses all over his face. 'Can we do it soon?'

He laughed. 'Well, there is protocol of course. I think you have to do a marriage guidance course and post the banns or something, but I am sure it can be done as quickly as possible. Sr. Lucija will probably be able to help.'

When Franco arrived home late that evening he was met by Jessy and Salvatore waiting for him, beaming with their news. He was ecstatic on their behalf and immediately rang their parish priest who set the formal wheels in motion, with no time lost. Like Salvatore, Franco also had had a realisation of sorts while on Gozo. For him it was being back at the Azure Window, where he had once taken Ana many years ago. While Billy and Neil had slowly walked around the periphery of the cliff face, Franco had sat on the steps of an old watch-tower reminiscing on the day he had spent with Ana there, making plans. Plans which never had come to fruition, when fate got in the way and irrevocably changed the course of their lives. These last few days she had been on his mind constantly. At his request, Neil had taken him to the small Carmelite convent at the foot of the hill beside the Citadel, where he had gone after the war to be reunited with his and Ana's baby daughter, Rigalla.

Sr. Regina, the same nun who had first handed his daughter to him was still there. In a wheelchair now, she had grasped both his hands in her own and shaken them up and down with tears in her eyes. Together they sat at the old kitchen table, almost completely scrubbed of its paint over the years and drank sweet red wine as they remembered his parents, Margarita and Nikola, calling with him to collect baby Rigalla. Sr. Regina had met several times with Rigalla, now Sr. Lucija, over the years and she delighted in hearing about Jessica and her romance with Salvatore. It was to Sr. Regina that Franco divulged the feeling that he felt his time was near.

'It's an awareness in my body,' he explained. 'It is hard to explain. Not like an illness or anything, but a knowing. I suppose it must be like when a woman *feels* she is pregnant before even being told. Sometimes things feel sharper around me, like somebody turns on a light in my head and I see things that I hadn't noticed before. Not things as in objects, but realisations of why things happen as they do. What it is all about.' He shook his head. 'Like I said. I can't explain it. But I know what I feel.'

Sr. Regina was nodding her head all the time he spoke. 'I have heard that from many people over the years,' she said. 'Indeed I have had that experience myself. I am much older than you, remember. You know this convent is a nursing home for the elderly now?' Franco said he did. 'I have heard it said before, from those who feel that death is approaching, that they know it is soon by their own body gently telling them. It is God's fatherly way of telling us to prepare. You don't seem to be at all afraid Gianfranco?'

Franco shook his head. 'No. I am ready. I have seen enough now. Would I like to see Jessica and Salvatore married and bounce their children on my knee? Yes. Selfishly so. But, I don't think it will happen.'

'You think you will be watching from above?'

'No,' Franco replied. 'I don't think they will ever marry.'

So the news the young couple imparted on his return that evening stumped him a little, but their joy was contagious. As Franco Vella went to sleep that night he dreamed only of weddings and wondered if he would fit into his old suit.

Jessy also went to sleep thinking of her wedding. Finding it impossible to switch off with dozens of plans running around in her head she sat up, turned on the bedside lamp and rummaged in her locker drawer for a notebook and pen. Skimming through the book until she came to a number of blank pages together, she wrote on the top of a page – WEDDING PLANS, underlining it with two straight lines. On a sub-line underneath she wrote - BUY. First on the list Jessy scribbled, wedding dress. She woke the next morning with the notebook still in her hand and her white bedspread and hands dotted with ink. The list had grown onto three pages. Already Jessy began to wonder if it would be possible to organise and buy everything in three weeks. Also, she wondered if her savings would cover the cost of the long list she had created. It was highly improbable. Secretly wondering if her father Jimmy would help with the costs, Jessy lifted her mobile to ring him and give him the good news. He would need to be given some warning of an imminent trip to Malta as soon as they had set a date, as would Joyce and her friends in Ireland.

Unusually, Salvatore was still in the house that morning when Jessy went to the kitchen in search of her charger. On most mornings he was out before she was up, eager to get started on the breakfast rush for Malta's busy workers and holiday-makers, even on a Sunday.

'Morning hubby,' she giggled, planting a kiss on his lips and squeezing her arms tightly around his waist. 'I'm just going to ring Jimmy to tell him about the wedding. And Joyce. Oh, I hope the girls can get over. Even just one of them. Tina hopefully.'

'Whoa,' Salvatore said, tipping her on the nose with his finger, as you would a bold puppy. 'We haven't discussed anything about the wedding yet. I presumed we'd be thinking something small?'

'Sure,' Jessy replied, plugging her charger into the wall socket and inserting the mobile. 'But my father will have to be there to give me away. And we can't not invite Joyce or my best friends.'

Salvatore ran his fingers through his hair. 'No, I guess not,' then added, 'Let's keep it a secret. A surprise.'

Jessy widened her eyes and looked incredulously at her fiancé. 'But why?'

'Oh, I don't know. I mean, if we are going America, we will need all the spare cash we can find. The fare over will cost a fortune alone. Why don't we just go off to the church, or even a registry office and do it quickly and quietly, then come back and tell everybody afterwards?' Salvatore grabbed her hands hopefully. 'What do you think?'

'I think you are mad, or joking. At least I hope you are joking?' Jessy felt as though her stomach did a summersault. Suddenly breakfast didn't seem very appealing. 'What is the big rush?'

'I thought you agreed last night to do it soon?'

'Yes,' Jessy answered, taking a seat at the kitchen table and beckoning for him to sit next to her. Salvatore remained standing. 'But, I want my father there and my friends from Ireland. And a registry office? No way!'

Theatrically Salvatore threw his hands in the air, just like Franco when he was vexed or worried. 'Right then. Get them all over if that's what you want.' He turned to leave, then leaned down and dutifully kissed Jessy quickly on the cheek. 'I have to go.' Jessy looked up. There were tears in her eyes. 'What?' he asked, impatiently.

'You. That's what,' she answered, miserably. 'Last night and this morning I was so happy and now … now once again you are going off to work when you have just told me that you don't want me to have my father or my friends at our wedding. And now, suddenly you are talking about us marrying in a registry office. I feel like you are bullying me into agreeing with you, when it's not what I want. Not at all. And now you are just going to walk out, leaving me upset.'

And he did just that, without a reply, banging the front door shut while Jessy put her face in her hands and wept, completely at a loss as to what had just transpired between them. That was how Franco found her a few minutes later. Not hearing his approach, Jessy jumped when she felt his arms around her shoulders.

222

'Tell me,' he said, quietly. 'Tell Franco.'

Chapter 20

Malta. October, 1944.

~

October, 1st, 1944.

La Casa di Sabbia,
Viale Regina,
Bellariva,
Rimini
Italy

Carissimo Margarita,

I know you once said that you would repay the favour my family did for you and Nikola, now I need that promise to be fulfilled.

I need your help. My daughter Serenella has been gravely ill. But not only this, I am ashamed to say she is to have a child out of wedlock. I need a safe place for her to stay until the child is born. I will come to Malta in time for the birth and the matter will then no longer concern you.

If you are in agreement, please return a letter to me as soon as possible. I will forward arrangements.

I trust in your good word.

Tuo amico,

Maria-Angela Inglima.

~

'What do you think?' Margarita asked her husband, who sat at the long kitchen table. To her exasperation he had it strewn with a smelly fishing net.

'There is nothing to think,' was the reply. 'You reply immediately that yes. Send the girl.'

Margarita sat next to her husband on the simple wooden bench. She indicated with her head a curtain that separated a sleeping area from the living area. Behind this curtain was a small cot in which their first grandchild, Rigalla, lay sleeping.

The letter was dated 1st October. It had taken almost a month for it to reach Malta. The young man who had delivered it to their home on this last day of the month, had explained when they brought him inside that it had passed through many hands prior to being given to him two nights ago, before he sailed from Sicily to Malta.

'I was given it at the port,' he explained, swallowing another spoonful of the *Soppa tal-armla* which Margarita had placed in front of him, along with some of that morning's freshly baked bread. The simple local dish, known as Widow's Soup, was welcome sustenance after his long journey. The various types of vegetables together with fat broad beans were already filling the young man's hungry stomach. 'The man who gave it to me said he received it along with several other letters from a priest at Ragusa.'

Margarita and Nikola looked at each other. 'I wonder how they got it from Rimini to Sicily. It's a long way. This information is not something the Inglimas would want to fall into the wrong hands.'

The young man shook his head. 'There are ways and means of getting anything or anyone out of Italy or Sicily to anywhere in the world, if you know the right people.'

Nikola spoke then, 'I think it is best we don't ask any more questions,' he said.

'But I have another one,' Margarita asked. 'Where will we put her? There is absolutely no room upstairs.'

Nikola put down his fishing nets and affectionately kissed his pale wife on the cheek. 'God will provide,' he said. 'He will make room.'

His wife sighed. It was a typical reply from Nikola, but unfortunately not a very practical one. Despite two of her children now living away from home with families of their own, there were still twelve people living in this two bedroomed house, as well as a toddler. She and Nikola slept in the little area curtained off from the kitchen with their grand-daughter, Rigalla. Franco shared a room upstairs with six younger brothers. The other small bedroom housed their three daughters. They could not put a sick pregnant woman in there.

'We will have to hang another curtain,' Margarita said wearily, getting up to search through their large antique wardrobe for material she could use. Standing on a chair to reach to the top shelf, she felt her legs tremble once again.

'*Simu*,' Franco called. 'Let me,' and her son helped her down from the rickety chair before jumping up easily onto it himself. 'What are we looking for?'

'A roll of material, flowery … with maybe pink roses,' Margarita answered, 'at the back I think.'

As he handed it to her Franco asked what she was making.

'Another curtain,' Margarita replied. 'We are having a visitor and we need to make another room. Here I think,' she said, gesturing to where a very old desk was pushed against a wall. She had been given it along with some other expensive furniture from her luxurious home in Ragusa Ibla, Sicily, after her marriage to Nikola Vella, a humble Maltese fisherman. 'We can move this desk into our area and string a curtain up here.' She pointed to a wall on each side. 'It's good there is a window, to let in some light.'

'Who is the visitor?' Franco asked, already beginning to drag the heavy desk out from its place. 'Gosh *Simu*, what have you got in here?'

Margarita laughed. 'Everything,' she answered. 'The visitor is Serenella Inglima, daughter of my old friend Maria-Angela.'

Franco looked aghast. 'I thought you said she was a bad-tempered snob and her husband is a Fascist bully,' he said, surprised. 'Why is she coming to this lowly abode? Don't they have a palazzo in Ragusa and one in Italy too?'

Margarita nodded. 'Yes, but their daughter is in trouble and we owe them a favour. If it wasn't for Signore Inglima's assistance, your father wouldn't have been let out of prison in Sicily that time.'

'I don't understand why he was arrested in the first place,' Franco replied.

'Because if you remember, we were in Sicily when war was declared,' Margarita explained, 'visiting my family. Any known Maltese people there at the time were arrested as an enemy aliens. Nikola was arrested trying to board the boat home. I went straight to Ragusa to plead with the assistant to Giovanni Inglima, because he was the Town Mayor after his father died and he obtained a special dispensation. I promised them I would repay their favour in the future. And that time has come. Somehow our families always seem to end up owing each other favours.'

'What kind of trouble is she in?' Franco asked, making his way to where he could hear his baby daughter beginning to chatter happily to herself, letting them know she had woken from her afternoon nap.

'She is going to have a baby. And she is unmarried,' Margarita replied, 'and for the sake of their name being associated with scandal and the life of their daughter, the Inglimas asked to send her here. We can't say no.'

Franco nodded. Lifting his blond-haired giggling daughter out of her cot, he kissed the top of her head. He thought of Ana, his child's mother and agreed with Margarita. 'No. We can't say no.' If there had have been somebody to help his fiancée, his *former* fiancée he thought with a grimace, then maybe she would not have ended up thousands of miles away from him and now married to another man.

When Serenella Inglima did turn up that windy November morning she did not look very pregnant to Franco. Muffled in an expensive fur coat, she blinked her eyes as she entered the warm bright room. Despite the time of the year, the sun still shone strongly and the four windows allowed the sunshine to fill the room with both heat and light. Removing her coat, Franco's sisters gasped at her classy clothes. She was dressed as a noble woman, even down to the black diamante clasps on her cream leather shoes. Like most Maltese, children and adults alike, the Vellas were dressed smartly and cleanly but their clothes were old, worn and well-mended. This young lady's clothes looked shop bought and new, if a little dirty and dusty after the journey. She also had a stylish hat, complete with a feather on the side, which Rigalla from her perch in Franco's arms tried to grab to everyone's laughter.

Serenella also had a small case with her, which Franco carried behind the rose-patterned curtain. She arrived without parents, but in the company of a young doctor who introduced himself as Dottore Moretti. All the Vella children including baby Rigalla were ushered outside the house, while the adults sat down to talk.

Nikola brought out a simple bottle of homemade red wine. Terms were set out by the doctor and agreed upon by Margarita and Nikola. Serenella was not to go outside. She would help Margarita with light household duties and could sit in their small courtyard for fresh air. A few weeks before the baby was due, which was in April, Signora Inglima would arrive in Malta. Dottore Moretti could not be sure of his whereabouts at that time, but if possible he would assist the birth. If not, Margarita Vella would use her midwifery skills to deliver the baby.

The Vella family's involvement would end there. Margarita raised an eyebrow at Dottore Moretti who shook his head. Margarita knew this meant that the baby would be sent to an orphanage. Most likely Serenella would be forced to enter a convent. An enclosed convent no doubt, where she would never be seen again. It was probable that her family would be told she had died and Margarita wondered, guiltily, if it would be better if she did.

Franco was enraged when his mother voiced her sad premonitions to him and Nikola later. Serenella had retired behind the curtain and for privacy, the three elder family members had moved to the courtyard out back.

'But that's monstrous,' Franco said, angrily. 'She did nothing wrong. She was attacked, raped … by a Nazi according to that Doctor Moretti. Why should she and her baby suffer or be cast out like some criminal? It is the soldier that did it who should be suffering. Didn't they find the man responsible?'

Margarita nodded her head. 'Yes. A Franz Schmidt. He was hung. Her brother Angelo found out who he was. I believe he did suffer Franco,' she added. 'He was apparently dipped in hot tar then strung up on a scaffold in Rimini's town square.'

Franco shuddered. 'Jesus,' he whispered. 'Barbaric. But,' he added, 'it's no more barbaric than the kind of life Serenella's family have planned for her.' He beat his fist against the rough limestone wall. 'It is as though it is the worst of crimes for a woman to fall pregnant, when it is the most natural thing in the world. It is disgusting.'

Margarita and Nikola looked sadly at each other, aware that he spoke about Ana in his outburst. They had been both horrified and heart-broken to find out too late, that their son's fiancée had been pregnant at the time he had been exiled to the Orkney Islands in

1942. To save their distress Ana had hidden the pregnancy from them and was then forced into marriage with a man chosen by her Wing-Commander father – the same man who had sent their son away. She had also been cruelly lied to and told her baby had died. Afterwards Ana had left Malta with her husband when the war in Malta ended. She gone to live in England, unaware that her little daughter was alive and living in an orphanage in Gozo, where thankfully Franco had found her just a short time ago.

Franco noticed his mother shiver. '*Simu*,' he said gently. 'Why don't you go back inside? See if Serenella needs anything?' His mother nodded, trying unsuccessfully to hide her cough.

She found the young woman already asleep. Her suitcase lay unopened on the floor and her fur coat was lying across her body. She had taken her shoes off, but nothing else. The journey must have tired her, Margarita thought. Doctor Moretti had told them how it had been almost a week since they had left Italy, travelling sometimes by train and even once with Serenella as a patient in an ambulance. Finally last night they arrived via a military boat returning Maltese citizens who had been arrested in Sicily on the outbreak of war. No wonder the young woman was exhausted. Checking the window was closed, Margarita pulled the light curtain behind her and crept silently to the other end of the room, where her bed looked inviting. As her husband and son were still outside, she didn't want to use the small hut the family used as a privy. Instead she pulled the tin pot from under the bed and used that instead. Margarita thought of the sumptuous bathroom facilities she had left behind in Ragusa after her marriage to Nikola. She remembered the maid whose job it was to dispose of toiletry waste, the huge cast iron bath and high feather bed she once took as her due as the daughter of the wealthy Sacca family.Margarita fell asleep easily in the secure knowledge that she had made the right decision that time, many years ago, when Nikola Vella had asked her to be his wife.

Chapter 21

Malta. October, 2004.

'What do you think it will be like after you are married?' Franco asked, placing a cafeteria of coffee carefully on the table.

Jessy lifted it, putting a folded tea-towel underneath and mentally reminding herself to buy a pot stand. This was just one of the many small changes she was still making around the house she shared with Franco and Salvatore. Silently she poured the thick brown liquid into two cups, adding milk to hers and sugar to Franco's. As usual he had made it very strong and Jessy knew she would probably have palpitations after drinking it.

'How do you mean?' she asked, blowing on the coffee before taking a sip. Yes, definitely palpitations today, she thought.

'After your wedding.' Franco also took a sip, grimaced and added another spoonful of sugar. He had learned his coffee making skills from both his wife Serenella and mother Margarita who, like all Italians, liked it strong-tasting and sweet. 'When the big day is over and you go home together. What do you imagine?'

Jessy shook her head. 'We don't have a home. I mean,' she added, not wishing to offend Franco, 'not our *own* house. But I presume we will continue living here for a while?'

Franco shrugged his shoulders, 'You are welcome here for as long as you want. This is your home *hanini*. It's normal that you'd stay here.'

'But Salvatore has talked about us going to live in America, with cousins of his over there.'

Franco raised his eyebrows. 'Why?' he asked. 'Why do you want to go and live in America when you both have a home here? The restaurant? Good jobs? Family?'

This time it was Jessy who shrugged. 'For a change. Because we are young and want to see the world. So Salvatore can paint and have his own art gallery.'

'And what about you? Who do you know in America?'

Jessy took another long drink from her cup. 'Nobody. But like Salvatore said, we can always come back if we don't like it. If we don't settle.'

'Sure,' Franco agreed, drumming his fingers on the table. 'And is that what you want? To go to America?'

'I think so.' Actually the thought of going to America had never entered Jessy's head until Salvatore mentioned it. If she was going to go and live somewhere else, she would have liked to try Italy for a while, or even just England, to be nearer Jimmy and Neil. She had also toyed with the idea of going to University and studying languages and history. Suddenly, she was twenty-five and getting married and moving to America. A prickly feeling began on the top of her head. It moved slowly down her whole body, as though somebody was gradually pouring freezing water over her. Jessy shivered and shifted in the seat. It didn't go unnoticed by Franco who saw the look of anxiety shadow her face, like a cloud suddenly covering the sun.

Franco gripped Ana's little ring through the shirt he wore, where it dangled on a long chain. Ana, he quietly said in his head, give me some wisdom now. Let me know what to say to your girl. You know her better than anybody else. I need you to tell me what to say.

'I remember what Ana always said when faced with a quandary,' he said, his eyes suddenly lighting. 'Do you remember?'

She nodded. 'When you don't know what to do,

do nothing. And just wait for guidance.' They both grinned at each other as they simultaneously voiced it together.

'You weren't going to wait though. You and Gran. To get married,' Jessy reminded him.

He shook his head slowly. 'No. But there was a baby coming. Then when I proposed again and Ana accepted the night before she died, well, we didn't exactly have a lot of time to waste on planning a wedding. We would have done it as soon as possible. So it was different for us. On both occasions. But you and Salvatore - you have your whole lives in front of you. There is no big rush. If what you want is to have a wedding with all your family and friends there, in a church, then that is what you should have. I am sure it is what Ana would have wanted for you too. If you want to go to live in America, then go. But not because it is just to please Salvatore. If he loves you like he says, that will be okay with him. I didn't know he was so eager to get out of the restaurant?'

Jessy knew she had to be careful what she said. On one hand she didn't want to worry Franco or be dishonest. On the other hand, she wanted to let him know how Salvatore felt the strain of running the restaurant alone. Which is why he was so grateful for his eldest brother, Marco, unexpectedly coming on board.

'He misses his painting. He wants to make you proud too and he does love to cook. I think he is torn between what he wants to do and what he feels he should do. Perhaps the America idea is a way for him to make the break. Let Marco take the reins off him and maybe for Salvatore to do something just for himself.'

Franco smiled sadly. 'Yes. I understand that. I need to talk to him. What I have to say, my opinion, may seem a bit extreme to both of you. But, I really feel it is good advice. If I say so myself.'

'Go on,' Jessy said. 'I know whatever you say will be out of love for both of us.'

'I think perhaps Salvatore should go to America, like he wants to. But on his own. Or, if you really want to go, because it is what *you* want then you go too – but I do think you should at least postpone the wedding. Not break off the engagement. Just not get married right now. Like you are planning.'

It upset Jessy that his suggestion made her feel as though a weight had come off her shoulders. I don't know my own mind, she thought worriedly. This morning and last night I was planning our wedding and now I feel relieved that it could be postponed and Salvatore might go to America on his own. And what about me? Would I stay here with Franco? Should I go and live with Jimmy and Neil for a while? All of a sudden her life and the world seemed full of possibilities and she wasn't sure if America was on the top of her list.

Sensing her distress Franco got up, put his hands on each side of her face and kissed the top of her head in his paternal fashion. 'You don't need to make any decision today about anything *hanini*,' he said. 'Have you got any plans for the day? Weren't you supposed to be staying in that fancy hotel last night? In Gozo?'

Jessy nodded, 'Yes. I think I will go and see Neil. He and Mia are due to fly back soon and I've hardly seen him. Them, I mean.'

'And Salvatore is working I presume?'

'Yes. He said he needed to chat with Marco I think.'

But Salvatore wasn't working today. Already he was driving his new car onto the ferry to Sicily and he wasn't intending on driving it back.

***

'We did tell you we might need a favour someday and I believe your exact words were, *Sure no problem*. Is there going to be a problem?' Manuel asked. He raised his eyebrows and with a steely glare looked straight into his cousin's eyes. 'Because ... today is someday,' he added menacingly.

Salvatore felt as though he had been kicked in the stomach. He swallowed. His mouth felt as dry as a desert. Feeling the blood rush to his face, he tried to think of his feet which was a trick his mother had once taught him. As a young boy he used to blush easily and it caused him huge anxiety in school if the teacher directed a question at him. First his face would feel hot, then the more he thought about it, the hotter it became. So much so that he could feel his cheeks pulsate, causing his eyes to water. Each time it happened his classmates would laugh and pointing their fingers at him would say 'Salvu is going to cry. Cry-baby, cry-baby.' Serenella, after coaxing her young son to give a reason why he hated going to school, came up with the solution that put an end to his embarrassing blushes. She told him that if he thought of his feet submerged in ice cold water, the blood would rush from his face down to his feet instead. Salvatore now heeded his mother's advice once again as he tried to keep his voice steady.

'But that is crazy. You are asking me to store drugs in the restaurant. How can you ask that of me?'

Manuel came closer. He came so close in fact that Salvatore could feel his older cousin's breath on his face. He smelled of alcohol and cigarettes. Salvatore willed himself not to draw back in disgust and instead stood his ground, staring right back at the man in front. Manuel smiled, but it wasn't a pleasant smile. He clicked his tongue. Patting Salvatore on the arm he lowered his voice almost to a whisper.

'I think you misunderstood *cousin*. I am not asking you. I am telling you.'

This time Salvatore did stand back and looked at the faces of the men flanking Manuel. They had treated him completely with scorn and not the family member that he was.

'You are my family,' he said. 'How can you put this on me?' He was not in any way prepared for what came next.

'Family?' Manuel snarled, baring his teeth as though he were a dog about to attack. 'You need to act like you belong in this family. Instead of coming over here as though we are a holiday camp, whinging about the restaurant and bills. When have you ever earned the right to be part of the *famiglia Inglima*? You can't even speak our language correctly. Instead you sound like a tourist, putting words back to front like a school kid. You need to earn the right to call yourself part of our family. At least Marco takes his responsibilities as an Inglima seriously.'

Salvatore reeled at the words. Manuel was right, but he had no idea his cousin had felt such contempt for him. He believed that it was his birth-right, always to be made welcome in Sicily and his mother's family. As a child he would come over every holiday and be spoiled by loving aunts, uncles and cousins. To him the stately palazzo built high on a hill in Ragusa Ibla, the old part of the historic city, was another home from home. Did the other family members believe the same as Manuel, he wondered? Did they also think of him as a leech, somebody who used the palazzo as a holiday home and had never given anything back? Salvatore's face burned with shame. It *is* what they think, he believed. They don't think of me as one of them. He needed to talk to *Zio* Angelo and hear from his lips if he felt the same way about his nephew.

Chapter 22

Ragusa, Sicily. 1914.

Margarita had always hated the water. As a young child she had had a terrifying experience when her best friend, Maria-Angela, thought it hilarious to hold her head under as they played in the Mediterranean Sea, off the coast of Marina di Ragusa. This had made her vow that never again would she go into water above her ankles. She had flailed her young arms about frantically, until finally she had no more strength. It had been a young fisherman coming into shore who had roughly grabbed Margarita above sea level by her hair and carried her almost unconscious unto the beach, where he literally breathed life back into her body. Afterwards she still felt the stinging sensation of her head being pulled and had a severe migraine until the next day, but she was just thankful to be alive.

Ever after, Margarita avoided the water. While her older brother and friends frolicked in the sea on summer vacation, she sat instead on the beach, reading and watching the others play. No amount of coaxing would cajole her into going back out there. To her, the sea was a monster, ready at any moment to suck you under and spit you out, dead, like the jellyfish and crabs lying lifeless on the sandy shore.

By the age of fifteen, Margarita's marriage was already arranged. Giovanni Inglima was a respected up and coming young politician. His family, like hers, was wealthy and while the Inglima family lived in the older part of the town, in Ragusa Ibla, Margarita's family lived in the newer part of town. They could see each other's homes from where they were both situated. The Inglima palazzo loomed over the Piazza San Giorgio, where Margarita and her family resided, but theirs was just as resplendent and also newer. Indeed, their stately home ran the whole length of one street, complete with extravagant baroque balconies. There were twelve balconies in all. Each balcony was situated on the outside of the six ornate shuttered doors on the second floor of the building and the same on the third floor. The six higher balconies bore variations of the Sacca family coat of arms. The six balconies on the second floor were more notable for the different corbels which supported them. Each was elaborately carved with images of musicians. The two central balconies, divided by columns and supported by images of grotesque faces provided the focus, humouring passers-by. Some even whispered that they were the faces of Signora Sacca's former suitors, whom her husband now scorned for having won the hand of the coveted Sarah Margarita Schwarz – eldest daughter of the most honoured and revered man in Ragusa – His Excellency, Giuseppe Schwarz.

It was important to the Inglima and Sacca families that they kept close ties. With large families being the norm, marriages between both first and second cousins was widely acceptable. If there happened to be a situation where one was of a different religious background, on marriage the woman would automatically take on the faith of her husband.

But, unknown to the parents of both Margarita Sacca and Giovanni Inglima, Margarita had already decided that she was going to marry the brave fisherman who had so gallantly saved her life. She had seen him twice since that fateful day. Once had been in Punta Secca, the small fishing village near Marina di Ragusa and the second time had been on a family day trip to Malta, where she now realised he lived. The Inglima family had invited the Saccas to the opening of their restaurant in the beautiful city of Valletta. As usual Margarita's best friend, Maria-Angela

Notarbartolo, was also invited. Margarita had begged to be left at home as she dreaded travelling by sea, but had not been given permission to do so. As the Saccas' luxurious yacht sailed out of Marina di Ragusa, Margarita sat in one of the small cabins indoors while the others lay on deck, soaking up the warm sun and enjoying the sea views. Not until the boat had safely docked at Valletta did she eventually venture outside, blinking as her eyes adjusted once more to the light. There was a protest of some sort going on at the harbour. A lot of rough looking fishermen were shouting as people came on to shore. Margarita was shocked to see one of the yachtsmen punch an older fisherman who fell to the ground, amongst the outraged yells of his friends.

'They don't want our boats coming into this side of the harbour,' her father explained, pointing to another wharf in the distance. 'They want us to moor our boats there instead, but it is more convenient for us to disembark here.'

'Why don't they keep their boats at the other wharf?' Margarita asked.

'Because …' her father replied, helping her as she nervously walked the narrow board from the yacht onto terra firma, where the rest of her family were getting into an open topped horse carriage, '… see where those buildings are?' Margarita looked to where her father pointed and saw rows of different coloured doors. Women sat outside some of them making lace and children played.

'Yes,' she replied.

'That is where they live and they want to be able to see their boats from their homes,' he told her.

Margarita nodded. 'But that makes sense. So why don't people respect that?'

Her father laughed, haughtily. 'Because they have money. People with money always get their way in the end Margarita. So be grateful that you come from a family where it is plentiful.'

Margarita nodded, but privately believed that what the fishermen requested was both fair and made perfect sense. As she passed the small homes, Margarita couldn't help but notice how happy the children looked. They were playing among the fishing nets and boats scattered across the busy fishing harbour. The boats were being repaired by the older men as children looked on, often getting in the men's way. They looked so carefree. Even the women whose voices could be heard laughing and chattering as they called out to each other from one end of the long waterfront street to the other, seemed to be enjoying themselves as they worked. Washing was strewn on makeshift clotheslines hanging from outside one narrow upstairs window to a neighbouring one next door. Some windows had more elaborate drying racks that could be folded down against the house wall when not in use. Margarita guessed with the amount of children running around that was not very often. Ashamedly she realised that the actual process of what happened to her own clothes once she discarded them on her bedroom floor had never occurred to her. They just magically reappeared in her clothes closet, washed, ironed and smelling fresh – due to one of the family's many servants.

Before getting into the horse carriage, Margarita glanced once more at the picturesque domestic scene full of colour and life, just a short distance from where she was. And there, in the midst of the melee, barechested and helping an older man to turn over one of the vibrantly painted *luzzu* boats was her mystery Maltese man.

For the entire afternoon Margarita could think of

nothing else, or nobody else. She had to get down to the waterfront somehow and find him - speak to him - thank him personally for saving her life. Yes, she thought, so that is just an excuse, but at least I have a *bona fide* one. Her legs twitched impatiently as they all sat at the new seats in the long narrow restaurant with views over the magnificent St. Elmo's fort. The sun shining through the glass windows made the room quite hot and even with the door open, it was stifling inside.

'Sit still, girl,' her mother Sarah implored. 'And please put your gloves back on.'

'It is too hot,' Margarita moaned. 'I feel faint Mama. I need to go out for air.'

Sarah sighed, calling Maria-Angela over. 'Please, accompany Margarita out for some air,' she asked, to her daughter's delight. Maria-Angela was also delighted to get out of the boring function. They could not eat or drink until the silly speeches were over, talking about how the restaurant building dated back to the times of the Knights of Malta - how the Inglima family were so esteemed in Sicily and therefore given the restaurant as a token of the Maltese Government's respect and so on and on. The girls motioned to

Giovanni to join them and he readily agreed, jumping up eager to have an excuse to leave.

'I will escort the young ladies,' he volunteered, winking at them as he snatched a bottle of wine on the way out the door.

'Do you mind if I get some time to be alone?' Margarita asked. 'I have a slight headache.'

'Of course,' Maria Angela replied, she was dying to get Giovanni to *herself*. 'Meet us at the front of that convent,' she suggested, gesturing at the building situated on the top of a hill not far from the restaurant door. 'In say, half an hour?'

Margarita promised she would, then took off at a very brisk pace back to the waterfront. Eventually she broke into a run, her hair flying loose from its clips and caring only that she saw her fisherman again.

Nikola Vella saw the tall skinny girl running down the slope towards where he was now about to climb into his family's own *luzzu* and stopped to stare. He recognised her immediately. She had long jet black hair that he remembered pulling out almost by the roots, when he had hauled her out of the sea that memorable day. For a young girl she was very tall and he recalled that her long thin legs had seaweed wrapped around them, as though the water had already decided to claim her as its own. His father and a family friend had been there too on that day. As they shouted instructions to turn her over and let the sea run out of her lungs, he had instead sucked the water from her body. At least that was what it had seemed like at the time. As his lips pressed onto hers, his own mouth had filled with salty sea-water and she began to splutter while he spat out what had once been inside her.

Margarita ran right until she got to his boat and Nikola could see perspiration wetting her forehead and upper lip. 'It's you,' she panted. 'You are the man who saved me.'

Nikola blushed, for several reasons. One was that she called him a man, which by now he was. The other reason was that the other men around him had started to cheer and shout and the third reason was because he suddenly knew without any doubt, that he was going to marry this tall, dark haired Sicilian beauty.

The Saccas obviously had other ideas, but with Margarita's careful scheming they, and everybody else apart from Maria-Angela, were completely oblivious of her budding romance. Margarita's best friend had been a willing confidante during the courtship, providing an alibi when needed and encouraging the young woman in her clandestine plans to marry the man she loved. But Margarita was under no illusion that there was no way on earth her family would allow the marriage between their daughter and a fisherman. Her older brother had already broken his parents' hearts by declaring himself an atheist, even going so far as to legally change his name and renounce his Jewish birth. Margarita marrying a Catholic man would destroy their family's reputation completely.

It was on another Sacca family holiday in Malta, that Nikola Vella won the hand of his bride. Returning to their yacht at French Creek in Grand Harbour to board for their journey home, Signore Sacca was outraged to see that their boat had been seized by British sailors. He was even more outraged when he was informed that he and his wife and children were to be taken back to shore for internment. For it was on this day that Britain had declared war on Germany and the Great War had reached Malta. All entrances to the island had been closed by boom defences and nobody could sail in or out of the country without a written pass. The Saccas had none.

Refusing to leave his yacht, Signore Sacca, his wife

and children were duly arrested and manhandled onto shore. All protestations of his prestige in both Sicily and Malta were ignored by the military and within the hour the Sacca family found themselves at the Verdala Barracks, in the Cottonera area of Malta.

It was Nikola Vella's father, who hearing of the family's internment, bravely approached the Barracks and bargained with them. Nobody ever knew what had transpired between himself and the military he conversed with. Some say that he knew the men guarding the Saccas and persuaded them to set the family free. Others say that he was a spy for the British, many even said that money changed hands. What everybody did know, was that the day after her eighteenth birthday, Margarita Sacca sailed to Malta from Marina di Ragusa, with Nikola Vella on his small fishing boat, as his wife. It was His Excellency Francesco Giovanni Inglima (father of Giovanni) who performed the marriage ceremony in his role as *Guidice* at the *Municipio* at Ragusa. Nobody was more delighted than Margarita's best friend, Maria-Angela.

'She was *my* intended Papa,' Giovanni Inglima had said with disbelief, when he heard the news that Margarita was married early that morning. 'How could you marry her when you know I had wished to?' His father closed his study door and gestured to the crestfallen young man to sit down. Taking a seat opposite, Francesco Giovanni Inglima put his elbows on his desk and making a steeple with his fingers, he leaned forward towards his son.

'She is a Jew,' he stated.

The younger man raised his eyebrows. 'Yes. But Margarita could become Catholic if I married her.'

'But she was born a Jew,' his father stated once again. 'And times are changing Giovanni. There is a new wave of ideology sweeping Europe. Jews are safe for now, they live among us and are rich, but soon this will change. It has to change.'

Giovanni shook his head, not understanding a word. 'But what has that to do with me and Margarita?' he asked.

'It is best that you marry a Catholic girl,' his father replied. 'One who is one hundred per cent Catholic, with no Jewish blood. Trust me. I have your best interests at heart and I know the perfect bride for you.'

'Who?' the young man asked.

'Maria-Angela Notarbartolo. She is the heir to a fortune.'

'But she is self-centred and precocious.'
'Then you will have to correct that,' his father answered. 'But the match is ideal for both our families. And at least she is of the *correct* faith.'
'And Margarita? What faith is *she* now, married in a registry office? You married her to a *fisherman* Papa. How could you?'
'Enough.' His father rose angrily from his seat. 'She is no longer your concern. I am head of this family and I make decisions I know to be best for this family. I had to prevent you marrying Margarita Sacca for your own sake. And for the sake of any children you might have had. You will thank me one day.'

Chapter 23

Malta. October, 2004.

'Jess, how are you?' Neil asked, smiling as he pulled the doors of his hotel balcony closed so he could hear Jessy better on his mobile phone. Immediately the noise of the busy Sliema waterfront was drowned out, where never ending traffic passed by and the tourists who were walking in the Sunday morning sunshine could be heard chattering loudly.

'I'm grand,' Jessy replied, making his smile even wider. She hadn't lost her Irish colloquiums yet. 'I rang to see what you are up to? You and Mia I mean?' she added, not wanting to make it obvious that she knew anything was up between the couple.

'I was actually just going to ring you,' Neil answered. 'Have you had breakfast yet?'

'No. I wasn't hungry before but I am starving now,' Jessy told him. 'Where and when?'

'I thought you were a veggie?' he teased. 'How about now and downstairs, here at The Regent? I can smell a fry wafting up the stairs and I could murder a good old English breakfast this morning.'

'Okay. Sounds good. See you soon,' and Jessy

ended the call before dashing upstairs for the world's quickest shower.

'Your hair is wet,' Neil commented, lifting damp curls from where they clung to her back like wet seaweed.

'No!' she exclaimed. 'We'd better call the *pulizija*. I should be arrested for indecent exposure.' Sticking her tongue out playfully at him Jessy snapped the menu shut and began theatrically counting on her fingers. 'I will have one pot of coffee, two eggs, three of those potato cake things, four slices of toast and five tomatoes please.'

Neil laughed out loud. 'You will never eat all that,' he exclaimed.

'Watch me,' Jessy answered cheekily, as Neil rolled his eyes and made his way to the self-service counter.

'I need to tell you something,' Jessy said, pushing her empty plate across the table and wiping her mouth with a paper napkin.

'Is it that you saw Mia kissing Salvatore's brother, Marco?'

Jessy looked aghast. 'You know?'

'Yes. Mia told me. She said she wanted to and I quote 'Tell me before your bloody sister got there first'.

So yes I know.'

'I'm sorry. That she cheated on you. Are you okay?'

Neil shrugged his shoulders and poured another coffee into both their cups. 'I couldn't care less, to be honest,' was his candid reply.

'But why not? And where is she now?'

Languorously, Neil lay back in his seat. 'Why not? Because I don't love her and where is she now? With Marco en route to Sicily.'

'How do you know? Were you talking to her this morning?'

'Yes, on the mobile. And she told me that Salvatore was also on the ferry, on his way to Sicily too.'

Jessy sat up, her face growing hot. 'But he's at the restaurant.'

'Nope,' Neil answered. 'He was on the ferry. He was driving because apparently Marco tried to get a lift and he was ignored by your fiancé. Marco wasn't too happy I believe.'

Jessy was raging. 'But why didn't he tell me he was going. For goodness sake!' Annoyed, she threw her napkin down on the table and asked Neil if he had a cigarette.

'You know I don't smoke,' Neil replied, 'and I thought you'd given up?'

'Not when I am annoyed,' Jessy retorted, picking up her bag. 'I'm going to the shop. Are you coming?'

'I've never been on one of those ferries around Malta. Have you?' Neil asked, trying to lighten the mood. Jess looked furious. He noticed she hadn't even said thank you to the man behind the tobacco shop counter. Instead she grabbed the cigarette pack and lighter and lit one as soon as she got outside.

'Yes. No. I mean, I've just been on the one over and back to Valletta, but not the tourist one. No.'

'Let's go then,' he said, guiding her arm across the busy street.

Apparently it was necessary to go to Valletta first, to catch the next boat which was leaving soon for a day long cruise around Malta and the Blue Lagoon. As the *dghajsa* bobbed up and down on the short journey, Neil could tell by the stony look on her face that Jess was in no mood for chit-chat. Once again she was trying to ring Salvatore but kept losing signal.

'Wait until we get to Valletta,' Neil suggested. 'What's the rush?'

'What time were you talking to Mia?'

Neil thought, 'It was about nine this morning.'

Looking at her watch Jessy replied, 'Well it is nearly one now, so he will definitely be in Sicily by this time. And since he has his car, he is probably also at Angelo's in Ragusa.'

'Who's Angelo?'

'His uncle,' Jessy answered sourly. 'His mother's brother. He has this big huge palazzo over there, you should see the size of it and that's where Salvatore always goes.'

'Oh, have you been?'

Jessy nodded her head. 'Yes. For his Uncle Marius's funeral, just before you arrived over. But I don't think he really wanted me there, to be honest.'

Neil looked ahead as Valletta's impressive harbour came into view. What a view it was! Approaching this ancient fortified city on a boat was a whole different experience. Immediately he took out the camera he always carried and began snapping photos quickly before they had to disembark. Later he would find one of Jessy among the many he took on that trip, her dark hair blowing in the wind and a heart-rending look of disillusionment in her face.

'Salvatore. Finally,' she said, trying to keep the

vexation out of her voice. 'Why did you go to Sicily?'

Salvatore swore to himself. Bloody Marco had obviously spilled the beans to Franco. 'It was a spur of the moment thing.' He could tell by Jessy's silence that it wasn't an acceptable reply. 'What are you doing?'

Jessy took a few seconds to answer. 'I'm just getting the boat to the Blue Lagoon. With Neil,' she added, knowing this would annoy her fiancé. For some reason anytime she mentioned Neil it seemed to stir something up in Salvatore.

It did once more. Salvatore bit his lip. 'I need to sort some family stuff with Angelo, so will stay here tonight and maybe even tomorrow. Marco is going back this evening after he leaves Mia to Catania airport, so he can look after things with the builders till I return.'

Jessy nodded. Holding her mobile tight between her shoulder and ear she took the cigarette packet out of her pocket and tried to light one. Instead, Neil took the lighter out of her hands, flicked it and held it up for Jessy to light her cigarette. Giving Neil the thumbs up, she rolled her eyes while motioning towards the phone, then walked away with her back to the water's edge.

'Right. So I will see you Tuesday then?' she asked, trying to keep the note of annoyance out of her voice.

What she actually wanted to do was yell at him. Why hadn't he taken her? Once again he had gone off to Sicily without her, when he knew how much she hoped to return to the island with him and under better circumstances than a funeral.

Salvatore could hear the long slow exhale she made as she blew smoke out and realised if Jessy was smoking, this meant that she was really annoyed with him. He took a deep breath and moved further away from where Angelo was sitting, not wanting to be overheard. 'I will try and get back early tomorrow love,' he said, 'and maybe we can make more plans for the wedding. I won't go into the restaurant at all. Just come straight home.'

'Sure,' Jessy replied. 'Ciao,' and with that she ended the call.

'Neil,' she said, beckoning him over. 'Let's skip the boat to the Blue Lagoon and get ridiculously drunk instead.' Neil didn't take much coaxing and happily agreed.

'Just look at that view,' Neil declared, taking in the panoramic scene in front. Huge cruise ships were anchored in the extensive harbour, over which towered Valletta's magnificent bastion walls. 'You are so lucky to live here.'

Jessy nodded her head. 'Yes. It is beautiful. I always try to imagine how it was when Gran first came here as a young woman. But then of course it was just before the outbreak of war. It must have looked quite different.'

***

'How did you meet Salvatore?' Neil asked. 'Tell me.'

Jessy tucked her hands under her chin and leaned towards him, elbows on the table. 'It was in May, 2001 and my very first night in Malta. We were in the little church in Sr. Lucija's convent, Gran and I, that is. He was at the window and I thought I was seeing things. He looked ... too perfect almost. So handsome. Then later I went out for a sneaky cigarette and he was in the courtyard, watering plants.' She giggled and Neil was happy to see a smile on her face once more, even if it was due to talking about Salvatore.

'He told me afterwards that he was loitering, hoping to catch me on my own. I think I fell for him right there and then and he said he did too. After that we spent every minute we could together. At first I tried to keep it from Gran. She was so protective. Then the night we all went to L'Artiste he was there and that was the night too that Gran realised the restaurant belonged to Franco. And the next day she saw him, at Floriana where the Pope was. The two of them just took off together like bold children. Imagine!'

'And I guess once your grandmother realised Salvatore's relationship to Franco she gave her approval. Right?'

Jessy nodded. 'Yes. She thought he was the bee's knees because he was Franco's son. Then … well, after Gran died I went to stay in Franco's and I just never left. And then I met you and Billy. You know the rest. How did you meet Mia?'

Neil sighed. 'Nothing as romantic as that I'm afraid. I met her in a bar. I was lonely. She was lonely. She started staying over more and more. I liked the company. Billy was still here in Malta and I guess I missed calling to him in the evenings for chats. Mia filled a gap. All her stuff strewn around the place drove me mad and my tiny bathroom drove her mad, so we moved into her bigger place together. Before I knew it, we were cohabiting. Though somehow I ended up paying all the bills, including the rent.'

'Your little love-nest,' Jessy joked, 'as she called it.

What will you do now? Will you stay or move out?'

'Move out for sure,' Neil said. 'I'll either move in to Billy's or stay at Dad's.'

'Have you thought any more about changing jobs and doing architecture like you said?'

Neil looked over, impressed that she had remembered what he had told her many months ago. 'Actually, I am thinking of doing just that when I go back. The R.A.F. is great, but to be honest, I kind of joined it really just to please Billy and Dad. But when I am here in Malta, I am blown away by the buildings, both old and new. It really infuses my passion for drawing and making plans, but that's not enough for me. I'd love to actually see something I've designed being built. I can't think of anything more satisfying than seeing a picture in your mind translated into a real life structure in front of you. There forever. Well, unless somebody comes along someday and knocks it all down of course.'

Jessy laughed. 'Yes, well at least you will have seen it standing first. Hmm, well I would love to build something too, but nothing as grand as what you have described. The picture in my head is much simpler.'

'Go on,' Neil encouraged. 'Tell me.'

'I want to build a family. A home,' Jessy answered, quietly. 'I never had that. A Mum and Dad, kids, just family stuff you know.' Neil nodded. He did know. 'I want to put my excited kids to bed on Christmas Eve and watch their faces as they open presents from Santa. I want to bake my children cakes for birthdays and make a house full of memories.' She bent over to pick up her handbag and rummaged inside while Neil watched, a million desires running through his mind. 'Look,' Jessy held up a small hook in the air, as though it was something precious and not just a piece of bent rust. 'See this?'

Neil took it out of her hand. 'A nail?'

She laughed and poured more of the white Maltese wine into her glass. 'Yes. But it is not just a nail. Do you want to know where I got it?' Neil nodded his head, wondering if she had maybe too much to drink.

'Sure, tell me,' he said, intrigued.

'It used to be on our front door at home. Me and Gran's house. It was where we hung stuff like the Christmas wreath, balloons for birthdays, even shamrock on St. Patrick's Day. It signifies home to me. Family. Traditions and memories. I took this out of the door the last time I went home, to empty the house after Gran died and I decided I will hang it on a door someday. My door. For my family. Do you think that is silly?' Neil gulped and taking the cork out of the cold wine bottle he liberally poured another drink for himself. 'Not silly at all,' he replied, honestly. 'Not one bit.' And he fell another little more in love.

Chapter 24

Malta. April, 1945.

Salvatore was correct in understanding that Marco had never felt wanted by his mother, Serenella. He wasn't. His conception, her pregnancy and his birth were all incredibly traumatic events for the young woman, who felt only despair when her son took his first breath. When the nurse had held the squalling baby to her breast, Serenella pushed the newborn away. Primarily this reaction did not cause concern. Many mothers, particularly after a difficult birth, could not bond with their child initially. Then, nature took over as she often does and even the most hardened hearts are melted. It didn't happen in this case. Dutifully the young mother nursed her child, wincing each time his little mouth found her breast and not from pain, but from disgust. To think *his* mouth was on her breast was too much to bear. He had the same eyes, the same stocky build. His greedy little fists punched the air while he suckled, as if in victory of also claiming her body for his own pleasure. It was all Serenella could do not to hold the muslin cloth firmly over his plump lips while he slept and silence his breaths forever.

Franco, her husband, was as pleased with the birth of her son Marco as though he had been his own child. At least he appeared to be. After the deaths of both his parents in the last few months, a new life had been welcomed by the whole family. It had been at his Uncle Father Cauchi's suggestion that he and Serenella had married, reluctantly on both parts. The priest could see no other solution.

'You most definitely cannot stay on at this house without being married,' he had insisted to Serenella. 'And I can't see how Franco is going to look after his young daughter on his own.' Some of the younger children had already gone to live with older siblings and their families. Just Pawlo, Franco and his daughter Rigalla – and now Serenella, remained in the Vella family home. 'You will have to move out otherwise, as it is immoral for you to live here alone with two grown men.'

Serenella had nowhere to go and no money. On a sunny March morning the young couple had been married in the nearby church of San Girgor il-Kbir. Afterwards they went straight home and unknown to Franco his bride had wept as she did her housework that day. Unknown to Serenella, Franco had also shed tears, remembering that he was to have married Ana in that same church.

***

'He's dead,' Pawlo cried, running in through the open front door and brandishing 'The Times of Malta' newspaper in his hand.

'Shush,' Serenella whispered, putting her finger cautiously to her lips and waving in the direction of the small cot. 'Who is dead?'

'Mussolini,' Pawlo declared, handing her the paper. 'He and his whore, Claretta Petacci. Strung up like a side of meat at a petrol station.'

Serenella felt bile rise to her throat. Taking the newspaper from Pawlo's hand she sat down numbly at the kitchen table, laying the newspaper out flat on the table in front of her. The photo took up most of the front page with words **IL DUCE IS DEAD** written in black capital letters across the top. The image was shocking and she was surprised that it had even been printed. Benito Mussolini, the leader of the Fascist Party had indeed been hung like a piece of meat by his ankles, but she could tell it was definitely him. His mistress hung next to him and that image shocked Serenella even more. It was barbaric. Claretta Petacci, whose name had caused so much conflict in Villa Carpena, had also been strung up by her ankles, her skirt tied around her knees. A bit late for modesty now, Serenella thought.

Pawlo gave a running commentary on what was written in the newspaper, as Serenella tried to read the words herself. Her English was not fluent and this paper was an English language one.

'I can't read it all either,' Pawlo said, 'but the Maltese ones are completely sold out. This is the only paper I could get. But from what I can gather, the Partisans shot him and Petacci, then dumped their bodies, along with other Fascists at a petrol station and the locals strung them up like that. Good enough for them. They'll probably slaughter the whole family if they can find them.'

'No!' Serenella cried. 'They wouldn't. Not Rachele and Romano and Anna-Maria!'

Pawlo looked surprised. 'You speak as if you knew them?'

Serenella shook her head. 'No. Of course not. I just mean that they are not responsible for his actions.'

'Then you could say the same about Claretta,' Pawlo replied candidly. 'Why kill her and not Mussolini's wife? What is the difference?'

Serenella turned angrily to face her brother-in-law. 'Rachele is nothing like Claretta Petacci. She is a good mother.'

Pawlo looked suspiciously at the young woman. Her eyes flared with fury. Why would she know so much about the Mussolini family, or care so much. Then he recalled his mother saying that Serenella's father was a Fascist.

'Are you happy that Mussolini is dead?' he asked.

A slow smile spread over Serenella's face. 'Happy?' she asked. 'Yes. Just unhappy I wasn't the one to pull the trigger.'

But Serenella was very concerned about her family. If they were hunting out Fascist supporters then her father was at risk, as were her mother and brothers. Her concern was for Rachele and her children too. She wished there was some way she could contact home to enquire, but she had vowed when she left Rimini that October night, that the next time she wanted to see her mother was when she was dead. That part of her life was over now. Although Angelo had promised to protect her, she had not seen him since the day after she had taken that morphine. Contrary to what her brother and mother had believed, Serenella had not wished to die. She merely had hoped that if she took enough of the morphine powder that the baby might not survive. It hadn't worked.

There had been an almighty row between Angelo and Mama that evening after Doctor Moretti had left. She had accused her son of turning his back on Mussolini and his father by joining the *Partigiani*. Due to what Serenella could make out from her bedroom, it had sounded like he didn't deny it. In her rage Maria-Angela was obviously throwing items around the house, because Serenella could hear dishes being smashed. Then she heard Angelo slam the front door and a truck speeding noisily off. So much for his promise to look after her. Mama hadn't even got out of bed to say goodbye, when Doctor Moretti had wakened Serenella during the night and they had both crept out of the house to a car waiting outside. Her outfit and a packed case had been laid out by somebody while she slept, so Mama had obviously known she was leaving that night - but she hadn't tried to wish her daughter a safe journey and say farewell.

As Serenella looked back at the house before the car drove out of their gates, she saw a light come on in her mother's bedroom window and curtains twitched. Serenella bit her lip and stubbornly refused to cry. Surely whatever she faced in Malta could be no worse than life under the control of her own mother.

'I know you are going to ask my dear, but no, I am afraid I have heard no word from Giorgio,' Moretti said quietly. He sat next to her on the back seat of the motorcar. She could not see the face of the driver, just the back of his head. She could only make out a red scarf tied around his neck and he wore a black hat with a dark jacket.

'If you find him, will you tell him where I am?' she asked quietly.

The doctor nodded. 'Of course.' But he didn't hold out much hope. What he had kept from the young woman, was that the priest who was to marry her and Giorgio, had told him that the young partisan had been dragged roughly along Rimini's town square and thrown into a truck by German soldiers. He was roaring Serenella's name, then was hit on his head by the butt of a gun. That was the last the priest had seen of Giorgio Cavallo. Doctor Moretti decided that in the young woman's current situation, no news was better than bad news.

Chapter 25

Mtarfa, Malta. October, 2004.

'Graveyards are the same the world over, aren't they,' Jessy whispered, wiping her hand over the engraved stone, dusted with sand blown from some nearby beach.

ANA MELLOR-McGUILL

1926 – 2001

Dearly Loved

UNITED KINGDOM - IRELAND - MALTA

Served as a nurse in Mtarfa Military Hospital

WWII

'You mean because they are full of dead people,' Neil answered, frankly.

Jessy tut-tutted. 'No! Gosh, sometimes you are just too … too annoying. I mean, they are so quiet. Peaceful. You know.'

Neil wanted to retort that maybe that was because everybody was dead, so they weren't exactly going to be having some wild party, but decided to keep his mouth shut.

'Look,' Jessy pointed to where earth had recently been moved and fresh soil planted. 'Franco has already planted daffodil bulbs, but I bet they won't come up. They never seem to over here. They were Gran's favourite. And mine.'

Neil had visited the cemetery in Mtarfa previously with Billy, but to him personally, he never saw the point in making a pilgrimage to the place where a loved one was buried. Much better, he thought, to go somewhere that had meant something to them when they were alive. However, it had been Jessy's wish to visit her grandmother's grave a week ago on her birthday, but Salvatore hadn't had the time to accompany her. Neil hoped that the alcohol consumed in Valletta had left his bloodstream by the time they'd picked up his car in the underground car-park. They then made their way to the hilly Maltese town where Jessy's grandmother was buried and also Billy's wife Katie and their babies.

'Today is one of those weird thinking days,' Jessy said, kissing her hand then placing it on the marble headstone, before turning around and linking her arm companionably into Neil's, as they made their way towards the entrance gate. 'Do you think it is going to rain? I think so,' she said, pulling a light raincoat out of her bag. 'It always rains in graveyards. Doesn't it?'

Neil laughed. 'Which question will I answer first?' he asked. 'The one about do I think it's going to rain, or do I think it always rains in graveyards? Actually, I would like to know what you mean by this being a 'thinking day' as you so eloquently put it. And, what else do you keep in that bag? Nails, raincoats ... dead bodies by any chance?'

Jessy pinched him teasingly on the arm. 'What I mean is, one of those days when you just can't stop thinking about everything in your life. How you ended up where you are, who you are with and stuff. Like, with Ana, being here makes me think of her, obviously. All those years she lived in Ireland with Ernie, she must have been so lonely wondering what happened to Franco and Billy. She didn't know that all that time they were also thinking about her. Missing her and still loving her. Life is just so ... out of our control sometimes.'

'Out of our control?'

'Yes. We believe things are as we think they are, but sometimes they are not really that way at all.'

Neil guffawed loudly. 'You actually are totally

nuts you know,' he chortled. 'What the heck does that mean?'

'Take you and I for example,' Jessy tried to explain, 'if somebody saw us they would probably think we are a couple. But we aren't. We are half-brother and sister. With a whole crazy, unbelievable story behind who we are and how we got here and found each other. It is like soap opera stuff. Ana kept big secrets all of her life. So did Ernie and Billy. Even Franco. Why? Because of other people and what they might think or do or say. Because of fear, loads of reasons. Yet, in the end, all their secrets came out. Didn't they? So Neil Wilson, if you have any big secrets, out with them now or forever hold your peace.'

'I am not your brother,' he said, continuing to walk with Jessy's arm linked into his. Then suddenly it wasn't. He felt Jessy roughly whisk her arm out from under his and although he knew she had stopped walking, he continued to. His was heart beating ninety to the dozen at every step.

'Are you joking with me or are you serious? Because if you are serious then you better explain why you just said that to me. Right now,' she demanded.

He turned. 'I found out when I went to San

Francisco that Jimmy isn't my Dad at all. Mom has no idea who is.'

Neil walked on, until stopping abruptly as he felt something small and hard hit the back of his head.

'What the ... ? Did you just throw that at me?' he asked in disbelief, pointing at the stone which landed at his feet.

'Yes. I did,' came the reply. 'And I'll fire another one if you don't tell me what is going on!' Because now Jessy knew for sure, that something definitely was.

It was getting chilly. Jessy untied the rain jacket from around her waist and slipped it over her head, then zipped it up. She dug her hands into the pockets on either side and looked over at him. He was leaning with his back against a wall and was looking out towards where Mosta Dome could be seen in the distance. He had his sunglasses on, more to keep out the wind than in protection from the sun. She knew that the wind always caused his eyes to run. It wasn't so sunny now. The sky was becoming darker by the minute and Jessy looked at her watch. It was already after six in the evening. This is ridiculous, she thought. We can't just sit here in silence.

'Neil.'

He turned around. Because of his glasses, Jessy couldn't see if he was looking at her or not, but she presumed that he was. He lifted his chin.

'Hmm?'

'Will you talk to me?'

He looked back towards Mosta again. Jessy sighed and stood up, brushing the small stones and dust off the back of her jeans. Her movement caused him to turn around again.

'Where are you going?' he called, seeing her beginning to walk back towards the road.

Jessy didn't answer. She kept walking. But, just as she knew he would, Jessy heard Neil run up behind her. He swung her around.

'Where are you going?' he asked again, holding on to her arm. She shrugged him off.

'What's the point in me staying here if you are just going to stand there, ignoring me?'

He hung his head.

'I'm sorry. I just … I was imagining this scene since I found out and now that I'm here … we're here, it isn't turning out like I had thought.'

'And what did you think it would turn out like?'

she asked, half turned towards him.

'I don't know. I guess I thought you would be shocked, then pleased. I didn't expect you to be so bloody angry to be honest.' He *was* being honest. He was fuming. 'Your reaction was definitely not what I was expecting.'

'I can't believe you didn't tell me as soon as you found out?' Jessy was seething.

'I tried to. I mean I planned to. That was the reason I asked you to meet me at Gozo that day, but you started telling me about your engagement and you were so excited. I just couldn't do it. It didn't seem the right time and then I went back to the U.K. I couldn't tell you by phone.'

'Why did you make such a big deal out of it?' Jessy demanded. 'Why ask me to go the whole way out there? To Gozo? It's not the easiest place to get to you know!'

Neil nodded. 'Yes I do know. I guess I thought that …' he gestured around them, '… it meant something to you and me and …'

'And you thought there'd be some big romantic reunion or something? Isn't that it? Isn't that what you meant?' Jessy cried.

'Yes. Damn it. Yes, that is what I'd thought. But now I know I was a stupid fool.'

'I don't believe you.' Jessy cried. 'What did you expect?'

Neil looked at her, standing there. She had her hands outstretched, tears were in her eyes. Her hood was up, but didn't quite cover her hair which was blowing all around her face. He stepped closer towards her, reaching out to move the tendrils from her eyes. To his surprise she roughly pushed his hand away.

'Don't,' she cried. 'Don't you dare try and comfort me.'

He sprang back. 'Comfort you. Comfort *you*. What about *me*?' he cried in return. 'Every single time you are in trouble or upset you ring me and I have always been there for you. Jessy opened her mouth to reply, but Neil put his finger in the air and she obediently stayed silent. 'I have been going through hell for months, longer even and I never said a word. I listened to all your wedding plans and all your concerns about Salvatore and only ever treated you *exactly* like a big brother would. Even though all the time it was killing me. Now, *you* are angry with *me*. For what I would like to know. For *what* exactly?' Neil glared at her, his eyes flaring in maddened exasperation.

'For not telling me,' she wailed. 'For not telling me you weren't my brother. Do you think I would have confided in you like I did, if I'd known you weren't my brother? You *lied* to me. All this time you knew and you didn't tell me. How *could* you?'

Neil wanted to shake her. He didn't want to hurt her, he just wanted to shake the anger out of her and have her listen to him.

'It was a huge shock to me too Jess. It's not just all about you, you know. I thought all my life that Jimmy was my Dad and now I know that he isn't and it has really hurt me. I haven't even told him yet. Or Billy. You are the first person I have told, but the one I've dreaded telling the most.'

'Why?'

'Because I didn't want anything to change between us. I didn't want you to treat me like some stranger.'

'I wouldn't have treated you like a stranger,' she wept. 'It changes everything.'

'Exactly,' he replied, dejectedly. 'It has changed everything. Look at us.'

Jessy had her head in her hands now and was sobbing. He moved his foot in her direction and she put out a hand.

'Don't,' she whispered quietly. 'Just don't.'

He didn't know what to do. Should he leave her? Just get in the car and go? Go where? Back to England? Then what? How would they ever reconcile then? And how could he leave her here alone in this state?

'Jess,' he whispered. 'It's getting dark. We need to go.'

She nodded. Then turned around and began to walk away slowly.

'Jess,' he called, after her retreating back. 'Where are you going? Don't be silly.'

She continued to walk. He saw her take the mobile out of her bag and put it to her ear. She's ringing *him*, he thought and turned his back, walking in the other direction.

But Jessy wasn't ringing Salvatore. Instead she rang another number and not too far away a mobile phone was picked up from a side table and answered.

'Yes,' Jessy heard.

'Jeany?' she asked. 'Is it okay if I call?'

'Of course darling,' came the concerned reply. 'Where are you? I will send a car.'

Jessy looked ahead. 'I will be at the foyer of the

Sands Hotel', she answered. 'Thank you Jeany.'

Unsteadily, the older woman got to her feet. 'I will see you very soon darling,' and she hung up the phone. 'Antonio,' she called. 'I need you.' And it felt good to know, that right now she too was needed by somebody.

The driver didn't say a word during the whole journey. He had one of those black peaked caps on and in the darkness Jessy couldn't make out if it was Antonio or the other driver, Samuel. But she was glad at not having to make small talk, because she didn't think she would be able to manage it, without making it obvious that she was upset.

The splendour of the palace never failed to take Jessy's breath away. From the outside you would never guess at what lay beyond the austere wooden gates. They were discreetly situated in the middle of a long limestone wall, which ran along the opposite side of the quiet harbour of St Julian's. The wall was extremely high and the gates were painted emerald green but were now quite faded due to the sea winds. One would never imagine the opulence and grandeur that lay on the other side of the wall. In the sixteenth century, the palace had been constructed in this manner, as a form of defence. The bastion enclosure had been built purposely higher than the palace itself, to conceal the structure from outside. It was also further screened by an abundance of tall pine trees and other foliage on the far side of the wall, lining the driveway to the palace's decorative entrance doors.

Jeany was waiting at the main doors and came out to meet Ana's grand-daughter. Unusually she opened the back door of the car before the driver had a chance to get out.

'Love,' she said quietly, putting her arms around the young woman who stepped out. 'Let's have a little cocktail,' and Jessy smiled.

'That sounds good' she answered.

Jeany was wearing a cream linen trouser suit and long gold necklaces hung around her neck. Her fingers were adorned with gold rings and some had large diamonds and other gemstones, which glittered in the soft lighting of her drawing room. There was an oak sideboard against one wall displaying an array of various alcoholic beverages, but Jeany didn't help herself to a drink. Instead she rang a little bell which tinkled delicately. Within minutes, a young woman dressed in a black pinafore and white blouse entered, while Jessy settled herself on the cream leather suite.

'Two Bellinis please Chiara,' Jeany ordered, then taking a seat next to Jessy she patted the young woman on the arm. 'Now talk,' she said kindly.

'I don't even know where to begin,' Jessy mumbled. 'I've just been told something that shocked me and I didn't know who I could talk to, that wouldn't be just as shocked as me.'

She paused for a moment while Chiara returned to the room with their drinks on a silver tray and placed them on the small round glass table next to them. Along with the two glasses, a silver cocktail shaker sat in a small glass bucket of ice which was decorated with slices of peaches. 'Oh, this looks very posh,' Jessy said, accepting a glass from Jeany. 'Yum, it's delicious,' she added after taking a sip.

Jeany nodded her head in agreement. 'My favourite. Now tell me. What was the shock?' she asked, tentatively.

'Neil just told me he is not my brother. He said that when he was in San Francisco last year, his mother told him that Jimmy is not his father and she doesn't know who is. He has known all this time and never told me.'

Jeany simply nodded her head. 'And you are upset because you don't have a brother, like you thought? But your father Jimmy still brought him up, with Billy, so technically he is still your brother, or half-brother. Of sorts,' she added. To be honest it was a bit confusing, she thought.

'I'm upset because he kept it from me. I am upset because yes, I thought I had a brother and now I don't. But really, I am upset because I might lose him now. He has no reason to stay around. Be around *me* anymore I mean.'

'But he won't just suddenly disappear and stop seeing Billy or Jimmy,' Jeany said. 'He has known those men all his life and loves them as a grandfather and father. Wait, do Billy and Jimmy know this?'

'No. He said he hadn't told anyone yet and dreaded telling me the most.'

'Oh, why is that?'

'He said he didn't want anything to change between us and for us to become strangers.'

'There you are dear,' Jeany said, comfortingly. 'He doesn't want anything to change either. So don't worry, everything will be alright.'

Jessy took another mouthful of the Bellini. 'I hope so,' she said. 'Because he means the world to me.'

Jeany could tell. 'And Salvatore, how are things with him?'

Jessy leaned back against the plump cushions and crossed her legs. 'He has been talking about us going to America for a while, to live.'

Jeany raised an eyebrow. 'To America? Why?'

'A fresh start. Just the two of us. Franco thinks I should let him go alone though. He thinks we need some time apart to think about things and not rush into marriage. Salvatore suggested we get married very soon and then he changed his mind.' She felt tears coming to her eyes and tried to blink them away, but it didn't go unnoticed by the older woman.

'And how do you feel,' she asked, 'about your relationship?'

Jessy shook her head sadly. 'It's sometimes really hard. It's just not straightforward anymore, like it used to be. I find myself second guessing everything. Everything that I say to him takes lots of thinking about first. It never used to be like that. It used to be really easy and natural. We just talked, about everything. Now, well now, he finds my words are attacks – I find his words are just ... words.'

'Go on,' Jeany coaxed, re-filling both their glasses with the thick peach-coloured liquid.

'When I went to Sicily for his uncle's funeral, I felt so unwanted,' she said quietly. Just the memory of it caused her tummy to somersault. 'It made me realise that he has this whole other life that I am not part of and he doesn't seem to want me to be part of. I spent most of the day with people I'd met on the boat over, then went home. He didn't even take me to the ferry. He got a driver to.'

Jeany was listening intently, watching every expression on the young woman's face. All it showed was sadness and not the look of a woman in love, or a happy bride-to-be. She had a concern of her own, just something she had heard of the day before. She wondered if this was the actual reason why she presumed Jessy had come to see her. But Jessy was obviously in the dark about the situation and Jeany needed to be certain of the truth before she could impart this information.

'I don't know where it all started to go wrong. I think back and the last time I can remember feeling normal with him was ... probably around the time we got engaged. The first time I realised that I was feeling anyway different about him was just before Christmas. I was in a restaurant at St. Julian's and was really annoyed after I sent him a text. I tried to ring him, but he didn't reply and his phone just rang out. I'd wanted him to pick me up and for us to go somewhere to eat. I guess I was annoyed that it was just another occasion when I was all dressed up and feeling happy that it was the holidays and just … just wanting to be with him. But as usual he didn't answer. As usual he was too busy.'

At that moment Jessy heard a ping as a message arrived on her mobile. She glanced at the handbag lying on the floor by her feet.

'Read it,' Jeany said. 'It could be important.'

Jessy picked the bag from the floor and lifted out the phone. It was Neil. 'Are you okay?' it read. She showed the message to Jeany, who needed to put her glasses on to see the small print. She nodded her head. 'See. He isn't going anywhere like I told you,' she stated. 'Now continue what you were saying, love.'

'I kind of felt I was finally beginning to feel I belonged here, in Valletta, in my job. I was one of the team. But when I sat there in that restaurant on my own and all around me were couples doing Christmas shopping and families out together, I felt so lonely. But yet, I had a fiancé. I called to see him at the restaurant the next day, but he was too busy to talk to me. I offered to help, but he gave me some money instead and told me to get a Christmas gift for Franco. I had wanted us to go around the shops together and both of us pick something nice.'

'Lots of men work long hours and their partners or wives find themselves socialising alone or shopping alone, even at Christmas.'

Yes. I know. But even just our talking like this about him and everything isn't right - I should be able to talk to *him*.'

'Why don't you?'

'He clams up. He gets defensive and then storms out. I end up feeling like a silly little girl having a tantrum. Not like his partner and definitely not like somebody who is going to be his wife. I hate this. It all feels so terribly wrong.'

Jeany sighed. She had to agree with Jessy. But more than anything it confirmed that the news she had heard yesterday might just be correct. A huge wedding was planned for next spring in Ragusa, Sicily. Jeany had heard this from her Sicilian maid Chiara, as the agency she worked for had requested all their temporary staff to be available over the Easter weekend. Francesca, the only daughter of Marianna and Ernesto Inglima, was getting married to a Maltese man, a third cousin no less. Chiara didn't know his name, only that he was a nephew of the renowned *Padrino* of Ragusa, Angelo Inglima.

Chapter 26

Malta. September, 1946.

Serenella needed to get in contact with Doctor Moretti, but had no idea how to go about it. When he had left her here in October 1944, he had simply embraced her and promised to be in touch, but she had never heard from him since. Also her mother hadn't arrived for the birth of her grandson as she had said. Although Serenella pretended to herself that she was glad - really she felt hurt at being cast out so easily. She was just like a piece of furniture nobody wanted anymore. Giorgio was on her mind day and night and she had shed many tears worrying about where he could be and wondering if he was alive or dead. The only link she had with him were the empty envelopes, or what he had used as envelopes. Not even his hand-writing was on the front, but just to know he had once held them was enough. Another memento was the white headscarf she had used several years ago to wipe the blood from Giorgio's face on the day he had defended her. Grubby now, the blood long since dried and faded, Serenella kept it along with the envelopes inside a white linen pillowcase, taken that last night from her bedroom in

Rimini.

The baby whimpered from his place in the middle of the bed and Serenella replaced her hidden treasures in the case she had retrieved from under the small bed. She and her son Marco still slept in the same space, curtained off from the rest of the downstairs area, where she had spent her first night in the Vella household. Franco slept upstairs with his daughter Rigalla. He had confided in Serenella after the death of his parents that the little girl was his own. She had been shocked, then saddened when he explained about the child's mother, Ana. She could understand his pain and somehow his own sorrow made her feel closer to him. But Serenella did not confide in him about Giorgio, or who the father of her own child was. Mussolini and any known Fascists were ostracized in both Italy and Malta, with many of their followers being hunted out and killed. So Serenella went along with the story that her mother and Angelo believed, that the German soldier Franz had forced himself on her and left her expecting his baby. Franz having been killed so horrifically was something that Serenella could not bear to acknowledge. At night she often woke up, her heart racing after yet another dream where she saw his body hanging from a rope, just like so many others she had seen that horrific day in Rimini.

On these mornings, when she woke terrified by the horrors she had seen in her dreams, Serenella would lift Marco, putting him into the old perambulator which had been used for several of Margarita's children. Then she would walk for miles and miles. Pushing the pram down the cobblestone hill to where fishermen were setting out in their *luzzu* from Balluta Bay, she would sometimes think about asking where a person could get a boat to Sicily. But she knew it would be pointless. Who would take her with a baby? Where would she get the money? It would be useless to try and return to Italy. In a country that size she would never find Giorgio. Nevertheless, Serenella was sure if she could just get to Marina di Ragusa in Sicily, to where Valentina and Carlo possibly still lived, then she would be alright. Wheeling the perambulator along the dusty coast road in the direction of St. Julians, she kept stopping at various points to watch boats as they sailed in the distance. Squinting in the sun, Serenella looked longingly across the wide expanse of water, thinking of all the seas between her and the man she loved.

Usually by the time she got back to the house in

Sliema, Franco would be pacing about waiting on her return. Although it was never officially discussed between them, it was more or less taken for granted that Serenella would care for Rigalla as though she were her own while Franco worked. It was an arrangement which she privately begrudged. It was difficult enough to look after her own squalling baby, never mind a toddler as well. Nobody seemed to be aware of the fact that Serenella had never in her life had to do the slightest domestic chore. She had helped with looking after her siblings, but they were not babies. Until she'd had her own she had never changed or dressed a baby in her life. It had been Franco who had shown her. After Marco was born the nurse had simply handed the child over, tidied Serenella up a bit and promptly left. The young mother had no baby clothes prepared and except for Franco giving her the clothes his own daughter had outgrown, the baby would have remained as naked as he was born.

It was also Franco, who to Serenella's distress, had shown her how to place the baby to her breast and it was also he who had washed the blood from the sheets which she had stained during childbirth. All of these things Franco did without being asked, or without saying a word. He could see how the young woman struggled. As the eldest of many children and having watched his mother over the years, Franco had the expertise that Serenella did not. However, he had to be free to work. Roads, bridges and homes needed to be repaired and he and his brother Pawlo were busy from morning until darkness fell. Serenella was required to run the home and look after the children. It was the only demand he had made on her as his wife so far.

The household was usually chaotic when Franco and Pawlo arrived home. Dinner was rarely prepared. Rigalla was often wearing soiled clothes and Serenella looked completely exhausted. As soon as the men came through the front door she would retire behind the curtain and stay there until they had gone to bed for the night. Franco was worn out and Pawlo was sick of living in squalor.

'What's wrong with her?' he had bawled at Franco. 'What woman doesn't know how to cook or look after a child?'

But Franco would just shake his head and complete the chores that needed to be done.

When, several weeks later, Pawlo announced he was getting married and bringing his new wife to live with them, Franco didn't know if he should feel relieved or concerned. Two women in the same house never mixed well, especially if one hadn't a clue how to run a home. As the wife of the eldest son, Serenella should by right have the upper hand. However, when the young bride moved into the house, Serenella was eager to hand the reins over to her new sister-in-law. From then on it was Inez who ran the household capably and with pleasure.

Serenella spent more and more time at the seafront, frequently leaving Marco with Inez. Often Franco had to search for her and bring her home on his horse and cart. He knew he would find her at some bay looking out to sea and silently she would climb up beside him. Franco wondered what she had left behind in Italy, or Sicily. All he knew was that she was from the wealthy Inglima family and had spent the war in Italy, where her father was well connected with the Fascist Party. It was a German soldier who had forcefully impregnated her and it was to save her from being executed as a whore that her family had sent their daughter to Malta. Franco didn't know what had happened to Serenella's family or the doctor since she had arrived. There had been no communication from the Inglima family, even though a letter had been sent by him to the address in Rimini – the address Franco had found written on top of the letter his mother had received from Signora Inglima before Serenella arrived. Franco didn't know how to contact the doctor either.

Sure that his wife was simply homesick for her family, Franco suggested that she write to them. To his surprise she had simply clicked her tongue and shook her head, without giving any further explanation. Then one Sunday morning, a surprise visitor turned up at their doorstep. He was dressed in a formal dark suit and was Sicilian. It had been Inez who answered the door and showed the important looking man into the large kitchen, where she'd called her husband who was in the courtyard brushing down their horse.

'My name is Gianluca Russo,' he said in English and bowed respectfully. 'I am here to speak with Signore Franco Vella and his wife, Serenella.' Franco was already coming down the stairs with Rigalla in his arms on hearing the guest arrive.

'My wife is out for a walk,' he said quizzically. 'What can I do for you?'

Inez gestured for the gentleman to sit down and summoned by her husband, she took Rigalla from

Franco's arms and went outside with Pawlo.

'I am visiting you today on behalf of the Inglima family in my role as their lawyer,' Signore Russo imparted, as he pulled a document from a brown leather briefcase. 'You are requested to sign these papers.'

Franco took the sheets which were passed over. 'They are in Italian. I can't read them properly. What does it say?'

'Signora Maria-Angela Inglima is giving you ownership of their property in Valletta. A restaurant.'

'What? Why?' Franco asked, confused. 'And what has become of the Inglimas? We haven't heard anything from them since Serenella arrived. They didn't reply to the letter about their grandson's birth or my parent's deaths.'

Signore Russo waved his left hand in the air dismissively. 'Signore Giovanni Inglima is dead,' he sniffed. 'Killed by partisans.'

Franco gasped.

'Signora Inglima is currently abroad with her son Marius. The other two sons are also dead. Angelo is now head of the Inglima family.'

'Oh my God,' Franco cried. 'How did they die?'

The lawyer ran his hand under his chin. 'Assassinato' he replied. 'This restaurant is being given as a gift, from Signora Inglima to you and her daughter. She said it is a wedding present.'

Franco was speechless. 'But I don't know anything about running a restaurant,' he implored. 'I am a fisherman.'

Signore Russo shrugged his shoulders. 'You can learn. You can sell. But it is yours when you sign this paper,' he said, offering the astonished Franco a pen.

'Can you tell me anything else about my wife's family?' Franco asked, still holding the pen after he had signed the document. 'Or can you wait until she returns? I am sure she will have many questions.'

The lawyer shut his briefcase and held out his hand, which Franco shook. 'Angelo Inglima will be in contact upon his return.'

'Return?' Franco asked. 'Return from where?'

Signore Russo simply tipped his hat with his hand and strode towards the front door. 'He wished me to give a message to Signora Serenella but she is not here, so I will tell you and you can pass it on.'

Franco nodded. 'Of course. What is the message?'

'Stay out of Sicily until he sends for her. No matter

how long that will be.'

Chapter 27

Malta. October, 2004.

Salvatore found his Uncle Angelo in his usual spot, on the wide pillared veranda with its impressive views of Ragusa. The view stretched far and wide. On one side, the flat roofed buildings and majestic churches apparently arranged haphazardly, clung precariously onto the hillside. On the other side, tall cypress trees towered above green fields and hedging, where in the distance goats could be seen grazing on scorched grass.

It was literally like living in two different worlds. In Malta there was Franco's extended Vella family and their descendants. There was the restaurant and his friends, his work colleagues and now Jessy. Money had always been tight, or at least used to be before L'Artiste became so popular. There was his painting and jaunts out fishing with his father on their small *luzzu* – not that he had done either in the last year since taking over the restaurant from his father. His older brother Marco, who had previously shown no interest in L'Artiste and had been busy with his successful accountancy business in America, was quite happy when Franco had relinquished control of the restaurant to Salvatore. His twin sisters who were married with their own families had no interest in the running of Ristorante L'Artiste.

The restaurant had never made much money. Franco had been quite satisfied with having just enough to live on and he was neither ambitious nor materialistic. Once he had achieved ownership of a house for Serenella away from the restaurant, he was happy and his wife had seemed quite content with the moderate household allowance he brought home. She seemed to be able to manage on very little. Franco had always been amazed at how economically she budgeted for the fashionable clothes she liked to wear and dress her children in.

In Sicily money was never an issue. The Inglima home, an actual eighteenth century palace, was almost like a museum. Famous art adorned the walls and everybody seemed so free, not tied down to jobs or businesses. Days were spent lounging around the private courtyard and swimming in one of its pools. Indoor for winter, outdoor for summer. Wonderful meals were prepared for the family by professional chefs. Salvatore loved joining the others as they took their yachts from Marina di Ragusa, sailing to Sardinia or Malta for long weekends of fun and parties. Manuel was right. For Salvatore it was like visiting his own holiday camp. But until now, he didn't realise that he was expected to earn his place there.

As far as he was concerned his mother had already done that for him, simply by being born into the respected Inglima family. He had presumed that it was her love for Franco which made his mother leave the luxurious lifestyle of Sicilian nobility and live out her life on the small island of Malta. The restaurant, on a prominent street facing Valletta's waterfront, had been gifted to Serenella and Franco on their marriage by her parents as a wedding present. For the first several years of their life together the couple lived above the restaurant. Following years of diligent saving by Franco they finally bought a three storey house nearby. Serenella had never really helped at L'Artiste. She had attempted to, but had no idea about working in a kitchen, or working at anything apart from adding some feminine touches and advising on the decorating. It was Franco who did the cooking and running of the business, which when the busier summer season began was manageable with occasional help from his younger siblings.

His menu consisted of simple local Maltese dishes

of rabbit, or fish which Franco caught himself. Having no mortgage on the building made it possible to get by and save for the new house Serenella desperately wanted. Unable to afford one with a garden, she had made do with the large terrace at the top of the house where she grew an assortment of beautiful flowers and shrubs.

Even as a young child Salvatore was aware of a sadness in his mother's eyes. The only time she seemed to be alive was when they holidayed in her favourite Sicilian seaside town of Marina di Ragusa. The Inglima family owned a luxurious villa there, just a stone's throw from the sea. Once a small sanatorium, the house had been remodelled and was now a seven bedroomed villa with extensive gardens back and front, including a wide wrap-around balcony with stunning views over the Mediterranean Sea, directly facing Malta. Until Serenella's early death, Salvatore spent many happy times with his mother there, with whole days spent on the beach. In the evening, long tables would be set up under the wisteria covered pergola inside the walled garden. A little gate-house with emerald green shutters at the end of the property, just before the tall black electronic gates, was where he and his mother shared a

310

room together. Despite the villa being very modern and comfortable, for some reason Serenella preferred to sleep in the place she called, *la mia casetta*. She said it was cooler, which it was, even without the air conditioning available in the villa. The thick yellow limestone walls were cool in the summer months and the high ceiling on which an old fashioned fan whirred, offered a haven out of the harsh Sicilian sun.

Nobody except Salvatore and his mother ever went in to the little house. Everything was white, from bed linen to the hand woven rugs on the floor. Not wanting to change the layout of the *casetta*, Serenella had a bathroom installed in what used to be a small bedroom. The only other room was the large living area that also doubled as a bedroom. Their high oak bed was the dominant feature and they kept their clothes in an old renaissance style antique wardrobe beside it. One wall was decorated with chipped blue and white Sicilian tiles above where his mother told him used to be a small kitchen area. They didn't spend much time in this little gate-house during the day. Once they woke, they went straight to the beach and after nightfall, when even the cicadas stopped singing and the moon hung above the navy shimmering sea they would go indoors.

Just the two of them, where Serenella would make up stories about the type of people who might have one time lived in the small house.

Aware as a child that he was the favourite, Salvatore endured the teasing and jealousy of his older siblings. His brother Marco, a man when Salvatore came into the world, was studying as an accountant in America and later married a woman from New York – who divorced him at a huge cost ten years later. His sister Rosalia was already married with twin boys when Serenella embarrassingly became pregnant with Salvatore, and his other sister Mari (short for Margarita) was engaged. On his arrival home from college for the summer holidays, Marco was absolutely appalled to find their mother pregnant at her age and fired disgusted glances at Franco, who only look amused at his reaction. Serenella's early death had been a devastating loss to Salvatore. Franco's demonstrative love did not make up for the close bond he had shared with Serenella. Even now, tears came easy to his eyes any time he thought of his mother and he only wanted her family, the Inglima family, to see him as their own.

Angelo was asleep. One of his many Borsalino hats covered his face. Tan was the colour of choice today.

Looking down, Salvatore wasn't surprised to see that his uncle was also wearing tan leather loafers and a matching belt. Cream chinos and a cream shirt complimented the outfit, showing off his weathered dark brown skin, although well lined now in his eightieth year. Even just relaxing at home his uncle always looked stylishly dressed.

'*Zio*,' Salvatore called quietly, placing his hand gently on his uncle's shoulder. Immediately a hand went up removing the hat and Angelo's face broke into a wide smile, showing teeth extraordinarily white for an old man.

'*Salvucio, il mio ragazzo*,' Angelo exclaimed, opening his arms for Salvatore to lean down and hug him, kissing his nephew on both cheeks which was reciprocated by Salvatore. Somehow just hearing his beloved uncle call him *my boy* brought tears to Salvatore's eyes. He had no doubt that this old man loved him, regardless of what Manuel had said. But, he wanted more than love. He wanted more than anything to have *Zio* Angelo's respect and he would do whatever was necessary to earn it.

'I knew you'd come to see me,' his uncle said, patting Salvatore on the back and offering him a chair closer to the edge of the veranda railings. Salvatore took the one opposite beside the glass-topped table between the two men. Angelo sat back in his chair and regarded his nephew.

'Your brother was arrested at Catania Airport.'

Salvatore sat up. 'What? Why?'

'*You* tell *me* why you think he might have been arrested?' Angelo asked conspiratorially.

Salvatore felt the heat rise to his face. 'Was it anything to do with drugs?'

Angelo smiled and nodded his head slowly up and down. 'He sang like a choir boy.'

Salvatore felt the sweat break out on his brow. 'I came here to talk to you about that.'

'I know,' Angelo replied. 'I am aware of everything that has gone on. I know about your argument with Manuel earlier. I know about the drugs that Manuel and Marco tried to shift through Franco's restaurant. It was I who had Marco arrested.'

Salvatore's eyes widened. The Inglima family never involved police in family matters.

'They were working for me, those *carabineiri*,' Angelo explained. 'I just needed to put the frighteners on Marco and it worked. I had had my suspicions about

314

your brother since he came back from New York with Manuel and mysteriously began helping out at the restaurant. I've had my associates on their tail for months.'

Salvatore was speechless, scarcely able to believe what he was hearing.

'He had big ideas when he came from back America, thinking he was going to be next Inglima *Padrino* and bring our family into the filthy drug trade. However, he was a very tiny fish in a very huge ocean. Under normal circumstances, in the idiotic way he behaved, carting bags of flour around thinking it was concealing cocaine - getting you to mind packages for him – he wouldn't have lasted a week in that game. When the *carabineiri* hauled him in for questioning Marco wasted no time in naming Manuel. And you.'

'Me?' Salvatore jumped up.

'Sit down, Salvu. Relax,' Angelo said, waving his hand at the chair in front. 'As I said, they are working for me, so you will not get in any trouble. I needed to separate the wheat from the chaff. Now I know that you are the wheat and that Marco is the chaff. And Manuel ...' he made the sign of the cross in the air, which Salvatore understood meant – he was dead, or as good as.

Salvatore felt as though he was part of some crazy dream. Either that or he almost expected somebody to come out with cameras and tell him that he had been set up in some elaborate prank. In part he was relieved that the whole nightmare of Marco and Manuel and the drugs, was over. Yet it was unbelievable the extent to which his uncle was involved from the side-lines - watching everything that was going on. It was as though Salvatore was part of some examination and he was being tested.

Angelo leaned over the table towards Salvatore and cupped his nephew's face with one hand. 'You have had a lot to take in today *Salvucio*, but there is more for you to know. Much more.' Reaching into his inside pocket, he pulled out a long gold chain with a small gold locket hanging from it. Salvatore took the locket and opened the clasp. Inside was the faded black and white photograph of a young man. He had never seen the man's face before.

'Who is it?' he asked his uncle.

'Giorgio Cavallo,' Angelo answered. 'The man your mother had planned to marry.'

Salvatore squinted his eyes. 'Then why didn't she?'

316

Angelo sighed and threw his hands into the air. 'The war started. Your mother was in Italy at the time. She got pregnant over there.'

Salvatore sat up. 'Pregnant? Was Pop over in Italy during the war? I thought he had been exiled to Scotland.'

'She wasn't pregnant to Franco, Salvu. She had got pregnant to somebody else and was sent to have the baby in Malta where nobody would know her. Franco married her before she gave birth to your brother Marco.'

Salvatore swore. 'Then who got her pregnant?'

At this question Angelo stood up. 'This is going to be a shock to you Salvu, so be prepared. Our family had been staunch Fascists during the war, then we turned our backs on them and everything that they stood for.'

'I never knew that. You always spoke out about what bullies the Fascists were.' Salvatore had a sick feeling in his stomach - aware that by the way Angelo was looking and speaking, whatever he was going to say must be something terrible. His uncle's face was ashen.

'My father, Giovanni Inglima, was highly involved in the Fascist party. In fact, he and Mussolini (his uncle spat on the ground, as he always did when Il Duce's name was mentioned) were very close friends. As children we spent all our summers at their home at Villa Carpena in Forli. I was sickened by the bullying tactics of my father and the Fascist party. I left. I joined the partisans early on in the war. My father never knew, but Mama did.'

Salvatore gasped. This was unbelievable.

'After the war ended we returned here to Sicily. We said that our father voted against Mussolini in 1943 and that our family turned against the party. We made up a story of how my father had been shot as a traitor by Il Duce's administration. That's not true. My father stuck by Mussolini (he spat again) till the end and he was captured by the allies who hung him like they did every other Fascist they found trying to escape Italy. It was after his death that the Inglimas destroyed the evidence of ever having being involved with that man. That tyrant.' Angelo clenched his fists in anger.

'But who was Marco's father?' Salvatore asked. He had no interest in the rest of the story right now.

'Let me get to that in my own way,' Angelo declared firmly. 'Your mother stayed at Villa Carpena for most of the war with her family. Later on they all moved to Rimini. Rachele Mussolini and her children went between Forli and their residence in Rome. In secret, Serenella kept up correspondence with Giorgio Cavallo who was by now a partisan fighting in Italy. He'd been sent there to fight against the Fascists by his commander, a Doctor Moretti, to avoid conscription.'

Salvatore felt as though he was holding his breath, waiting on the name he wanted to hear – the person who had got his mother pregnant. Suddenly another thought occurred to him.

'Does Marco know who is father is?' he asked quickly.

'Yes. He does just very recently.'

'And where is he now? Marco?' Salvatore asked.

'On his way back to America,' Angelo answered. 'He thinks I arranged that he can avoid prison on condition he never returns to Sicily, but I really did it for his own safety. I am telling you, because as Serenella's son, you will soon be head of the Inglima family. Marco has relinquished that role by his own actions.'

Now it was Salvatore's turn to stand up. '*Zio*, please, will you just tell me who got my mother pregnant in Italy and whatever else it is you are holding back.'

'Marco's father was ...' and when Angelo spat with disgust – Salvatore cried out with dismay. 'No!'

Chapter 28

Malta. March, 1946.

Serenella was delightfully tipsy. Lifting the gramophone arm, she removed the black record and replaced it with another. This time it was Bing Crosby's, "Don't Fence Me In." She twirled, then put her hand out to steady herself on the wooden table. The warm March sun was beginning to set behind the city of Valletta, casting shadows of nearby buildings onto the roofed terrace where Serenella Vella was having her own private party. Unknown to Franco, Inez had offered to take Rigalla and Marco for the night, giving his wife plenty of time to prepare. It was the least Inez could do after the shocking remark she had made to the other women, as they shopped at the vegetable market in Valletta on that Friday morning.

Unaware that her sister-in-law was within earshot, Inez gossiped with the locals about her in-laws' recent move to the newly named, Ristorante L'Artiste, on the waterfront.

'It's wonderful to have the house to ourselves at last,' she'd gushed. 'I am totally re-decorating each room, starting with the kitchen.'

'Is it a large kitchen?' a woman asked. 'Maybe you could make two rooms downstairs.'

'The kitchen is enormous,' Inez replied. 'Especially now that I've taken down that partition curtain.'

'Partition curtain?' another voice asked. 'What was that for?'

Inez threw her hand in the air dramatically. 'For Serenella.'

'Serenella?'

'Yes. She doesn't sleep with her husband you know. She slept downstairs with her baby and Franco slept upstairs with his baby sister. It's the same now in their new home.'

Serenella's cheeks burned as she heard the audible gasps of the chattering women.

'Well, she must have slept with him at some stage,' a cackling voice added, 'if they have a baby.'

'It is not for me to say,' she heard her sister-in-law reply, happy to be the focus of attention. 'But all I *will* say is that when she turned up at the Vella's house that winter, she already had another passenger. If you know what I mean.'

Serenella felt weak with embarrassment. But what surprised her more than anything, was that she was more embarrassed for her husband than herself. She could just imagine that gaggle of clucking geese running home to impart this remarkable gossip to their husbands, men who were friends of Franco's. These men, would no doubt, also spread this piece of news and taunt her husband, just like Inez had belittled her. She could not let that happen. Franco was a decent hardworking man and a good husband and father. No words had been spoken between them about the lack of physical contact since they married. Indeed Serenella was well aware that they were not properly man and wife in the eyes of the church, or law probably. But to think that now it was public knowledge was humiliating to them both. She would have to do something to remedy the situation.

The perfect occasion came about just two days later. Calling out, *'Bongu'*, as was her usual habit on arriving at the Vella house before entering her previous home - Serenella pushed the perambulator into the airy room, with Rigalla toddling in behind her. Inez was feeding her baby in the courtyard, while laundry flapped around her on several rows of clothes-lines. She made to stand up, but to her surprise, Serenella told her to stay seated and began to unpeg the dry sheets from where they hung, throwing them into a straw basket lying on the ground. Inez bit her lip, not wanting to cause insult by telling the other woman that she should fold them first to save on the ironing.

'I need to ask you a favour, Inez', Serenella said, flinging yet another sheet onto the pile, ignoring the fact that it was still damp.

'Oh, what is it?' Inez asked, removing the child from under her dress and closing the buttons with one hand, while she expertly held her baby with the other.

'It is our wedding anniversary today,' Serenella stated.

Inez looked up in surprise.

'Yes. I know, hard to believe it is a full year,' her sister-in-law replied. 'I want to ask you if you would take the children for the night. So I can celebrate with Franco.'

Inez opened her mouth with astonishment.

Serenella continued, noticing how the other woman looked taken aback by her remark. 'I was going to ask you on Friday at the market, but when I approached you, you were so busy *gossiping*, (she stressed the word) with your friends, that I didn't like to disturb you.' She gave Inez a knowing look and to her satisfaction the young woman's face coloured. She couldn't refuse Serenella's request.

What to wear for her little ruse was Serenella's main concern when she returned alone to their apartment above L'Artiste. Franco usually closed the restaurant on a Sunday as soon as it was dark, which in March was around seven o'clock. He preferred to be at home at least one night before the children went to bed. Serenella didn't have many clothes. What she had brought from Sicily in her small case where all things he had seen before and she had no money to buy anything. It had to be something different, something that made her *look* different. Being able to buy the latest fashions was the luxury she missed most. Serenella pulled various bits of clothing out of her wardrobe, then sat on her bed in despair. The other room, where Franco slept, held another large wardrobe which she remembered still contained old clothes from the previous owners.

However, on opening the wardrobe door she was disappointed to see all that hung there now where garments belonging to her husband. On top of the wardrobe were two suitcases. One large, one small. The large one contained drawings, lots of pencils and a few torn shirts, with some just having a few buttons missing. Shirts she noticed that Franco had left out in the hope of her mending them, which she never had. Serenella sighed and threw them beside her on the floor. The other case held more drawings, a medical book and a bit of ribbon, but on the bottom she gasped to see a dress folded up. She pulled it out and held it towards the light, then excitedly tried it on. It fitted, almost. The dress was a bit tight around the chest and a quite short also. Whoever it belonged to must have been both small and skinny she guessed. But it would do.

Next, she dragged the tin bath into the kitchen from its place on the large terrace, then filled it with the water she'd been heating for an hour on the old stove. She tipped some cologne into the water. Her mother had packed the bottle into the case, before she left Italy. She had never used it in Malta, until now, and the scent initially made her catch her breath - reminding her of a different life. Serenella sniffed from the bottle and immediately felt transported back to the last time she had worn the fragrance, the day she had hoped to marry Giorgio Cavallo.

Once washed and dressed, the next chore on her

list was to prepare the table. Franco always brought home food from the restaurant for their meals as Serenella was a terrible cook. As she placed candles on the table, covered with the yellow and blue check cloth, she had recently bought on their move to Valletta, Serenella sipped from a large glass of strong Maltese wine. That was not something that was hard to find. In their small courtyard cellar were bottles of wine stored for the restaurant and Serenella had lifted a few of them that morning.

The very first glass of wine went straight to Serenella's head. She had almost slipped while carrying the heavy gramophone onto a table closer to the terrace doors, so she could hear the music better. Giggling, she thought of the people below in the restaurant, where they sat enjoying one of Franco's delicious fish dishes - and how would they react if they could see his quiet wife, drunk and wearing a figure hugging skimpy dress and dancing just above their heads? The first record she put on was, 'You Are My Sunshine,' which Franco often played over and over again for Rigalla, spinning her around the floor as the little girl squealed in delight. The toddler could sing every word of it perfectly in English, even if she didn't understand the words. After liberally pouring herself another glass of the red coloured liquid, Serenella now sang along to the latest record she had picked up a few weeks ago at the market – Nella Colombo's song, '*In Certa Di Te*'.

The first time she had heard the song on the restaurant radio, Serenella had had to leave the children in the kitchen courtyard, where they were helping her to fill pots with soil for the small lemon trees they were planting. She had to rush upstairs to their apartment where she composed herself by dipping her head under the water pump. The shock of the cold water made her catch her breath and stop the tears which had threatened to come to her eyes. The last time she had cried was when she had begged her mother not to send her away from Italy and away from where she had any hope of being reunited with Giorgio. But her tears were ignored and Serenella had decided from that day that she would never let anybody see her cry again. It was just a few days later when, on wandering around the outdoor market with the children, that she heard the sultry tones of the female singer again. She followed the sound, until she reached the stall where a smartly dressed man, wearing a funny looking English bowler hat and necktie was calling out for people to choose a record to listen to.

'This one,' she requested, pointing at the record currently turning on the gramophone, without even wanting to know the price first. Frustrated by the spectacle the seller was making, by lifting the record with a flourish, then pretending to shine it with his spotty necktie before placing it into a paper sleeve and theatrically writing the name of both the song and singer across the front. Serenella handed over the money, ignoring the man's flirtatious wink and snatched the change hurriedly out of his hand. That afternoon she had played the song over and over until she knew each word by heart, feeling as though it had been written just for her.

In Certa Di Te' - Looking for you

I walk on my own in the city,
Passing through the crowd that does not know,
who does not see my pain,
looking for you, dreaming of you,
that I have not you anymore.
Watch- it's not you
Listen, it's not you
Where have you been lost my love?
I will see you again, I will find you again, my poor love!

I try uselessly to forget you
the first love cannot be forgotten
it's written by name,
a unique name at the bottom of the heart,
I know you are the love
the real love, the great love.

Everything was set, like a stage awaiting its audience. Candles flickered seductively in the dusk and soft music played in the background, as Serenella heard the apartment door open. She pulled the last clip from her hair, allowing it to tumble in dark waves around her face. With her heart thumping in her chest, she stood ready to welcome her husband home as he walked through the door, in one hand thankfully carrying an aromatic dish of something for dinner.

Franco didn't notice her at first. Instead he looked around the large room with a puzzled expression on his face. Where is everyone, he wondered? Usually he would walk in at this time of the evening to the chaos of children either crying at not wanting to go bed, or playing happily in the tin bath with clothes strewn untidily around the room. Why was it so dark? Walking further into the kitchen area, he heard the music playing first and noticed that the narrow doors leading out onto the large terrace were open. A feeling of fear gripped his chest. Placing the hot dish quickly on the table, Franco ran out to where a shocking sight met his eyes. Serenella was standing with her arms open towards him, her hair cascading like Medusa's around her shoulders. The table was set with candles and music was playing on the gramophone, but it was what she wore that made Franco Vella's heart feel as though it had hit the floor.

The blue dress! Ana had later adorned it with a white lace collar, made by his own mother's hands as a Christmas gift to her daughter-in-law to be. She had been wearing the dress at the 15th of August celebrations, when Malta was in the early days of war. The night when they had first climbed together to the top of Mosta Dome. The night he had kissed her for the first time. A clumsy, innocent but perfect kiss. That was the dress she had worn on that warm, starry night. It had exactly matched the colour of her blue eyes and Franco knew that night, that he would love her for the rest of his life.

It looked so wrong, so terribly wrong on somebody else.

'That dress does not belong to you!' he roared, in

an uncharacteristic show of temper.

That night both husband and wife lied to each other. Franco lied when he said the sight of Serenella wearing the dress which his mother had been working on before she died, had caused him to yell out like he did. He didn't tell the truth, which was that the dress had belonged to Ana. Serenella lied and said that she had grown to love him and wanted to be physically close to Franco, as his wife. She didn't say what she had overheard in the market, or that she had to get drunk to allow him close to her. She cried, which shocked Franco – he had never seen her show emotion about anything up until now. Sobbing, his wife told him how she was lonely. How she missed her family, how his avoidance of her had hurt her. So Franco took her for the first time to his bed believing it was out of pity. When, a few months later, Serenella proudly displayed her growing bump, Inez had to endure the disapproving looks of the local women, who sneered at her fibs about her obviously happily married and pregnant sister-in-law.

Chapter 29

Malta. October, 2004.

Jessy groaned. Reaching for a glass and finding none she sat up and wiped the smudged mascara now caked onto her eyelashes. 'Oh, my head,' she mumbled out loud, looking around the sun dappled room. 'Oh no,' she cried, noticing on her phone that is almost midday. She had also missed a call from Neil, but puzzlingly there were *seven* missed calls from Salvatore. Creeping gingerly out of her bed and slipping feet into fluffy slippers, Jessy pulled a blue cotton nightgown over her naked body before padding to her en-suite.

'Ah, you are awake,' Franco laughed when Jessy ventured into the kitchen. He handed her a mug of steaming coffee which she gladly accepted, this time thankful that it was both strong and sweet. 'You had a good time with your brother?' he asked, guessing from her long sleep and bleary eyes that it was also a good time with some strong alcohol.

'Yes. But my head is banging. I had too many Bellinis on an empty tummy,' Jessy moaned, sitting slowly on the kitchen chair. 'Did you speak to Salvatore?'

'Yes,' Franco replied, 'and he was just getting the ferry back from Sicily. He said he tried to ring you several times.'

Jessy squinted her eyes and looked at Franco. 'You are dressed very smartly this morning,' she commented. 'Is it a special occasion?'

Franco nodded his head. 'Yes and also I had a good sleep. Very good and nice dreams.'

'Oh? What about?' Jessy asked, getting up and rummaging in her handbag on the table for some headache tablets.

'I dreamed about a lot of people in my life who have died,' he replied with a wistful smile. 'My parents, Ana, Serenella – everybody. Even our old dog who died was in my dream. But when I woke I wasn't sad. I feel happy and younger,' he added with a chuckle. 'Today I feel like a young Franco Vella again.'

'Well for some,' Jessy replied, knocking back two painkillers with a long mouthful of coffee. Then, seeing him wearing what he called his 'posh' fishing hat, she added, 'Where are you going?'

'Today Rigalla has a surprise for me,' he replied happily, 'and she has asked me to call up to her convent. You are welcome to come along too.'

Jessy grimaced and shook her head. 'Sorry. I really need a long hot shower first to feel human again. But I will call afterwards if that's okay?'

Franco nodded, 'Yes. Join us when you are ready.' Then, before leaving, he leaned down to kiss the top of her head. 'You are my sunshine you know, *hanini*.'

***

Jessy was applying her makeup when the call came.

'It's me,' Salvatore said.

Jessy giggled. 'Yes I know that, silly. You do realise that your name comes up on my phone when you ring me? You sound just like Franco,' she continued. 'He always says – *'This is Franco Vella speaking'*, when obviously I know it is him.'

Salvatore joined in her laughter, despite the nervousness he was feeling. 'Can you meet me at St. Julian's? At that restaurant you like there?'

Jessy's forehead crinkled. 'Yes, but why?'

'Well, you always say we never do anything spontaneous, so I'd like to take you out to lunch before I go back to L'Artiste and see how the builders are getting on. That's spontaneous isn't it?'

'Okay. Or we could meet Franco and Sr. Lucija at the convent,' she suggested. 'They are meeting up there now.'

Salvatore pulled a face. 'No. I want us to have a private talk.'

Jessy didn't answer for a second, wondering what was up. 'Sure, okay. Are you there already?'

'Yes.'

'I'll leave now but you know yourself how long it might take with traffic, but about ten or fifteen minutes okay?'

'Sure,' and he put down the phone, signalling the waiter to bring him a double brandy. He was going to need some Dutch courage.

'The buses are so slow,' Jessy huffed as she pulled a chair out next to Salvatore, about a half an hour later. 'Thank God we will be driving back.'

Salvatore leaned over to give her a kiss on the cheek. It didn't go unnoticed by him that she hadn't greeted him with a hug on arriving. 'We'll have to get the bus back I'm afraid,' he said, beckoning the waitress to come over to their table.

'Oh! Where is the car?' Jessy asked, removing her sunglasses and placing them on her head.

'Wine?' Salvatore enquired.

Jessy was about to reply no, having just barely recovered from a hangover, then instead decided to be spontaneous also. 'Yes, red wine would be lovely,' she answered.

'I have returned the car,' Salvatore gave their order and watched Jessy's face for her reaction.

Her eyebrows shot up immediately. 'Really? Why? Oh, did Manuel ask for the money for it?'

'No. He was expecting a different kind of payment apparently.'

'How do you mean?' Jessy asked, then as she noticed the empty brandy glass added, 'Is everything alright?'

Salvatore shook his head. It was lowered. 'No.'

He studied a scratch on the table and traced its curvature with his index finger. Over and over he traced the wood until the skin on his finger almost started to feel burned from friction. It was impossible to look into her face, but he could feel Jessy's gaze on him. She put out her hand and placed it over his fingers, stilling them. He noticed her engagement ring sparkling in the light. Just seeing it filled him with guilt. He recalled how excited she had been in Azzopardi's

Jewellery Shop that day in Valletta and had tried on virtually every ring in the establishment. He had taken great delight in her pleasure and afterwards had treated them both to an expensive meal in one of the city's most elite restaurants. Jessy couldn't take her eyes off the precious diamond sparkling on the third finger of her left hand. Childishly she had shown anybody who congratulated them how to make a traditional Irish wish with the ring.

'Salvu, will you look at me?' she asked quietly, her voice almost a whisper.

Again he shook his head.

Jessy lifted her hand. Salvu could still feel the heat of her palm, but now it was on his face which was dark with stubble. She gently tilted his head towards her.

'Just tell me. I need to know what is wrong.'

Salvatore stretched his legs out straight under the table and blew a long slow breath, finally looking at her. He cracked his knuckles. 'Sorry.' He knew she hated when he did that. She said it made her cringe.

This time Jessy shook her head. 'Sorry?' she repeated, quizzically.

He realised she had misinterpreted what he meant. What was he saying sorry for? It was all such a mess.

Salvatore knew two things. One was that if he told her, he would feel a huge sense of relief and the second was that once he did tell her, their relationship would be over. Some of Franco's sayings for when he was worried about something were, 'Will it matter a whole lot in a year's time?' and the other, 'If so, then what's the worst thing that could possibly happen?' Salvu felt he already knew the answer to both of those questions.

'When I met you, I already had a girlfriend. Well, she was more of a childhood friend really, but it was presumed by both our families, in Sicily that is, that we would get married.'

Jessy felt numb. 'Who was it?' she asked quietly, as the waitress placed two full glasses of wine in front of them.

He hesitated, very aware that Jessy had asked, *was*, instead of *is*. 'The thing is, she - and our families - *still* kind of assume that we are getting married.'

'Who is she?' Jessy demanded, then took a long gulp of her wine, her eyes fixed on his face.

'Francesca.'

She gasped. 'She's your cousin.'

'No. Not really. She is a third cousin – it is perfectly acceptable to marry a third cousin.'

'And are you going to?' Jessy couldn't believe how calm she was.

'I don't know what I am going to do,' he replied, also surprised at how composed Jessy was behaving. He at least expected her to burst into tears or shout, or *show* something of what she must be feeling.

'Do you mean you have been in a relationship with her the whole time you have been with me?'

He hung his head. 'Kind of. But not like you think.'

'Explain what *kind of* means,' she replied coolly, reaching again for the comforting glass of wine.

He sighed. 'Just that when I go there – to Ragusa – she is always around. She calls herself my girlfriend. So do the others.'

'But, they all seemed to know about me when I was over for the funeral. Who did they think I was then?'

'A family friend. A relation of Franco's from Ireland. I mentioned you and the story about Ana and her being Rigalla's mother. My mother had told *Zio* Angelo about it years ago.'

'That's why Francesca was so horrible to me?' Jessy asked. 'She thought I was moving in on you – yet she didn't realise I was your fiancée. That's why you kept me at arm's length isn't it? That's why I couldn't ever go to Sicily with you, or why I wasn't asked to sit next to you at the funeral.' He nodded.

'I can't believe it,' she whispered, almost to herself. 'All this time, you have been two-timing me.'

Salvatore lifted his head and looked over at the young woman. She looked incredibly cool. Her face was almost expressionless and she was looking quite serenely out the window at the bay in front. Her arms were flat on the table, with the palms face down. She didn't even look angry or upset. There were no tears in her eyes. Instead Jessy simply stared vacantly at the busy harbour opposite.

'I need to have a moment,' she said, slowly rising from her chair, then she lifted her handbag and made her way to the rear of the restaurant. In the bathroom Jessy splashed her face with cold running water and looked in the mirror. Her face was wet, but from not from crying. That might come later. Right now she needed to just get away from *him*.

She was out the door in seconds. Customers turned their heads with surprise as Jessy ran swiftly through the crowded restaurant obviously in a state of distress. The regulars glanced worriedly at each other.

Two of the waiters rushed out the back, one of them even lifting the fire extinguisher off the wall on his way. Marlena, the young waitress Jessy was friendly with, ran out the restaurant's front door, but Jessy was already far ahead in the distance, running as though in fear for her life. Marlena closed the door quietly and turned to the faces looking questionably at her. She shrugged at the customers, saying with a grin, 'Well, somebody must be late for work.' However, she was sure it was not something simple that had put the dreadful look of anguish on the Irish girl's face. Something was up with Jessy and her boyfriend, of that she had no doubt.

Chapter 30

Malta - Sicily. July, 1975.

Serenella bent down and picked up the letter which she had let fall from her trembling hands just a few seconds ago. It was from her eldest brother, Angelo Inglima. Their mother, Maria-Angela, was dead.

Franco argued that he should accompany Serenella on the ferry to Sicily, but she insisted that she wanted to go alone.

'You will just feel uncomfortable,' she told him, impatiently. 'I will be feeling self-conscious enough without also worrying about you.'

Wearing a black Chanel dress and heels, with black stockings and clutching a black Chanel handbag, Serenella Vella stepped off the ferry. Her hair was tied in a neat bun and by her feet was a small black weekend case. The only colour was the strand of pearls hanging around her neck.

Angelo Inglima was pleased. Serenella was obviously using the money he posted to her address every month, although no acknowledgement had ever been made. It was unlikely that Franco Vella made enough money at the restaurant to dress his wife in

Chanel. He wondered if Serenella's choice of designer was a deliberate snub to the country of her birth, by choosing French fashion over Italian. Mama would have been horrified, he thought.

She recognised him immediately - dressed head to toe in Gucci. Serenella didn't wave. Instead she waited for him to come to her. He walked just the same, long loping strides with his arms swinging. As he approached, she felt her heart beat rapidly. He was smiling warmly, then his arms opened and against her own resolve, Serenella sank into them.

'*Angelo, mia caro fratello,*' she cried.

Maria-Angela Inglima's body had already been removed to the Duomo of San Giorgio. Serenella was relieved she did not have to sleep under the same roof as the woman she had never learned to forgive.

'She was filled with remorse until the very end,' Angelo told her. 'Only now do I understand why.'

Serenella glanced at her brother. 'Why? What do you mean, why?'

'Before I answer that question dear sister, there are many other things that I need to tell you.' Angelo gestured for her to sit. They had been walking around the olive grove as they talked, with Serenella stopping at almost every tree, recalling how she had helped both Giorgio and his father Carlo to plant many of them. Now those small saplings had grown tall and were heavy with fruit, their numerous cream flowers showing promise of a good harvest to come.

Angelo put a hand in his pocket. His sister gasped when he lifted out a gold locket. Immediately she grabbed it and opened the clasp – Giorgio Cavallo's face looked back at her.

'Where did you get this?' she asked quietly, running her finger lovingly over the image.

'Mama found it - after you left. Doctor Moretti confirmed her suspicions.'

'Moretti? What happened to him? He and Mama never came to Malta for the birth as promised. Whatever happened after I left Italy, Angelo?'

'It was a terrible time to be in Italy,' her brother replied. 'Especially for Fascists and anybody involved with them. Not long before Mussolini was shot – to Serenella's disgust Angelo spat on the ground – Mama went to Villa Carpena to see Rachele. Their family had to go into hiding. She found the locket there and realised what had happened to you. I am the only person she told.'

Serenella shook her head in disbelief. 'So she knew. She knew and she didn't come to fetch me. To take me home.'

'You were already married,' Angelo replied. 'And we knew what would happen to you if word ever got out that you were the mother of Mussolini's son.'

'But nobody knew apart from the doctor, you and Mama. None of us would have told anybody.'

'And Giorgio knew,' Angelo added.

'Giorgio wouldn't have told anybody either. He was going to marry me and bring Marco up as his own child.'

Once again Angelo put his hand into his pocket. This time he retrieved a newspaper clipping. It showed the bodies of Mussolini and Claretta being dumped unceremoniously from a truck onto the ground, before their bodies were attacked by the angry mob and subsequently hung. He handed the page to Serenella who scrutinized it with distaste, then gasped.

'Giorgio!'

Angelo nodded. 'They say that before pulling the trigger he had shouted, 'This is for Serenella.'

Serenella felt faint. 'What do you mean?' she asked incredulous.

Her brother sighed and shook his head. 'Nobody is exactly clear who fired the shots that killed that pair. All that is known is that they were taken by partisans from the house in the countryside and killed, shot to death. Nobody has ever formally been named. The repercussions would be too great if the Fascists ever discovered who exactly was responsible for the death of their leader. But what has been reported is that one young partisan shouted those words before pulling the trigger. It is said that partisan was Giorgio Cavallo.'

Serenella stood up. She opened her handbag and placed the newspaper clipping inside, then undid the heavy pearl necklace from her neck and replaced it with her precious gold locket instead. This time she did not try to hide it underneath her clothes. Putting the pearls in her bag, she shut it tight.

'Do you know what happened to Giorgio?' she asked.

Angelo nodded.

***

Italy. September, 1944.

Giorgio Cavallo groaned as he lifted his aching head and in the darkness, tried to make out where he was.

He was obviously on a truck, as he could feel the movement of the wheels underneath. He was aware of others lying next to him. Some of them groaned, but some bodies lay too still and were most probably dead.

'Is anyone here alive?' he whispered.

'Here.'

'Just about,' another voice answered.

'Any idea where we are going?' Giorgio asked, pulling himself up and leaning on his elbows. He began to crawl across the bodies until he could feel the flap at the back of the truck and lifted it to peer out. 'I can't see a bloody thing,' he said. 'It's night. I must have passed out for hours.'

'You must be still passed out comrade,' a familiar voice replied, 'because it's still daylight and you are looking right out at it.'

Giorgio felt a terrible fear grip him. Holding his hand up to his face he cried out. 'I can't see. I can't see a thing.'

The camp doctor assured Giorgio that his blindness was temporary. 'It's from the knock you got on the head,' he said indifferently. 'You've a nasty cut across both eyes which has affected your vision, but it will come back when the swelling subsides.'

By April 1945, when Giorgio Cavallo and his comrades in arms were finally rescued from their internment camp on the Swiss border, he had become used to his blindness. But a blind man was no good to the cause. A blind man was no good for anything, or so he thought.

Giorgio believed it was providence that he happened to be in the small town of Giulino di Mezzegra when news came to where he and his friends were hiding. Mussolini and his mistress were spending the night in a nearby farmhouse. No longer able to be involved in the fighting, Giorgio was now in charge of planning manoeuvres. His initial request to be included with the men who were planning Mussolini's capture was refused. It wasn't until he eventually revealed his real reason for wanting to put the bullet into Il Duce that the others consented.

'You won't be able to see him. How the hell are you going to fire at him?' one of the men cried.

After the execution of Benito Mussolini and Claretta Petacci there were many speculations about who actually fired the mortal shots. The name Walter Audisio, a partisan who used the name, 'Colonel Valerio', was given by some, as the executioner. Some say it was an Aldo Lampredi and another partisan named Moretti who drove to the De Maria family farmhouse on the afternoon of April 28th 1945, to collect Mussolini and Petacci. Their vehicle then pulled up at the entrance of the Villa Belmonte, where Mussolini and Petacci were ordered to get out and stand by the wall. Some witnesses say that Walter Audisio shot them with a submachine gun which belonged to Moretti, as his own had jammed. But, there are other witnesses - that of the men belonging to the *Partigiani Siciliani* who spoke of it only in their own company. They knew a different account - one that they ensured was never recorded in any written form. What they saw was their trusted friend and comrade standing inches from Il Duce, with a gun pointed at his chest. When he shouted the words, 'This is for Serenella,' the Dictator tore open his shirt and cried, 'Aim at my heart.' Giorgio Cavallo fired.

Giorgio Cavallo was present when they dumped the bodies of Mussolini and his mistress at the Piazzale Loreto, the major town square in Milan. He could not see what the enraged public then did to the bodies - but he heard the shouts of hatred. Neither did he know that a newspaper reporter snapped a photo of him, as he stood inches from where Il Duce's body lay. He knew only that the man who had caused so much pain to thousands, including the woman Giorgio loved, was finally dead.

***

Serenella wept as Angelo told her the events which had occurred after she had left.

'What happened to him afterwards?' she asked. 'Is he still alive?'

'Yes,' Angelo answered. 'He is.'

'Where is he?'

'He lives with his sister in Ragusa Ibla. In the same house where he lived as a child and where I know you often visited.'

'I want to see him,' Serenella cried. 'I want to see him now. I want to know why he never came to get me.'

Angelo linked his arm into hers and they continued to walk once more around the olive grove.

'You know why he didn't,' he replied gently. 'You were married. He had been left blind after the beating from the soldiers. But also, he had much work to do here in Sicily after the war ended. In many ways another kind of war was just on the horizon. One we are still trying to fight.'

'What do you mean?'

Angelo sighed. 'Italy was a total mess after the war, Serenella. It was like anarchy. Nobody seemed to know who was in power – nobody knew who to trust. The country as we knew it in the 1930s was gone. Those who were once respected, were now being dragged from their homes and hung in the street like dogs. People who were wealthy just a few years before, now were destitute. Our family was fortunate – we might have lost all of the Saccas money, but our own was secure. Mama and Marius went to America for a few years to keep safe and away from those seeking out Fascists and their families.

'Why did it take you until now to send for me?' she asked.

'It was because of Mama,' Angelo answered. 'She was ashamed. But not just for how she treated you, but because of what they did to the Sacca family. She was afraid that you would find out and you were now married to Margarita Sacca's son. Also there are people here who know who Marco's father is – she feared for your life and your son's.'

'What they did to Margarita's family? I don't understand?'

'You know that our family and the Saccas were close friends?'

Serenella nodded her head. 'Yes.'

'You know also that they were Jews. Well, because of that they had to leave Sicily during the war – Margarita's father entrusted his jewellery businesses to our papa. He put all of their money into funding for the Fascist Empire and lost everything.'

'But Margarita said that the family money was stolen by Nazis, after her parents were sent to that awful concentration camp. Poor Margarita suffered so much over her parents' deaths and she never heard from her older brother again. She never gave up hope that he survived.'

'That's not true, Serenella. Papa had full control of the Sacca wealth and he lost it all. After he died I went to their former home and it was then owned by the Italian Government, including their businesses. The building is now a bank and financial centre.'

Serenella could hardly take in all her brother was telling her. She had so many questions to ask but for the moment, there was only one foremost in her mind. For now, the others could wait.

'When can I see Giorgio?'

Chapter 31

Ragusa Ibla, Sicily. October, 2004.

Salvatore jumped quickly out of his seat as Jessy ran past.

'Jessy,' he called. 'Where are you going?' Lifting his wallet off the table, he hastily retrieved some notes and threw them down, then noticed Jessy's phone and picked it up. Ironically, his own phone began to ring and he put it to his ear, as he began to hurry down the busy street, trying to keep Jessy in his sight. She's going to Billy's, he realised.

It was Francesca.

'Have you told her yet?' she questioned in Italian. He could tell by her voice that she had been crying again.

'Yes. I will have to ring you back,' Salvatore continued.

'No. I need you tell me *now* what is going to happen Salvu, because my parents are here with me. My father wants to speak to you.'

Salvatore stopped walking. Ernesto Inglima was not a man to mess about with – and especially not when it concerned his only daughter.

'*Salvucio!*'

Salvatore let his breath out. Ernesto didn't sound too cross.

'Ernesto,' he replied. '*Come stai?*'

There was a second or two of silence and Salvatore felt his heart rate quicken. Eventually, Ernesto replied.

'How am I, you ask?' Ernesto repeated. 'I am fine. My daughter is not fine, unfortunately. You know how silly girls can get before their weddings. She seems to have an idea that you changed your mind about marrying her. She says that you have another girlfriend.'

'Ernesto, I …' Salvatore said, but was interrupted.

'*Non ti preoccupare,*' Ernesto answered. 'Don't worry. I explained to her that it is different for us men. We must sow our wild oats before we settle down. I told her that you would never dishonour the family by calling off the wedding. I reminded her of the high esteem your *Zio* Angelo holds you in - that you will someday be head of the *famiglia Inglima* and that Francesca would be your wife. Wasn't I right to do that Salvu?'

Salvatore nodded.

'I'm sorry,' Ernesto said. 'I did not hear your

reply.'

'*Certo*,' Salvatore answered. He looked ahead. Jessy was out of his sight.

'I knew you were a man of honour,' Ernesto replied. 'Francesca wants a word with you now.'

'Salvu.'

He could already hear the relief in her voice.

'Do what you have to do,' Francesca said softly. 'Then come back soon. I love you,' and she was gone.

Salvatore sighed. In his other hand was Jessy's mobile phone. The photo on the screen in front had been taken on the day of their engagement, at the restaurant where they went to celebrate. Jessy was holding her hand out so her sparkly ring was visible, and she had the biggest grin on her face. And he ... he too was smiling, knowing that he was making his father happy, by keeping a part of his beloved Ana close by.

Now he would break two hearts. Jessy's and Franco's. Or three – his own heart also.

***

The previous night in Sicily, as he sat on the veranda long after his uncle had gone to bed, Salvatore made his decision. It was the hardest one of his life. He had raged at first - at how his own mother had been violated by one of Italy's greatest persecutors. But the new-found knowledge of Mussolini's own personal persecution of Serenella had shaken Salvatore to the core of his being. He was completely consumed by hatred and the need for revenge. It had been Francesca who had eventually calmed him down.

'The greatest retribution you can have for your mother's name Salvu, is to continue doing what Angelo is doing,' she said wisely. 'Rid not just our Sicily, but Italy too, of the evil of corruption. The corruption that Mussolini and those Fascists brought into our country. And not just them – but those who have followed their footsteps, encouraging all that is evil in other countries to come here and bring their drugs, their human trafficking – for their own power. For their own wealth.'

Salvatore nodded. 'But how? Just me? Angelo has so many contacts – he is so respected and honoured in Sicily and Italy. How can I possibly take over from that?'

'Because it is your birth-right,' Francesca replied, her dark eyes gleaming with confidence. 'Angelo has chosen you and that will be enough. Enough for you to gain the respect you deserve as his heir. But not just the heir to all of this …' and Francesca waved her arms around the veranda and towards the palazzo, '… but also the heir to the Inglima name and all the authority that entails. But, you can use it as we know Marco would have, for his own personal gain and greed, or you can use it for good, as Angelo has tried to - to bring Sicily and Italy back to being a country of honour and tradition once more. It is up to you.'

But it came at a cost. Salvatore knew the first price would be Jessica. He had no doubt that Jessy would immediately move out of Franco's home when he told her about Francesca and what his uncle wanted. To his father, that would be almost like losing Ana all over again.

After walking Francesca to her family's luxury apartment at the palazzo, Salvatore took the stairs leading to the long gallery hall, where portraits of his family members were hung. As always, the painting of his mother as a sixteen year old girl made him catch his breath. She had been stunning. His older sisters looked very like her, but as everybody said, he had the same eyes as his mother and the same high cheekbones and the full lips. His sisters had a wider shaped mouth, like Franco's. He looked at his mother's hands – they were tiny. He got his hands from Pop then.

Gazing now at the portrait of his grandmother, Maria-Angela, he wondered how she had reacted to the news of her daughter's pregnancy. Somehow, his mother had ended up being sent to live in Malta and somehow she had ended up marrying Franco Vella. Salvatore realised now, that it had not been a case of his mother falling in love and running off to live with the poor fisherman, as he had been led to believe. His grandfather, Giovanni Inglima, had been a stern-faced man. Any photographs or paintings of him dressed in Fascist uniform had been destroyed. In this photograph, Giovanni was simply wearing a dark suit – and his chains of office, as Mayor of Ragusa. He had also been the only judge in Sicily at that time. There were single portraits of each of his uncles - Angelo, Lorenzo, Marco (for whom his brother was named) and Marius. Another portrait was a family one, with Salvatore's grandparents standing on either side of their children.

Walking along the hallway, Salvatore recognised other faces - his great grandfather, Francesco Giovanni Inglima, also one time the Mayor of Ragusa. Standing in the middle of the long gallery, he looked around and stretching as far as his eye could see, were images of other relatives - Ernesto and Marianna with their children, Francesca and Manuel. There were several photos of his own siblings, Marco, Rosalia, Margarita and himself - a photo of his mother and Franco on their last wedding anniversary before Serenella's death. Looking at the photograph of his father, Gianfranco Vella, Salvatore realised something that until now he had not fully grasped. Franco was also Sicilian. His grandmother, Margarita Sacca, was Sicilian. She had given birth to Franco here in Ragusa Ibla, the land of her own birth.

Salvatore understood. This was where he belonged. He needed to be here and make his mother proud. He needed to come back and reclaim her rights, in the land of her birth. A land where she had been so happy and from where she had been so cruelly evicted, through no fault of her own. Pulling the gold locket from his pocket, Salvatore squeezed it tight. *'Per te Mamma,'* he whispered. *'Per te.'*

Chapter 32

Malta. October, 2004.

Jessy leaned against the bus shelter and tried to get her breath. She felt a coldness in her veins, as though she had a sudden chill. It made her shiver slightly. She realised now too, for the first time, that she no longer felt that she would follow Salvu anywhere. She wasn't going to America with him. She didn't want to go and that realisation was like a stab in the chest – because it meant she was falling out of love with Salvatore and that made her gasp out loud. Her cheeks felt hot. Walking aimlessly on through the busy street of people now vacating businesses that were closing for the day, she stood still in her tracks. If anybody had been walking behind her, they would have collided with a young woman who suddenly stood like a statue in the middle of a crowded footpath, looking like she had just received some horrifying news. A man tut-tutted as he tried to manoeuvre around her. He glanced back to give her a scowl, but changed his mind when he saw the look on the pretty young lady's face. It was flushed. Her eyes were bright with unshed tears. A hand was clasped over her mouth which was open as though she was about to cry out.

The man stalled for a second, unsure whether to ask if she was alright. Then, another body bumped into his. After giving a quick apology he swung back around, but all he could see was the young woman running. She was running back down the street he had just walked up. Had she left something important behind, he wondered? A baby in a forgotten pram? It was not the look of somebody who had merely left a phone behind in some coffee shop. Jessy had no idea that she would pop up in a strange man's thoughts several times that evening, as he remembered the woman in the yellow dress with that awful look of distress in her eyes.

Jessy hadn't thought about where she was running until she arrived at the blue door. Why? Why had she come here? Panting for breath, she leaned her two palms against the coolness of the wooden frame, as though she was trying to push the door open. Her legs felt like jelly, unused as they were to running so fast. Beads of sweat ran down the front of her dress, as the strap of her brown leather handbag slipped from her arm. Pressing her forehead against the coolness of the door, Jessy gradually felt her heartbeat slow down. She waited until her breathing calmed, then picked up her bag. Opening the small zipped compartment inside, her fingers felt the jagged edges of a key. She pulled it out and inserted the key into the lock. It opened easily. The door creaked a little.

The hallway smelled instantly familiar. Jessy heard the click behind her as the bolt sprang back into place. She bent down and picked up the letters under her feet, holding them in her hand as she ascended the spiral staircase. Her breathing was normal now, but her mouth felt dry. Walking into the long narrow kitchen she reached onto the open shelf for a glass. There was bottled sparkling water in the fridge. She poured some in and swallowed it quickly. It made her splutter and cough. The water was freezing and felt like it burned her chest. She replaced the bottle and closed the fridge, then noticed the photo stuck to the front. She, Billy and Neil smiled back. Jessy ran her finger over the smiling face. His blond hair was shorter then.

It was probably for the best that Billy wasn't here. She needed some time to be alone. To think. To cry? Jessy didn't feel much like crying, not yet. If Ana hadn't died. If there hadn't been the connection between Ana and Franco - would she and Salvatore have continued with the relationship or would it have fizzled out as most holiday romances do? It was something Jessy pondered on a lot. No doubt there would have been tears when the trip was over and she had to return to Ireland. Salvatore, she was sure, would have taken her to the airport. Jessy imagined how she would have clung to him, upset at leaving and crying the desperate tears of a young woman in love, distraught at leaving her new boyfriend behind. Ana would have comforted her on the journey back to their little country village of Aghameen and patiently listened as Jessy talked about him non-stop when they were home. They would have written long romantic letters and run up huge phone bills. There would have been another trip. Either Salvatore visiting Ireland, or she returning to Malta. It would have been so exciting.

Jessy knew now that Salvu would not have left the island to move closer to her. He would never have left the restaurant or Franco. She also realised he had other reasons for not leaving Malta. Or Sicily. She, naturally, would not have wanted to leave Ana. Though leaving Ireland would not have been much of a wrench. Yes. It would have been Jessy that left her home. Salvatore most definitely would not. That thought alone caused a feeling in her that she didn't like. It was the same feeling that Jessy had each time she boarded yet another plane alone, while her fiancé stayed behind too busy to join her, or when he went on a trip to Sicily once more without inviting her. The feeling was one of sadness, knowing she did not mean as much to him as he did to her. For Jessy knew that she would have been by Salvatore's side no matter where he went, or where he lived. No hesitation. No doubts. But he did not, would not, do the same. But Neil, Neil would. Of that she was absolutely sure.

She had left her phone behind on the restaurant table. Damn! Walking into the hallway, Jessy picked up the landline phone and pressed the key for Neil's number that she herself had punched into Billy's speed-dial. By now he was probably on his way to the airport. Looking at her watch, Jessy said a silent prayer. Please God, let him answer.

Neil Wilson heard his phone ring. It was lying on his passenger seat. He glanced over and ignored it. He'd already said goodbye to Billy after dropping him off at Stephanie's house on the way to the airport. It wouldn't be Jessy, as she had already ignored his many calls and in his foul humour after a sleepless night, there was nobody else he wanted to speak to.

It rang again. He'd get it later.

As he waited at the traffic lights, Neil picked up his phone and glanced at the missed call number. It was Billy's Maltese landline. But he had just dropped Billy off at Stephanie's. So who..? Then he realised that the only people with keys to Billy's apartment at St. Julian's were himself, Billy's niece Ćesina and ... the only other person with keys was Jessy.

The phone rang loudly in the airy hallway. It was him.

'Jess, what is it? What's going on? Are you okay?'

Just hearing his voice unleashed a flood of tears. Despite all her brave intentions, Jessy's voice wobbled as she tried to answer.

'It's Salvatore ...' unable to say anything else, she continued to cry. Not little whimpers of despair, but instead noisy howls of anguish.

'I'm on my way.'

She nodded, but could say no words.

Neil looked behind him and swiftly did a U-turn on the busy Maltese motorway.

***

Jessy raised herself from where she had been sitting on the top step of Billy's winding staircase. She had left the door open and hearing the footsteps noisily climbing the three floors up, she looked down and gasped to see the dark haired man running quickly up to where she stood.

'Salvatore,' she cried, before he had reached the top. She staggered backwards, but within seconds he was in front of her.

'Jessy,' he said breathlessly, reaching out to the young woman who looked full of despair in front of him. 'Please. Let me talk. Let me explain.'

'I don't want to …' she mumbled. 'I don't want to hear …'

'Please. Jessy, I need to explain.' Salvatore followed her into the kitchen, placing her phone on the table. He took the seat opposite where she had sat down at Billy's kitchen table.

'Explain?' she asked calmly. 'Okay. Explain.'

'I don't know where to start,' he said. 'There is too much. So much. Family stuff. Stuff to do with Marco and drugs and …'

'Marco and drugs?' Jessy cried. 'What are you talking about?'

He sighed heavily and hung his head again, just as he had done in the restaurant. To Jessy's eyes he suddenly looked smaller. He looked dejected and shabby somehow. Even his skin looked unhealthy. Why hadn't she noticed that before?

'Salvu, I want you to tell me everything,' she said, firmly. 'Right from the very start. Right from the very first time that this all became part of your life.' Inside her heart was pounding and her legs felt weak, like they did when she had just finished a long walk, as if there was no strength left in them. But she needed to be strong now, not weak. This was too important.

He didn't reply. She waited. Then hesitantly, he began.

'I didn't suspect anything, at first. Manuel gave me a parcel to take back to Malta on one of my visits to Sicily. I didn't even ask what it was. He just said that he'd get it off me the next time he was over in the restaurant. It was something for a friend he said. I threw it in that cupboard where we keep all the old account books and forgot all about it. Then he gave me another one to take back too and before I knew it the cupboard was nearly full of these brown paper packages. They weren't that big, about the size of an A5

369

envelope. One day when I was on the phone to him, I mentioned kind of jokingly that they were taking up space. He said he was sorry and he'd get someone to pick them up. And he did. Some young guy came in one evening, said he was collecting Manuel's parcels, so I put them all in one of those recycling bags and handed them over. I didn't think about it again.'

'The guy came back about a week or so later. This time he handed me a parcel and said it was for Manuel. So, I put it in the same cupboard and brought it over with me the next time I went to Ragusa. I never asked what was inside and I'd no interest. It was just a parcel. Manuel seemed to be delighted with it though when I gave it to him. That was the night I told you about, when he'd been flashing money around and treated the whole family to dinner and drinks. He was always very generous to us all, but that night he kept slapping me on the back and saying I was *una della famiglia*. I thought it was strange as I am his cousin, well distant cousin, so I am already one of the family like he said. He is Francesca's brother by the way.'

On hearing this Jessy swallowed. Up until now she had been holding her breath, listening in horrified disbelief at what Salvatore was telling her.

'Then he gave me that car. He told me I could use it to come over and back to Sicily on the ferry and I could pay him back someday. I couldn't believe it. A brand new Alfa Romeo. I told him there was no way I could ever imagine having that kind of money and he said there was no rush and we were family. When I said I'd have to get insurance to drive it, he told me that he'd sort that all out for me and if I'd any trouble while driving it, to give him a call. It wasn't for days afterwards that I opened the boot and saw all the packages inside. I rang Manuel immediately. He told me that it was he who had paid that big tax bill on the restaurant. Over twenty thousand he said it was and that I owed him. Or Pop did. Also we owed him for the re-mortgage that Marco had taken out for L'Artiste.'

'I thought Franco owned the restaurant outright. Doesn't he?' Jessy asked, crinkling her forehead in confusion. 'So how can there be a loan on it? I don't understand?' She looked at Salvatore quizzically waiting for an answer. 'Well?' she prompted gently.

'I re-mortgaged it. Or should I say, Marco and Manuel did, I think,' he answered, ashamedly. 'For the new kitchen and all the fancy equipment, the big walk-in freezer ... the staff's wage increase.'

Jessy felt sick. 'But, I thought that was from the extra money you've been taking in, with all the additional customers recently. The place is packed from morning till night. You said yourself the restaurant was making a fortune.'

Salvatore took a cigarette packet and lighter out of his pocket, withdrew a cigarette and put it between his lips. Just as he flicked the lighter, to his astonishment Jessy whipped the cigarette out of his mouth.

'You can't smoke in Billy's kitchen,' she protested. 'What is wrong with you?'

This slight criticism immediately triggered an outrage in him and Salvatore jumped with indignation to his feet. 'For goodness sake,' he hissed. 'You worry about that.' Nevertheless, he yanked the door into the small balcony open and stomped outside, lighting the cigarette. He leaned against the black wrought-iron railings and looked up. Blowing out the smoke he already felt remorse. Jessy was standing at the shuttered door, watching him. Her eyes looked watery, like she was about to cry. Instinctively he wanted to rush over and put his arms around her, even moving his foot as though about to cross the short space to her side. Instead, ashamedly he stayed and took another deep drag of the cigarette.

Jessy spoke first, her voice wavering a little. 'I feel like you are a stranger to me.'

He sighed and smiled sadly. 'I feel like a stranger to me too.'

There was silence for a few seconds. Both of them looking at each other, as though trying to recognise the other. Tentatively Jessy walked towards him. Salvatore put out both his hands protectively, warning her off. He knew that if she came close, if she put her arms around him, he would break, because it was just what he needed most at this moment. To have her arms around him and say that everything was going to be alright.

'I found out yesterday that Marco was arrested, courtesy of my Uncle Angelo, at Catania airport. It turns out that Angelo had been watching Marco and Manuel for some time. He has exiled Marco to the States and Manuel ... well ... it doesn't look good for him.'

Jessy couldn't believe her ears. Once again she felt as though she was part of some Godfather movie. 'Are you telling me that your family are involved with the Mafia?' Jessy asked with disbelief.

'Don't be ridiculous. They are my family. Not the

Mafia,' he replied defensively, his dark eyes glancing around as though somebody was listening.

'Well they sound like they are to me. Some family - getting you to hide their drugs in Franco's restaurant.'

His eyes flashed angrily.

'How dare you speak about my family disrespectfully? You know nothing about them.'

Jessy gasped. 'Are you serious? You are telling me that your family were using you to store drugs and God knows what else in Franco's business and you expect me to show them respect? And actually Salvatore – it is *you* I know nothing about.'

Salvatore stepped closer to where Jessy stood, with her arms folded defensively and a look of disbelief and pain on her face.

'Please love. None of this is my fault. Can't you see that?'

'And Francesca. She is not your fault either?' Jessy shouted, finally giving vent to the anger she was feeling. 'We've been together over two years and all this time you had another girlfriend in Sicily.' By now Jessy was shaking with the hurt she felt.

'Jessy.' Salvatore put his arms around her shoulders and felt full of remorse once more as her shoulders shook under his touch. 'Please. Let me explain. There is so much family stuff that Angelo told me last night, my head is spinning with it all – but if you let me talk – you will understand. I think.'

'Stuff? What stuff?'

'About my family's past and how it is intermingled with Margarita's family. Franco's family I mean. How my uncle and his organisation have worked to help the Italian people after the war. How he wants me to take over from him and keep everything within the family the same. Continue the Inglima line. The family line.'

'But you are not an Inglima,' she cried. 'You are a Vella.'

Salvatore threw his hands in the air. 'I am also an Inglima. Angelo requests that I begin to add Inglima to my surname, Inglima-Vella.'

Jessy suddenly realised something and the knowledge made her catch her breath. 'And Francesca. She is an Inglima too.'

'Yes,' he replied. 'So of course Angelo thinks it is the perfect match. Her grandfather was his father Giovanni's brother. Francesca's father, also called Manuel, died when she was young, so Angelo took the family to live with him - and yes we are third cousins, but she is still an Inglima.'

'So … why did you do it Salvatore? Why be with me?'

He hesitated, aware that his words might hurt her. 'I didn't think it was going to last this long. I … when you moved into our house and I saw how Franco loved having you around … it made up for him losing Ana. I do love you Jessy, really I do and I want …'

'I can't …' she stumbled blindly back into the kitchen and leaned over the sink, feeling as though she might be sick. 'Go … please go.'

'I need …' Salvatore replied, putting his arms on her shoulders, attempting to turn her around to face him.

'Go …' she pleaded once again. 'Please … please just go.'

'You heard what she said.'

Salvatore swivelled around to face Neil Wilson as he entered the room, a look of absolute anger on his face.

'GO!' Neil roared at Salvatore, then ran towards Jessy who fell sobbing into his arms.

Chapter 33

Sicily. July, 1975.

To Serenella, this short journey felt like coming home, even more so than walking the familiar Inglima olive groves. As she travelled the steep incline of Ragusa Ibla's cobblestone roads, Serenella gazed over the high walls of the ancient town and looked down at the majestic view. In the distance she could see what used to be the home of Franco's mother, Margarita Sacca. This home had now been taken over by the government. The narrow pathway ahead looked deceivingly straight, but she knew from experience that the more you walked in Ragusa Ibla, the higher you climbed. A fact which puzzled many a tourist who didn't understand when they were sightseeing, that the paths down, sometimes unbelievably took you higher up. It was a trick. It was a known fact that the higher you lived, the poorer you were, as only the destitute would live so far away from town. It was said that if you lived at the top of Ragusa Ibla's lofty city, then it could take a full day to walk down and back up again. Who would want to do that? Below was the town, where you could get work, or food, or go to school.

Whether living in the Italian countryside or beside the sea, there was always easy access to food. Not so however, for those who lived in the steep streets and dwellings of Italy's highest built homes.

The Cavallos lived nearly at the summit. Their home was easy to miss. On the corner was a monastery. Next to it was a small door, which many mistook for a side entrance to the building. But it wasn't. It was the home of Valentina and Carlo Cavallo – one time gardener and cook to Serenella's family who lived at the bottom of the town. Now the Cavallo's daughter, the elderly and twice married Annunciata lived there. Her first husband had been killed in the war and her second had been flattened under a fat buffalo. Annunciata missed neither. Although birthing nine children, she now lived alone, apart from a brother - Giorgio Cavallo.

Serenella was glad she had taken flat tennis shoes with her, remembering how arduous the steep cobblestoned walk was in the heat of the afternoon sun. Before knocking on the Cavallo door, she discreetly sat on a low wall and changed once again into her black Chanel heels. Brushing dust of her skirt and smoothing her *chignon* with her palms, she took a deep breath and lifted the brass handle, letting it fall heavily against the brightly painted blue door – not yet weathered by the forthcoming winter storms, which sometimes battered the homes of these elevated dwellings.

The door opened immediately and Serenella guessed that news of her arrival back in Ragusa had already passed many lips and reached this home. When the small woman who barely reached Serenella's shoulders opened the door, Serenella was met by an enormous hug and many kisses.

'*Avanti, Avanti,*' Annunciata cried, ushering Serenella down a long tiled hallway into a large and surprisingly modern kitchen/living area.

Later Serenella thought it was the familiar odours that made her cry like she did. Or maybe it was the scent of flowers and Sicilian oranges when she was brought right through the kitchen and out into the huge garden at the rear of the house. Or was it the man who stood up from a low wicker chair? The man who stood stately with the long scar across his forehead, now faded but still visible and running into both eyes – not closing them forever, but forever depriving him of the image that he wished with all his heart he could see now.

As the sun set in the back garden of that little house high on top of Ragusa Ibla, Serenella Inglima-Vella listened without speaking as her love, her Giorgio, told her how he had fought, not just as a young partisan, but also as young man in love – to give her back the honour stolen from her.

'I waited,' he told her, 'for it to come back. My sight. But it never did. When I first got word of that man being there – so close to where I was – I had to avenge what he had done to you. So, I shot him. Yes,' he said. 'It was me. I shot that *bastardo*. But I didn't shoot her. I had no war with her.'

She told him of Marco, of her life in Malta and of her daughters. Giorgio listened without speaking or interrupting, just as Serenella had listened to his story. Sometimes things she said, just like things he told her – they hurt. But they both kept their counsel. Both had suffered, both had lost and yet both had survived.

'I have always felt so bad for that brave German soldier who helped us,' Serenella said. 'And how he was murdered so horribly in my name.'

She saw Giorgio nod his head. 'Yes,' he agreed. 'Fernando was a good man.'

'Fernando?' she replied. 'No, his name was Franz.

Franz Schmidt.'

'No. That was his given name – with the partisans – to protect his identity. He was from here. From Ragusa Ibla. His family were Jews but he had renounced his faith long before the war and was a Professor in Austria, when war broke out. Ironically, his new identity was so authentic that he was conscripted into the German army. But his loyalty was always to Italy – to Sicily. He was one of our very best spies. He did so much to deliver information to us about what those Nazis were up to.'

'He saved my life. And he was hung for raping me.'

'No. He wasn't – Angelo told me the name of the man he believed had raped you, but I knew it wasn't Fernando. I just told your brother Angelo that we had killed him, because I couldn't tell him who was really responsible, not then. Fernando didn't survive the war, but it wasn't anything to do with you.'

Serenella was speechless. On hearing nothing from her, Giorgio continued.

'You are eventually going to ask why I didn't come looking for you?'

'Yes.'

'Because by the time the war was over, you were married and I was blind.'

Serenella shook her head sadly. 'It doesn't matter now.'

Silence.

Later Annunciata came out to the garden with two glasses of homemade limoncello on a tray. She was happy to see that Serenella and Giorgio were reclining on their wicker chairs, holding hands across a low table. She felt guilty at having to ask them to move so she could place the tray down.

'Gianfranco Vella is a good man,' Giorgio said. Serenella looked across at him with surprise at this sudden revelation. She had never mentioned the name of the man she had married. But obviously he knew this from her brother Angelo.

'Yes,' she answered, taking a sip of the sweet drink and licking her lips. 'But you are the one I have always loved.'

He didn't answer for a few seconds and Serenella felt her heart skip a beat. Did his silence mean he had stopped loving her?

'I have learned in my life that it is possible to love and not have,' he replied quietly. 'I do and always will love you, but it is not for me to *have* you.'

She placed her glass gently on the table and took his hand in hers.

'I can only understand that now,' she answered, 'but up until now … no.'

'Love him,' Giorgio said. 'From what I hear he is good to you. His family have been good to you. His uncle was good to you.'

'His uncle?' she asked. 'Which one?'

'Fernando.'

'Fernando?'

'Yes. Fernando Sacca. AKA – Franz Schmidt. He kept the same initials. But yes. It was Margarita's brother, the one who studied in Austria. He is the man who I used as a go-between with us. He is the man who saved your life. A good partisan and a good person. I want this for you Serenella' – and he grasped both her hands waveringly in his own strong ones – 'I want you to try and love your husband, because he has kept you and your son Marco safe. He gave you a home and for that I respect and honour him.'

Franco Vella never knew what prompted his wife to come to his bed that night. He presumed it was a simple need for comfort after the death of her mother.

He also didn't know that after her admission of still loving the man of her youth for most of her marriage, it was his own admission to still loving Ana that had once more frozen Serenella's heart against him. She had been willing to finally fully become his wife – until her own confession had encouraged him also to do the same.

Hearing Franco say that he had loved Ana still and had done so during all their married life, had cut Serenella to the core. When she realised that at the age of nearly fifty she was expecting a child, she once more closed her heart towards Franco. Believing that Salvatore's conception was almost a trick of God's to give her something to love after Giorgio's blessing – Serenella felt an almost primal surge of love for this last child and poured every ounce of love she had left into him.

Free once more to return to her Sicilian home, Serenella took Salvatore there at every opportunity. She cocooned them both in the home where Giorgio had once lived before the outbreak of the war, in the little *casetta*, across from the sea in Marina di Ragusa.

Chapter 34

Malta. October, 2004.

Franco debated with himself whether to walk up the hill to St. Ursula's convent, or drive. It wasn't very far, but the hill was steep and he'd already been out for a walk that morning along the promenade, watching with interest as younger men took their boats out on the sea. The car was parked just outside and finding keys in his pocket, he waved at the postman who shouted out a cheerful greeting, then climbed inside, ignoring the seatbelt as usual.

The convent door was opened by a young nun who informed him that his daughter would be down in a few minutes, if he wanted to wait in the reception room. Franco said he was happy to stay in the hallway. He took a seat near the door and recalled how Ana had waited patiently here for him, the night that he had taken her to Mosta Dome. That was also the night he had proposed once more and she had accepted him, for the second time. The memory didn't cause him pain like before. He still felt a warm glow inside from the pleasant dreams of last night. Instead, through his shirt, he felt Ana's tiny ring on its chain and he smiled. 'I'm visiting our girl today, our own girl,' he whispered, then stood as he heard their daughter reach the top of the stairway.

'So for your surprise,' Rigalla said smiling. 'We are having lunch at that new restaurant at Sliema. The one opposite The Regent Hotel, at the spot where you first saw Ana.'

Franco's eyes lit up. 'Oh what a lovely treat,' he replied, gallantly opening the convent's front door for his daughter and feeling satisfied that he had brought the car after all.

The simple white painted restaurant was indeed situated on the very spot where Ana had once leaned against an upturned *luzzu*. She had been unaware that Franco was gazing at her from his own boat, awestruck on a night-time fishing expedition. Now, from their seat on a height overlooking a little jetty jutting out into the sea, Franco pointed. 'That is most likely the very same jetty that was there at the time. These fancy restaurants have taken up all the promenade, but the shoreline itself is largely unchanged. Let's go down there afterwards and sit in my boat.'

'I wondered if that was your one,' Rigalla answered, pointing at one of the many small fishing vessels which bobbed on the sea in front. 'I can't see the name *Anabel* on it from here.'

'Yes, that's my one,' Franco answered. 'Fancy a short sail after lunch?'

Rigalla smiled. 'That would be perfect,' she replied.

Having descended the stairway from the back of the restaurant which led down to the jetty, Franco waited patiently for his daughter. Women can't leave anywhere without saying goodbye to half the place first, he thought good-humouredly. The rear of the restaurant had wide windows looking out onto the sea, affording a wonderful view for the diners. Rigalla stepped onto the top of the steps and gazed down to where Franco was standing, looking out onto the water which separated Sliema from Valletta. She knew without asking that he was thinking of Ana and all the seas between, which had kept them apart for so many years.

'Franco,' his daughter called cheerfully, having never referred to him as anything else, since she'd been brought up as his baby sister.

Franco turned, looked up and gasped. He staggered, feeling his heart beating irregularly. Sunlight streamed through the floor to ceiling window behind where she was standing at the top of the stairway. It clothed the woman in an almost ethereal glow. Her white dress glimmered as if it was lit by a thousand stars, shimmering magnificently. He struggled for breath. The bright blue of the sunny sky outside the window glistened against the beautiful blueness of her eyes. It almost looked as though she walked on water, with the shafts of sunlight appearing like beams from heaven.

'Ana,' he whispered. She smiled, and her smile dazzled his eyes. He could not move. He could not speak another word. She held out her hand and shakily his own stretched out before him, moving without him even realising. She began to descend. Slowly his tired old legs lifted and he ran, like he used to as a young man. She too began to run towards him. He felt a warm enveloping heat from the rays of the sun which shone on them both, as Franco held Ana once again in his arms and finally, closed his eyes.

***

'It's Ana's ring,' Jessy whispered, her words barely

audible. She held it between the forefinger and thumb of her right hand towards the hospital's bright fluorescent ceiling lights. Just less than an hour ago, this little ring had hung next to Franco's chest, close to his beating heart. He didn't know, none of them knew, that it was soon to stop the beating it had done every second of his long life. How can it be, Jessy wondered? How can he not be here? How can his heart just stop beating, just like that? Just decide, this beat will be my last, then nothing. No more. No more life, no more breath, no more of the person who's body it had been a home in since conception. It just stopped. Without any warning whatsoever. How can that be?

Billy had taken her left hand in his after she'd opened the white napkin, finding the ring inside where it had been wrapped. How can something that meant so much, come wrapped so carelessly, in a hospital café serviette? Did nobody care? Did nobody know the significance of this ring and what it meant? That she was now the owner of this tiny gem studded ring meant that not only was Ana gone, but now also Franco was gone. This gold band was the last link to their story. It had been Ana's engagement ring and been entrusted to Jessy when Franco died - a ring that once belonged to Margarita and that many years ago, had promised so much to a young couple in love. Ana had taken it off her finger when she had been forced to marry Flight Squadron Ernest McGuill during the war in Malta, thereby ending the promise she had made to Franco.

Ana had removed the ring to replace it with a wedding band, her heart breaking and for the rest of her life the ring hung on her rosary beads, where she saw it every day. After her death Franco had worn it on a long gold chain, also once belonging to his mother, until now. Until today when somebody had removed it. Who had, Jessy wondered? Who had slipped it from around Franco's neck? How did the nurse know it was meant for her? Somebody must have given the order for it to be handed over to Jessy. Was it Salvatore? Where was Franco's gold chain? Was another family member somewhere here in the hospital now also unwrapping a white napkin, containing Franco's chain?

'Did you know that Franco proposed to Ana again, the night before she died?'

Billy squeezed her hand and let out a long breath. 'Goodness. No. I didn't know that.' He swallowed, feeling his mouth extremely dry. Death didn't get easier, no matter what age you were. It always made him feel both surprised and grateful that he was still here, but also apart from the sadness, it gave him every time a strong feeling of responsibility. There was still work he had to do. At his age this seemed unbelievable.

'Yes,' Jessy carried on. 'He'd taken her …' she sobbed a little, '… he'd taken her to the top of Mosta Dome, where they'd had their first kiss during the war. And he said that he'd even got down on one knee and Ana had told him to get back up.' Jessy smiled. 'But she'd said yes. They were going to get married.'

Billy stretched his legs out slowly, straight in front. They were feeling cramped, crossed over each other as he sat. His stick which had been leaning against the chair fell. Jessy bent to pick it up, but he shook his head.

'I'll get it in a minute,' he said. 'Jessica, that is tragic. To think they were so close to being married once again and it didn't happen. But can I tell you about something your grandmother told me? It was about how things all panned out and her matter of fact way of coming to terms with it all?'

Jessy just nodded, not even attempting to wipe the tears falling from her eyes and he continued.

'We spoke about it one time and this is what she

said. That we are not in control of our destinies. As humans we like to think we have control of our own life. That we make plans and try to steer our own course but sometimes, it is as if a hand comes down into our lives from somewhere and stirs it about. Then we spend the rest of our time on earth trying to get back on the course we had planned. We think of how everything went totally wrong and how unfair it all was and how happy we could have been if life had gone exactly the way we had planned. We talk about what-ifs and about people and dreams we had lost.'

'But Ana who lost a lot in her life, told me that whenever she felt sad and God she had reason to, she would think of her blessings. She would think of you and Maria, of how neither of you would have existed if she'd married Franco. She said she would think of the things she had been given, after so much had been taken away. Jessy, she said when she did see it, she always believed that she had been given much more than she had lost.'

Jessy shook her head. 'No. I don't believe that,' she replied vehemently.

'Which part?'

'Do you mean, that she accepted losing Franco and

the life she could have had with him, just to have had Mum or me?'

Billy nodded. 'Yes. That is what she said.'

'Would I have accepted losing Ana to have my life here in Malta and be with Salvatore?' Jessy sobbed, turning to look at Billy.

He was already looking at her. 'Or Neil,' he stated, looking into her eyes. 'You'd already met Salvatore when Ana was alive. But you hadn't met Neil. Do you ever think that maybe you never would have, only that Ana died?'

Jessy was silent. In her head she ruminated on what Billy had just said. She leaned back in the uncomfortable plastic chair. If Ana hadn't died. If she had gone back to Ireland with her … but they would still have got the letter from the convent saying who her father was. So she would have still probably gone to England to meet him and probably met Neil then anyway. So, it hadn't made a huge big difference. They would have been on the same course, okay maybe by a different route, but the same course. Isn't that all that mattered? But Neil. Hadn't he told her he'd been planning to move to San Francisco until he met her? So it might have been a while, a year or two maybe before they'd met. But, she could have married Salvatore by then. Had children. She rested her head on Billy's shoulder.

'Will you ring Neil?'

'I already have,' Billy replied. 'He's on his way.'

Chapter 35

London. October, 2009.

Jessy opened her laptop and waited for the screen to light up. With trembling fingers she hit the icon for her emails. She bit her lip when she saw that the one which had kept her awake all night worrying, had finally reached her inbox. She clicked, read it quickly and yelled loudly. 'Yes!!!' she squealed with delight. She had passed. She was now a Bachelor of Arts – specialising in international history and language.

'I can't believe it,' she said for the hundredth time, much to her father Jimmy's amusement. 'I am definitely going for my Masters now.'

'Where are you going to study?' he asked, thrilled to bits that his daughter was so delighted at her achievement.

'I don't know, but the world is my oyster, right?' she answered, once more sitting at the table to reply to friends' messages, asking how she had done in the exams.

Underneath the Sky email page she was on – a ribbon of news was displayed at the bottom of her screen. The name, Neil Wilson, caught her eye. She clicked on the ribbon, opening up a bigger image of the news outbreak.

'Exciting find for successful up and coming UK architect Neil Wilson. While excavating a 1930s building in Germany recently bought by Neil Wilson – builders uncover a hidden trove of Nazi treasures stolen from wealthy Jewish families. Of particular interest is a large assortment of jewellery by the once renowned jewellery makers from Sicily, Italy – the Sacca family – with an estimated value of millions of euro.'

Jessy couldn't speak. Instead she signalled for Jimmy to come over to where she was sitting, entranced by the words she was reading on the screen.

'My word!' Jimmy cried. 'That's our Neil.'

Jessy simply nodded her head.

Workmen were shown on screen emptying dozens of necklaces, bracelets and rings out of chests onto plastic sheeting, on the gravelled ground of a building site. The reporter held up a tray of what looked like a set of rings resting on a dark velvet cushion, under a glass fronted case. The reporter held the case in front of the camera.

'Here I have been told is a unique collection of rare

rings, a set of twelve, each one encrusted with a different colour of precious stones. The rings represent the twelve ancient tribes of Israel. There is much excitement by the Jewish Historical and Archaeological representatives who have travelled here to the site. As the viewer may see, one of the rings is unfortunately missing.'

The reporter pointed to the empty space – number eight.

'Experts have told us this missing ring is valued at possibly a million euro and the complete set could be anything between one and ten million euro. The ring would have eight stones, each set with a different gem and the word 'Nephtali' will be inscribed on the inside of the band. Nephtali is … as most of us don't actually know, one of the sons of Jacob.

Jessy began to laugh.

'What is it?' Jimmy asked. 'What is so funny? It's great that our Neil found all that. Not that he'll be allowed to keep it probably.'

Jessy slipped Ana's little ring off her finger and handed it to her father.

'Read the inscription,' she said.

He did. 'My word!' he exclaimed, excitedly. 'We

have to ring Neil.'

***

Stuttgart, Germany. October, 2009.

Neil Wilson was sitting on a large boulder, sipping from a steel coffee cup and deep in conversation with Isaac, the New York based lapidarist who specialised in Jewish design. 'I never even heard of a lapidarist till I met you,' Neil chuckled. 'So it's somebody who works with gems, is that right?'

Isaac shrugged. 'Yes. But I don't make them. I study them and I just had to come over here when I heard – this find – it is remarkable.'

'Hang on mate,' Neil said as he put his coffee mug down and stood to retrieve the mobile phone which was ringing from his jeans pocket. 'Jess! Did you see it? Did you see the news? Isn't it unbelievable?'

'I know,' Jessy squealed on the other side. 'I, however, cannot believe you didn't tell me and I had to find out on the news.'

'Hey - who is the one that said we stick to our 'weekend only calls rule' unless it's an emergency? I told you I'd be patient and I am being. God help me.'

'This *is* an emergency,' Jessy squealed excitedly

398

once more down the phone-line. 'Open the text message I just sent you.'

Neil hit the menu button, then swore as he realised that he'd just cut Jessy off. The red envelope sign was lit up and he pressed open, then swore once more when he saw the image pop up on his screen. He rang Jessy back immediately.

'It's the ring! Isn't it? It's the missing ring? The one that belonged to Ana?'

'Yes,' Jessy replied enthusiastically. 'It is the same ring.'

***

Two days later ...

'Do you miss it?' Neil asked, as he watched Jessy rub the empty spot on her finger.

She smiled. 'Yes. But I couldn't not give it back to them. Every time I looked at it, I'd think of the vacant space in that tray where it should be.'

'Everybody thinks you are crazy you know,' Neil said, his eyes twinkling mischievously at the woman sitting opposite him.

'Me? What about you? You are even crazier than me, but to be honest ...' she said putting her hand on his arm and squeezing it affectionately '… I wouldn't have expected anything less from you.'

'So Miss McGuill, next stop Rome eh?' Jessy looked around the elegant dining room of Stuttgart's Millennium Hotel. 'Does this place remind you of anywhere?' she asked, raising her eyebrow coquettishly.

'The Kempinski in Gozo,' he answered, 'where you ran away when I tried to kiss you.' She twirled the stem of the wine glass between her fingers, then looked up and whispered, 'I won't run away if you kiss me now.'

Chapter 36

Rome, Italy. December, 2009.

Jessy looked out at the sea of people in front. From their vantage point, on the temporary stage set up outside the Great Synagogue of Rome at Lungotevere Cenci, it looked as though thousands had turned out on this mild December day. Many of the Romans were wrapped in furs as though they lived in Siberia, but Jessy found the weather quite humid. She had even taken off her red winter coat and was quite comfortable sitting in her green woollen polo neck jumper, though she had kept her scarf tied around her throat. Ana's warnings of catching her death, if not wrapped up in the winter, still rung in her ears.

She glanced at Neil who was deep in conversation with the Rabbi who had introduced himself earlier at dinner. He didn't speak much English, but Jessy was happy to practice her Italian and Neil had been very impressed with her knowledge of the language.

'You two could be saying anything about me and I wouldn't know,' he joked, putting his arm proprietarily around Jessy's waist and playfully squeezing her.

'He said he could find me a good Jewish husband,'

Jessy replied with mirth, 'but that I'd have to convert first.'

'Oh yes?' Neil answered. 'Did you not tell him you already have one waiting in the wings?'

Jessy blushed. 'Actually, I did,' she answered.

Now as she watched Neil, dressed as he was in his best navy suit, she could tell he was nervous. His hands were clasped behind his back. Neil only did that when he said he didn't know what else to do with them. And when he didn't know what to do with his hands, it meant that he was nervous. She longed to go over and do what she usually did in these situations to calm him down. Jessy recalled when Neil was going for his interview at the University at Manchester to study architecture, he had been very nervous. Later he told her it was her gently holding his hand and joking about silly things that had helped him relax. She had done the same thing two years later when he went from there to ABK Stuttgart University. As he did with her, when she was up in front of the terrifying interview at Courtauld University in London. Both had got in to the Universities that they wanted. Neil had surpassed even his own hopes and expectations. After his year in Stuttgart, he had been snapped up by the renowned

Stern and Rippich Architecture Company, also based in that busy German cosmopolitan city.

***

Jimmy's lack of reaction to Neil's confession that he was not his biological father, had astounded him.

'Makes no difference to me,' he had said, shrugging his shoulders. 'I had my own suspicions at the time but sure who couldn't love a red faced, squalling thing like you were?'

Billy also had no major reaction. He had said much the same as Jimmy when Neil confided that he was not Jimmy's son.

'Still my Neil,' he old man had said. 'Still my lad. Still my best mate. But what I do worry about, is what you are going to do about Jessy?'

Neil had told him then how he and Jessy had talked. Oh, how they had talked and talked.

'Don't you see,' she had told him. 'How Ana, my mum, your mum – their heartaches and losses and pain, were all to do with men? No wait,' she said, as Neil defensively began to speak. 'They had not got the choices that I have. They were all strong women.

Women who loved so much. Too much. And they all sacrificed what they wanted to do with their lives, because of men they loved, or men they ended up with but didn't love. Because of babies and the rules of the church and the law laid down also by men.

Neil,' she said, crossing the room to where he had stood, leaning against Billy's balcony wall. 'What I think I feel for you now is love and yes …' she admitted, '… attraction and all that goes with it. But I just broke up with the man I thought I was going to marry. I just lost Franco. I can't jump from that to … well, to you.'

Neil understood. And so they talked. Jessy spoke of how she still hoped to go to University and get a degree in something to do with history and the arts. Neil spoke about how he had already been looking online at places to study architecture. Jessy said she wanted to travel. Neil did too. She didn't promise anything. Either did Neil. Instead they spoke on the phone every weekend, sometimes for a whole day at times. They met at Christmas at Jimmy's, where Jessy now lived. But not the Christmas that Neil had to go to some girl's house for dinner instead. That time Jessy had said nothing, but she burned the turkey she had cooked for Jimmy and Billy. Neil on the other hand had spent the whole time in Nottingham drunk and wishing he was in the small terraced house in London.

And there were holidays and sometimes Jimmy went too. Sometimes they went alone and that usually went very well. Until the week on the Greek island of Kos, when Jessy didn't come home after a night out with a guy she met at the bar there. When she had finally got back to the apartment, Neil was gone. They hadn't spoken for nearly six months after that. Then Billy had died and they both went to Malta to lay him to rest, next to his wife Katie and their babies.

And now they were here, in Rome. Neil caught Jessy's eye. She winked at him, mouthing the words 'Knock them dead' before the microphone was put in front of him and he began to tell of how he had found the Sacca treasure.

'And now ladies and gentlemen, I hand you over to the Mayor of Ragusa Ibla, from where the precious treasure originated.' Relieved, Neil stood back and made space for the Mayor to take his place.

'*Buonsera signore e signori.* It is with tremendous pride and pleasure that I present to you, the Jewish community of Roma…' The introduction was met with a huge round of applause from the swelling audience. 'Some people, I am aware who are here, may not know of the terrible atrocities the Jewish people in Italy suffered during World War Two. Just before the war began for Italy, in 1938, Benito Mussolini together with Hitler, signed a document known as 'Defence of the Race'. This document removed all civil rights from Jews in Italy and my grandfather, Oskar Sacca, was forced to leave his hometown of Ragusa Ibla where his family had lived for generations.'

'My grandmother and grandfather fled here to Rome, where they believed there was a safe haven for the Jewish community. When the Germans occupied Rome in September 1943, the Jewish community were told if they handed over 50kg of gold, they would be left in peace. My family were the only ones with that type of wealth. They handed over a large assortment of jewellery to save their own lives and that of their friends and neighbours here in Roma. Here in my hand …' and he held a yellowed piece of paper in the air, '… is the receipt my grandfather received for that contribution. But the Nazis did not honour that promise. I discovered recently that on 16th October 1943, the Nazis rounded up and deported over two thousand Jews for concentration camps. My family were with them and they perished in the camps.'

'In September of this year, Neil Wilson, who as you just heard, recovered my families gold, which had been handed over to the Nazis in 1943. It was found in what was once a Nazi Commandant's home in Stuttgart, Germany. It is of tremendous monetary and sentimental value. Neil Wilson has donated this entire find to the Jewish Museum here at the Great Synagogue at Roma. Also, Jessica McGuill, was the owner of a precious ring which was missing from a collection of rare rings, signifying the twelve ancient tribes of Israel. Jessica is here with us tonight, but I believe is too modest to come to the stage.'

This was followed by another outburst of applause.

'Finally,' Salvatore Inglima Vella continued, 'it is with great pleasure that I now award Neil Wilson and Jessica McGuill Honorary Citizenship of Roma.'

***

Over nine hundred miles away, two people sat in their cosy armchairs. One had his eyes peeled towards the old Panasonic television set on top of an ancient oak bureau. The other also sat in front of the TV, while he listened intently to the speech being given by the Mayor of Ragusa, Salvatore Inglima Vella.

'How does he look?' Giorgio asked.

There was silence for a few seconds, then Giorgio heard his old friend and comrade breathe out a long slow breath. 'Like his mother. He looks like Serenella,' he answered.

Giorgio nodded. 'Your old eyes can at least see that. What I wouldn't give.'

Dottore Bartolomeo Moretti heaved himself slowly out of his seat and reached over to clasp the hand of the old man sitting next to him. 'We did good *mio amico*,' he said. 'We did good.' And the old man began to softly sing a tune not heard by either for many years, '*Bella ciao, bella ciao, bella ciao, ciao, ciao.*'

Epilogue

Malta. April, 2018.

In St. Julian's busy harbour town, a girl shifts uncomfortably on the hot leather seat as the bus stalls at yet another set of traffic lights. Dusk is beginning to settle on the Maltese island. She squints her eyes to focus on the light to her right hand side. It is coming from one of those baroque bow windows that are everywhere here on this tiny Mediterranean island. A woman is leaning out over the balcony and she is throwing something down below. The girl sees little hands popping up over a colourful array of – is that daffodils? A man comes on to the balcony. He puts his arms around the woman – now they are both laughing as two blond haired children jump up and down trying to catch whatever it is the woman is throwing at them. Tiny chocolate eggs. Of course, the girl realises. It's Easter Sunday. Hanging from a hook on the blue front door is a flowery wreath. It has all the flowers of spring encircled together, with a love heart in-between. But the flowers and leaves look more like those you would see on an Irish wreath, rather than on a Maltese one.

Suddenly the woman stands up straight and looks

out across the busy traffic. She catches the eye of a girl on the bus and begins to smile. Then she waves. The girl waves back. The woman tilts her head and says something to the man standing next to her and he looks over too, then waves. The children turn.

'Who are we waving at?' Anabel asks.

'I don't know,' replies her little brother, with the dimpled chin 'but wave anyway. You never know who it could be. Mam always says, 'Strangers are friends we haven't met yet.'

THE END

By the same author:

Under a Maltese Sky

Being caught up in war is not what Ana Mellor expects when she lands in Malta to join her Wing-Commander father. In the midst of horror and destruction, the courage and resilience of the Maltese people is revealed as they struggle to survive.

Ana falls in love but treachery intervenes with catastrophic consequences.

Meanwhile, disillusioned with Ireland's fight for political independence, Ernie McGuill leaves home to join the British Army. Due to the outbreak of war he trains as a fighter pilot and is posted to Malta.

It is against this background that the characters of Ana, Ernie and many others are interwoven in a story of betrayal and intrigue. This is not unravelled until generations later when two women make a journey to Malta - a journey that is to have astonishing consequences.

PROLOGUE

~ Malta 2001 ~

Ana was very happy. Today she had met Pope John Paul II and as she told her grand-daughter, if she died now, she would do so contentedly. As the rest of the group were busy chatting and drinking wine, Ana gazed out the window. From her seat she could see down into Grand Harbour. Although it was dark, Fort St. Elmo was lit up as was the whole harbour below. She wondered what had happened to all the people she had loved on this island. Where was the man who had never been far from her thoughts for over fifty years? Where were the girls she had been to school with, the nurses she trained beside and lived with through those terrible war years? She remembered vividly the horror of the war. It was almost impossible to visualize battleships moored where there was now a pretty marina, or to imagine the frightening sound of an air raid siren, breaking the silence of the night to warn them of yet another air raid.

Sadly Ana knew the fate of some of the friends she had loved in her time here during the war. Looking over at her grand-daughter she smiled to herself as she realised that when she was Jessy's age, she had been here in this country of sunshine and sadness, of laughter and loss and love. Thanks to her grand-daughter she was now back in Malta. Although she had been shocked and excited when she realised she was to return to the island, Ana was happy now that she had come. The place she had tried to forget for years was still familiar and just as beautiful.

By the same author:

The Azure Window

PROLOGUE
Malta, July, 1943.

The wind whipped wildly around her head. Ana put an arm up, grabbed a handful of blonde strands and pulled. Opening her fist, she watched as the hairs blew away like ribbons in the air. Her scalp tingled and she felt her heartbeat accelerate rapidly, as though it was going to burst out of her chest.

The sea was rough. Angry waves danced into the air, green and blue and brown. Ferocious. Would it be quick she wondered? Will I die before hitting the sea, or will my heart stop on the way down, like what happened to people who jumped off high-rise buildings? Her mouth had a funny taste, as though even panic had a flavour. This must be what it would be like to face a firing squad or an axe murderer, when you know you are going to die soon and crazy thoughts go through your head. It was as though the whole world had stood still and it was just she, Ana McGuill,

414

poised in terror on the top of The Azure Window in the middle of the Mediterranean Sea, trying to find the courage to end her life.

Franco had brought her to this place of natural wonder. They had held hands as they walked across the arch in the sea, he gripping hers tightly to keep her safe. He had always kept her safe and she believed that he always would. But he was gone.

They had stood looking out over the blue water. It had been warm and sunny then. Not like today. Today the sky was much darker, like her heart. The pain in her heart was unbearable. It lay like a heavy stone in her body, gnawing at her like a beast. Unable to sleep or eat, she went through her days on auto pilot. Until today. Today she had said, enough. That word had brought her here, almost seven hours later. This place where she and Franco had stood and planned their life together. How did so much change in so short a time?

She turned at the sound. There was nobody. A bird perhaps, or some animal.

~~~~

In a crib just a few miles away, an infant whimpered fretfully. A kindly face looked down and clutched a tiny finger. 'Ssssh little one, all will be well.'

She heard it again. The sound of a baby's cry. Turning around quickly once more, her foot slipped and she tumbled. An immense feeling of terror gripped her. Opening her mouth to scream she found that no sound came and it seemed as though her whole body was suddenly engulfed in an intense heat. On her knees she saw a hand outstretched. She grabbed it, pulling herself to her feet. Looking up, Ana turned her head left and right. Nobody. 'Hello,' she called. Where could they have gone? There was no place to hide.

Ana tentatively stepped across the stony ground until she was off the arch.

The baby closed her eyes.

All was well.

All novels by Nicola Kearns are available to buy on Amazon.co.uk and at nicolakearnswriter.com (Paperback).

Nicola Kearns contact:

nicolakearnswriter.com

nicolakearns3@hotmail.com

Twitter: @nicola3mary

Printed in Great Britain
by Amazon